Jaked

SABRINA STARK

CHAPTER 1

My roommate was a screamer. Through the thin, shabby walls, I heard Maddie and the mystery guy going at it for like the third time since I'd gotten home from work two hours earlier.

The guy was quiet. Maddie, not so much. Then again, she seldom was. But this guy was eliciting sounds that even by Maddie's dubious standards were just a shade over the top.

Huddled under the covers of my own single bed, I squeezed my eyes shut and tried to block out the noises.

It's not that I objected to sex. And it's not that I minded Maddie bringing back some guy to our cheap two-bedroom apartment. What I minded was the fact that I had to get up in three hours for my other job, and hearing Maddie scream out, "Yes! Yes! That's it! Oh yeah!" for like the millionth time wasn't exactly the thing for a restful night's sleep.

I'd never met the guy, but I had a pretty good idea who he was. She'd been talking about him non-stop for the past week. Jay, the guy with lickable, washboard abs. Jay, the guy with the hot, tight ass that she wanted to grip with both hands and never let go. Jay, the guy with picture-perfect pecs and a muscle-bound back of cryptic tattoos.

According to Maddie, he was famous for something or other. But with Maddie, claims to fame weren't exactly credible. She tossed around that phrase the way some people toss spare change into deli tip jars whether they ordered a sandwich or not.

Supposedly, the guy was rich too.

If there was any justice in this world, he'd have the face of a bulldog.

Whether I'd seen his face or not, this *had* to be the guy going at it in Maddie's bedroom. Returning from my six-hour bartending shift, I'd seen that unfamiliar vehicle out front, some exotic sports car way beyond the budget of anyone in *this* building.

It could only belong to him. Parked on the narrow street across from the twelve-unit where I'd been living with Maddie for the last few weeks, the car was blazing red with wide tires and shiny rims. The wheels alone probably cost more than what I'd made last month at both of my jobs combined.

In our neighborhood, the vehicle would be hard to miss. Obviously, the guy was an idiot. If the car was still there in the morning, it would be a miracle.

Who cared if the guy had a hot body? And who cared if he was eliciting sounds that weren't quite human? And who cared if he had gobs of money and didn't mind spending it?

He was a giant dog-faced, dumb-ass. Or at least that's what I told myself an hour later when I heard the promise of round-four coming from Maddie's bedroom. Groaning in frustration, I wrapped my pillow around my ears and burrowed deeper under the covers.

I definitely needed my own place, and not only because Maddie wasn't exactly diligent about paying her half of the rent, even if her name, not mine, was on the lease.

By the time I drifted off to sleep, Maddie's screams had subsided into giggles and moans. Two short hours later, I staggered out of bed and opened my door just a crack. The place was dark, and Maddie's bedroom door was fully shut.

Thank God.

I was dressed for work in a crisp white blouse and a plain black skirt that showed way too much leg, especially for a cold Michigan morning. It was late March. Technically, it was spring. In reality, snow wasn't exactly out of the question.

Even our apartment was freezing, whether from a faulty thermostat or Maddie's habit of paying the bills five days after the shutoff notice. As soon as I had the chance, I made a mental note to call the gas company. Again.

Shivering in the cold apartment, I stumbled on high heels toward the small kitchenette and flicked on the dim overhead light.

That's when I saw him, sitting alone at our small kitchen table. Shirtless and tousled looking, the guy was everything Maddie had claimed and then some. He wore no shirt, revealing a broad chest of sharply defined muscles, set off by bulging biceps and shoulders cut so fine they were almost a work of art.

When our eyes met, my mouth fell open. My purse thudded to the floor, and I didn't bother to look down.

Casually, he rocked back on his chair, cradling his hands behind his head. The guy looked utterly at home, not just in his own skin, but in the ugly little kitchenette, with its peeling wallpaper and cracked cupboards.

We locked eyes, and the silence stretched out. His face was all angles and shadows, with a strong jaw, chiseled cheekbones, and dark, probing eyes that made me swallow with an audible gulp.

His wasn't the face of a bulldog. Good for him. Bad for me. And not only because he was sleeping – or whatever – with my roommate.

It was because of the other thing. The thing that Maddie wouldn't know. Couldn't know.

His was a face I recognized.

When he spoke, his voice was low, not quite a whisper, but the next closest thing. It might've been a caress, except for the note of surprise that was impossible to miss. "Luna?" he said.

I hated that name, even if it *was* the thing on my birth certificate.

I bit my lip. Why on Earth was he here? To help me? To hinder me? I wasn't stupid. I knew it had to be more than a coincidence that he'd shown up here, in my apartment, two hours away from where we'd both grown up.

I lifted my chin and met his gaze head-on. "Jake," I said.

"You've got five minutes," he said.

"For what?" I asked.

"To pack your bags."

I glanced around. "Why?"

"Because," he said, "you're coming with me."

CHAPTER 2

I stared at him. "I am not."

He rocked forward on his chair and pressed his palms to the table. When I didn't move, he flicked his head toward my bedroom, just a few feet away. "You want me to pack for you?"

I stood my ground. "No."

He shoved back his chair and stood. He strode around the table. Brushing past me, he headed toward my bedroom while I followed on his heels.

When he opened the bedroom door, he stopped and gave the shabby little room the once-over. He made a sound of disgust.

"What?" I said.

"You don't belong here."

"Why not?"

"Because," he said, "it's depressing as hell."

I glanced around, taking in the gray walls, the dingy carpet, and the narrow window that offered a cinderblock view of the neighboring building.

"And you just figured this out?" I lowered my voice. "What are you doing here, anyway?"

"I'll tell you in the car."

I glanced toward Maddie's bedroom. "And what about

Maddie?"

He turned his head in my direction, and his dark gaze bored into mine. "What about her?"

I crossed my arms and gave him a snotty smile. "Is *she* going with us too?"

He looked only mildly interested. "You want her to?"

"I'm not even going with you," I said. "What Maddie does is her own business."

He left the doorway and strode into my bedroom. I followed after him and shut the door behind us. At one time, forever ago, we'd been friends, or at least that's what I'd thought, right up until the moment he'd kicked me to the curb like yesterday's garbage.

I hadn't seen him in how long? Six years? Of course, I'd been seventeen back then, way too young to be hanging out with the likes of Jake Bishop.

Even back then, he'd been wild to the core, and dangerous as hell. But to me? He'd been that teenage girl's wet dream, the guy you couldn't stop thinking about, no matter how hard you tried.

Stupidly, I'd had this massive crush on him. But that was a long time ago. Now, I was twenty-three and a college graduate. Older, wiser, and mostly reformed, I was way too smart to be crushing on anyone like him.

Recalling the difference in our ages, I did the math in my head. Jake would be how old now? Twenty-seven? Twenty-eight? Back when I'd been in high school, the five years between us had seemed monumental.

Now, the difference would be nothing. A scoffing sound escaped my lips. Less than nothing, actually. Probably, I was a lot more mature than Jake was, at least where it counted.

He stopped to give me a look. "Something funny?" he asked.

No way I'd be sharing *this* joke with him. "That depends," I said. "Do you like knock-knock jokes?"

"No." He strode toward my closet. He flung open the door. He stopped short, staring into the mostly empty space. He didn't turn around. "Where's your stuff?"

I felt color rise to my face. "Actually," I said, "it's kind of a long story."

Jake pushed aside a row of empty hangers and reached for the few that actually held clothes. "You'll be telling me later," he said.

"That's what *you* think." I flopped onto my freshly made bed and watched him with morbid curiosity. A normal girl would stop him this instant. I *would* have stopped him, or at least tried to, except, honestly, there was nothing in my closet worth defending.

Pathetic, I know.

Plus, watching him move, I was more than a little distracted. I gave his naked back a good, long look. It was just like Maddie had described, a tattooed mass of hard muscle that tapered to a narrow waist, slim hips, and long legs, clad in expensive-looking black tailored slacks.

The tattoos were new. The body wasn't.

As if my eyes had a mind of their own, my gaze drifted to his ass. No wonder Maddie hadn't wanted to let it go. My hands, resting beside me, gave my bed-coverings an involuntary squeeze. The motion felt oddly unsatisfying. I cleared my throat and flattened my palms against the bed. Mentally, I gave myself a good slap to the face.

He was Maddie's guy, not mine, even if I *had* known him first. With an effort, I yanked my gaze upward and reminded myself to keep it there.

Good thing too. I'd barely looked up when Jake turned around to face me. His gaze flicked to the shabby wooden dresser that stood beside the bed. "The dresser," he said. "What's in it?"

"Clothes, mostly." Of the unmentionable variety.

"How many?"

"Not a lot." It was true. There were five drawers. Four were empty.

He gave me a good, long look. "Uh-huh."

"Like you should talk," I said, giving his bare chest a pointed look. "You're not even wearing shirt."

"Not my fault," he said.

"Why's that?"

"I had one," he said. "It ripped."

I was still looking at his chest. That long-lost shirt, wherever it was, wasn't the only thing ripped around here. Damn it. With an effort, I pulled my gaze upward yet again. "Ripped?" I said. "How?"

"Bedroom casualty."

I gave him a smirk. "That's nice."

"Nah," he said. "But I've got a spare in the car, so, eh, whatever."

"Seriously?"

Again, he turned toward my closet. "You think I'm gonna drive around with no shirt?" He pulled a suitcase from the top shelf. His muscles tightened, making the ink on his back shift with the smooth motion. Sure, he *could* drive around with no shirt, but with a body like that, he'd be a menace to any girl who wanted to keep her eyes on the road.

He tossed the suitcase onto the floor and said, "Here. Pack your stuff."

As interesting as this was, I had someplace else to be. That was probably a good thing, all things considered.

"Sorry," I said, glancing at my watch. "But I've got to work at eight." It was kind of a bummer, actually. Today was

Saturday. Somehow, I'd always envisioned that when I graduated from college, I wouldn't be working weekends anymore. But a lot of things hadn't turned out exactly the way I'd planned.

"So," I continued, "I'll just pass on the whole packing thing if that's alright with you."

"No," he said. "It's not alright."

This was getting ridiculous. "Excuse me?"

"And about that job?" he said. "You quit yesterday."

I gave a little laugh. "Sure I did." If only I *could* quit. It wasn't exactly my dream job, but a girl had to start somewhere, right?

"Yeah," he said. "By email."

I studied his face. Was he kidding? He didn't look like he was kidding. "Quit messing around," I said.

"I'm not." He flicked his head toward the suitcase. "So pack."

"You can't be serious?"

As an answer, he reached into his front pants pocket. He pulled out a folded sheet of paper. He held it out vaguely in my direction. I pushed myself off from the bed and snatched the paper out of his hand.

I looked down and scanned the sheet, a printout of some bogus email between me and my boss. By the time I finished reading, my blood was boiling. I looked up. "What the hell?" I said.

"You can thank me later."

"I'm not gonna *thank* you," I said, waving the paper in his direction. "You forged a resignation letter?"

"Email," he corrected.

"Whatever," I gave him a hard look. "Please tell me you're joking."

His voice was flat. "I don't joke."

"You do too," I said. The guy had a wicked sense of humor, or at least he *used* to have a wicked sense of humor – not that anyone would guess it now.

I looked down at the paper, zooming in on the originating email address. "And how," I asked through clenched teeth, "did you get into my email account?"

"I'll tell you later." His voice hardened. "Now, for the last time, get packing."

I glared up at him. "Why?"

"Because," he said, "if you're still here tomorrow, it won't be *me* you've got to worry about."

I shook my head. "What are you getting at?"

He reached into his pocket and pulled out a cellphone. His fingers skimmed across the smooth screen, and he thrust the phone in my direction. Silently, I took it and looked down. My eyebrows furrowed. "But that doesn't make any sense," I said.

"You're telling *me*."

From somewhere in the apartment, a door slammed. I heard soft footsteps coming fast. A split-second later, my bedroom door flew open. The doorknob slammed into the neighboring wall, sending bits of plaster tumbling onto the faded carpet.

I jumped to my feet.

Oh crap.

Maddie stood in the doorway. Her body was naked, and her eyes were blazing. Her long red hair was a wild mess. Either she'd just been attacked by a ferret, or – more likely – she'd just woken up from the best sex of her life.

Embarrassingly, I was rooting for the ferret.

Still, for someone who'd gotten lucky four times over, Maddie looked decidedly unhappy. "What. The. Hell!" she said.

It wasn't the first time I'd seen Maddie naked. She had a nice body, and apparently, didn't mind flaunting it. To me. To her boyfriends. To the maintenance guy, who surprise, surprise, always came the first time we called. Maybe that's why the thermostat kept breaking. Sabotage.

My gaze bounced from Maddie to Jake and back again. "It's not what it looks like," I said.

"Then why," she gritted out, "is *he* in your bedroom?" Her gaze flew to Jake. "And why the hell aren't you wearing a shirt?"

As if she didn't know.

"Because," Jake said, "you ripped the damn thing off. Remember?"

A choked sound escaped my lips, half snort, half laugh. This had to be a dream. No. A nightmare. I squeezed my eyes shut and pinched myself on the arm.

I didn't wake up.

Damn it.□

CHAPTER 3

Inside my bedroom, I opened my eyes just a crack. Maddie was staring at me with murder in her eye, as if I, not she, were flashing naked goodies all over the apartment.

When she spoke, her voice dripped venom. "And *this* is the thanks I get for letting you live here?"

"Well technically," I said, "I've been the one paying the rent so…"

"Shut up!" she said. She whirled to Jake. "And *you*."

Jake looked oddly unconcerned. "Yeah?"

"You're cheating on me?" Maddie said. "Already?"

Jake gave her a bored look. He didn't answer.

"And with *her*?" Maddie said. She said "her" like I was the Bubonic Plague.

"For me to cheat," Jake said, "we'd have to be a couple."

Her gaze narrowed. "What are you saying?"

"Nothing to say," Jake said.

I glanced from Maddie to Jake. She had been wild about him. And in spite of my own crazy mixed-up feelings, I hated the thought of causing trouble between them. Besides, I couldn't afford to make Maddie mad. Technically, this was her place, not mine.

"Uh, I'll leave you two alone," I said.

Maddie bared her teeth. "You do that."

Gripping the printout of that stupid resignation email, I snatched my purse off the dresser. The bus would be here any minute. If I hurried, maybe I could reclaim my job before it was lost for good.

"And Anna?" Maddie said.

Technically, my name wasn't Anna. But it *was* the name I'd been answering to lately. I turned around. "Yeah?"

She tossed a strand of tousled red hair over her bare shoulder. "Don't bother coming back."

I stared at her. "What?"

She put her hands on her naked hips. "You heard me," she said. "We're done, sister."

I blew out a breath. "Oh Maddie, come on." I turned to give Jake a pleading look. "Tell her."

"Tell her what?" he said.

I gritted my teeth. "Tell her that nothing happened."

He gave me a wolfish grin. "If you say so, baby."

The bastard.

Fifteen minutes later, I was lugging my small overnight bag down the dimly lit hallway. Behind me, Jake was carrying my large suitcase, mostly empty, in one hand, and my favorite reading lamp in the other.

I'd like to say I'd be going back for the rest of my stuff. But the sad truth was, this was all I had. Even the furniture in my bedroom, as craptastic as it was, belonged to Maddie's former roommate, who'd left on the quick side a couple months earlier when she'd been busted for prostitution.

On a cheerier note, she'd be back in six to twelve months.

Behind us, Maddie was screaming obscenities loud enough to wake the dead. Down the long hallway, apartment doors were swinging open, with heads on all sides peeking out to look. Maddie had thrown on a loose, silky bathrobe but hadn't bothered to tie it. It flapped loose behind her as she stalked down the hall behind us.

"Nice bush!" called the guy from 211, some college student who'd once helped me carry in some groceries. Maddie was a stripper. Technically, she had no bush. Or maybe that was the guy's point?

"Up yours!" Maddie said.

The guy shrugged. "I'm just saying."

"Well don't!" she yelled.

I turned around just in time to see Maddie make yet another lunge for Jake's arm. Like he'd done the previous ten times, he shook her off and kept on going.

"Please, Jay," she begged. "Talk to me, okay?"

He stopped and turned around. "It's Jake," he said.

"Yeah, I know," she stammered. "But it's a pet name. Jay. For Jake. See?"

"I'm not your pet," he said.

Her voice rose. "Yeah? Well you weren't complaining last night."

"Yeah," he said. "Because I wasn't listening."

Even to me, the words felt like a slap. Poor Maddie. Sure, she hadn't been the best roommate. And sure, she was kicking me out when I hadn't done anything wrong. Still, the way Jake was treating her, it almost hurt to watch.

Maddie glared at him. "You asshole," she said.

Glancing in my direction, Jake flicked his head toward the stairway. "Keep going," he told me. "And if you stop one more time, I'm dropping the lamp."

Behind him, Maddie made another lunge. With a guttural scream, she ripped the lamp out of his hands and hurled it straight toward me. I leapt to the side, and it whizzed inches past my head. It bounced off the door of 204 and clattered to the floor in three pieces.

A split-second later, the door flew open, and Julian, the building's undisputed tough guy, stuck his head out. "What the hell's going on?" he said.

"None of your damn business," Maddie said.

"Girl," he said, "you keep waking me up, and it's gonna be my business quick."

Her gaze narrowed. She turned toward me. She stuck out her arm and pointed a long finger in my direction. "She's stealing my stuff."

"Oh come on!" I said. "It's not your stuff. It's mine."

Again, Jake turned to face me. "Luna," he said through clenched teeth, "for the last time, keep moving."

"Or what?" I said. "You'll drop the lamp?" I glanced at the thing, lying in pieces just a few feet away. "You know what?" I dropped the overnight case. "I've had enough of you bossing me around."

"Hey!" Julian barked out toward us. "You stealing from my girl?"

Was he talking to me? Or Jake? Honestly, I had no idea. "We're not stealing anything," I called back. "And besides, she's only 'your girl' when she needs extra cash. You *do* know that, don't you?"

"Your ass," he said. "Julian Webster don't pay nobody for pussy."

Liar. According to Maddie, Julian paid for a whole bunch of stuff whenever he had the money, which granted, wasn't very often. As for Maddie, she bought condoms in bulk and went through them fast.

Maddie gave Julian a pleading look. "Baby," she said. "Stop her, will ya?"

Julian's gaze swiveled back to me. Between us stood Jake. Jake's gaze was on me, and his back was to Julian. Embarrassingly, Jake was still shirtless, with one hand now empty, and the other hand still clutching that giant suitcase.

I wanted to crawl into a hole and disappear. If the situation weren't so pathetic, I might have laughed. The whole thing felt like an old Jerry Springer rerun, starring *me* as the slutty, boyfriend-stealing hoochie.

It was ironic really, considering Jake and I had never so much as kissed.

"Anna!" Julian barked. "Get your ass back here." His voice ground to a low menace. "Now."

Slowly, Jake turned around, facing off in Julian's direction. "You got a problem?" Jake said.

Julian's eyebrows furrowed. "Hey, aren't you–"

"Holy shit," the guy from 211 said. "It *is* him." He turned to call into his apartment. "Wayne! Get your ass out here! Quick! You gotta see this!"

My gaze drifted from Jake to Julian, and finally to the guy in 211, who was gazing at Jake, star-struck, like he'd just seen his favorite movie star in the men's room.

This was getting way too weird. "Oh for crying out loud," I muttered. I picked up my overnight case and called out, "Forget it. Let's just go." I'd barely turned around when I heard a door slam. I whirled back just in time to see Julian lunge for Jake.

Well, this was just great.▯

CHAPTER 4

Like lightning, Jake dodged to the side. He blocked Julian's fist with a raised forearm. Faster than I might've thought possible, Jake dropped the suitcase and hit Julian with a wicked right hook that sent Julian sprawling backward.

Catching his balance, Julian lowered his head and charged again. Jake turned sideways and gave Julian an elbow to the neck, followed by kick to the stomach.

Julian flew backward and crashed into the opposite wall. His ass hit the floor, and he gave a low groan.

Maddie glared at him. "Julian, you pussy!" she screeched. "Get your ass up!"

"Screw you," he groaned. "No amount of pussy's worth this."

Jake turned toward me. "Luna," he said. "If you're not in the car in exactly one minute, I'm carrying you." His voice hardened. "And leaving your crap."

"It's not crap," I lied.

"Move it," he said.

Grumbling, I grabbed my overnight case and started walking toward the stairway. Behind me, Maddie was still chewing out Julian, who could barely get a word in edgewise. And the words he *did* get in? Well, those were mostly of the four-letter variety.

Carrying the case down the steps, I heard Jake following behind me. He *was* still bringing my big suitcase, right?

I turned to look over my shoulder. When I did, the small overnight case slipped from my grip. I whirled in time to see it tumble down the grubby stairway, bouncing end over end. Just before it reached the bottom, it flew open, leaving a scattered trail of socks, bras, panties and – as if it couldn't get any worse – my pink packet of birth control pills.

With a muttered curse, I plunged toward the mess, taking the stairs two at a time until I reached the path of destruction. Desperately, I started scooping up undergarments, wincing as I considered the grimy floor and what sort of unmentionable stuff might be sticking to my unmentionables.

I wanted to scream, but somewhere up the hall, Maddie and Julian were doing more than enough for everyone. When I glanced up to see if they were killing each other yet, all I saw was Jake, along with my giant suitcase, towering over me.

In his free hand, he held my packet of birth control pills, along with a black leather bra that dangled loose from his index finger. His gaze drifted to a pair of lacy red panties lying a few feet away.

I reached up and snatched the pills from his outstretched hand. I shoved them into my purse. "Now turn around," I said.

"Why?"

"Because I don't want you looking at my underpants. That's why."

He held out the leather bra by that same outstretched finger. "I *have* seen them before," he said.

Ignoring the bra, I dove for the panties. "Not mine, you haven't. And, just so you know, that bra's not mine."

The bra hit the stairs a split-second later. I ignored it. I hadn't been kidding.

Frantically, I snatched up the red panties and reached out

for the rest. With frantic scooping motions, I gathered up what remained, along with – as disgusting as it was – bits of random floor trash.

When my hands were overflowing, I looked down at the silky mess. Oh God. How many times would I have to wash this stuff before I'd ever considering wearing it again?

If only I had more money, I'd probably leave it all right here and be done with it. But I was dead-broke and now, apparently homeless. With a sigh, I dumped everything into my overnight case, slammed it shut, and stumbled to my feet.

Glancing up the staircase, I saw Maddie emerge from the hallway. With clenched fists, she started heading down the stairs toward us. Jake flicked his head toward the exit. "You first," he told me.

Hoisting my case upward, I bolted for the double-doors that led to the parking lot. With Jake behind me, I plunged outside and headed toward the place the sports car had been parked last night.

It was gone.

I whirled on Jake. "Where's your car?" I demanded.

"It'll be here," he said.

"It *will* be here?" I said. "Please tell me you're joking."

Suddenly, I heard the squeal of tires and the roar of an engine. An exotic-looking sports car – the same one I'd seen earlier – roared into the turnaround and skidded to a stop.

"See?" Jake said.

In front of us, twenty-something guy with sandy-colored hair jumped out of the driver's seat. He used the keyless remote to pop the trunk. Jake strode toward the trunk and tossed the giant suitcase into it. I followed suit, tossing in my smaller case and stepping out of the way. Jake slammed the trunk shut and strode around to the driver's side.

As I watched, the other guy dove past Jake and crawled into

the tiny backseat, leaving Jake to claim the driver's spot. Not knowing what else to do, I dashed to the passenger's side door, flung it open, and dove inside. I slammed the door just in time to see Maddie bolt out of the building, still mostly naked, with Julian on her heels.

Frantically, I looked to Jake. He held out his hand toward the guy in the back seat. "Keys," Jake said.

No keys appeared. My heart racing, I turned toward the back of the car. The guy was digging around in his front pants pocket. I glanced out my car window just in time to get a full-frontal of Maddie as she launched her nearly naked body against the passenger side door.

Hurling a stream of obscenities, Maddie reached up to smack the window with both palms.

Desperately, I whirled again toward the back seat. The stranger was staring, dumbstruck, at Maddie's naked breasts, squashed up against the glass.

"Keys!" I yelled.

The guy jerked back and gave a quick shake of his head. Finally, he yanked the keys from his pants pocket and tossed them to Jake, who caught them with one hand and turned to start the engine. With a soft chuckle, Jake shifted the car into gear and squealed out of the lot.

Looking out the back window, I saw Maddie and Julian, standing in the pitted parking lot, each flipping us the double-bird. Other tenants were streaming from the front doors – some looking at our car, and more looking at Maddie, who still hadn't tied the sash of her robe.

Modesty aside, wasn't she freezing? An unwelcome image snapped into my brain. Yes. She *had* been freezing, if her nipples had been any kind of indicator. Groaning, I turned around and sank back in my seat.

The guy in the back spoke. "Oh man, that was just gross."

What a liar. I'd seen the look on his face. He hadn't been grossed out. He'd been mesmerized. "Yup," I said. "Utterly disgusting."

"You got that right," he said. "Total loogie."

"What?" I glanced at the passenger's side window. Sure enough, something wet and slimy was dripping down the glass.

Somehow, that was the final straw. I whirled toward Jake, sitting shirtless in the driver's seat. He was navigating city traffic with one eye on the road, and the other eye on the rearview mirror.

"What the hell!" I yelled.

"Hey, she was *your* roommate."

"Oh come on," I said. "That wasn't Maddie's fault. It was yours."

His eyebrows rose. "So, you're saying there's a problem?"

"You could say that." There were so many problems, I didn't know where to begin. I had no job. I had no place to live. I had no money. I gave Jake a withering look. And once I killed him, I had no place to bury the body.

"Some day," Jake said, "you'll thank me."

"Yeah, right." More likely, I'd be digging a Jake-sized hole in someone's cellar. I glanced out the car window and counted to ten. And then, I counted again. Finally, taking a long, deep breath, I made myself ask, "So where are we going, exactly?"

"My place."

Sports car or not, visions of a slumlord's dream skittered across my brain. I turned to the stranger in the back. "Do you know where he lives?"

"Sure," the guy said. "*Everyone* knows where Jake lives."

"Well, I don't."

"No shit?" the guy said. "You been living under a rock or something?"

I turned to Jake. "Why am I supposed to know where you

live?"

Still driving, Jake shrugged. Again, I turned toward the guy in the back. "And who are you?" I asked.

The guy grinned. "I'm Trey. His assistant."

I turned to Jake. "You have an assistant?"

"Apparently," Jake said.

Apparently? What did that mean? I turned to Trey. "What do you do, exactly?"

The guy slid a wary look in Jake's direction. "Whatever he wants."

"Well that's a pretty broad job description," I said.

Trey's grin widened. "Don't you know it."

Jake, with his left hand still draped over the steering wheel, reached toward the back with his right. He opened his hand, palm up. "Shirt," he said.

Trey reached down into a thick black satchel. He pulled out a cream-colored dress shirt with the tags still attached. Pulling a small pair of scissors from his pocket, Trey snipped off the tags and draped the shirt over Jake's open palm.

I glanced down at the fallen tags and caught my breath. If that shirt was the real deal, it cost nearly as much as my rent. I gave Jake a sideways glance and instantly regretted it.

Still shirtless, he leaned back in his seat. He looked like sin and sex and something a girl like me would be smart to avoid. I hadn't always been smart. I straightened in the seat. Well I was smart now. I felt myself nod. Yup. Utterly reformed.

Next to me, Jake was shrugging into his shirt. His ab muscles contracted, making the washboard shadows twist and shift in the morning light. My tongue brushed my upper lip. I sucked it back in and clamped my lips shut.

Annoyed – half with him and half with myself – I opened my mouth to ask, "Aren't you gonna pull over to do that?"

"Nah," he said. "I do this all the time. No big deal."

I glanced back at Trey, who gave me a solemn nod. "It's true," he said.

I leaned back and closed my eyes.

"If you're planning to sleep," Jake said, "forget it."

I didn't bother to open my eyes. "Why's that?" I said.

"Because," he said, "you've got some explaining to do."

My eyes flew open, and I whirled to face him. "Me?" I said. "*I* have some explaining to do? Well, that's rich."

"You can start any time," he said. ☐

CHAPTER 5

Inside the car, I gave Jake a murderous glare. "Let me get this straight. You barge into *my* place—"

"Technically," he said, "I was invited."

"Not by me," I told him. "And what about Maddie? She really liked you, you know."

Jake's jaw tightened. "Did it sound like she was complaining?"

Did he mean last night? God, what a bastard. I stared over at him. "In case you forgot, she *did* complain," I said. "Remember? On the way out?"

Jake gave something like a shrug. "Eh, I'm used to that."

I made a sound of disgust. "So what'd you do this morning? Did you wake up and say to yourself, 'Hey, I think I'll ruin someone's life today.'"

"Whose life are we talking about?" he asked.

As if he didn't know. "Mine," I said. "Obviously." True, Maddie wasn't happy right now either, but at least she still had a job and a place to live.

"I had to get you out of there," he said.

"Is that so?" I said. "Why?"

"You know why."

"Actually, I don't." Aside from that strange text on his

phone, he'd offered up no good reason for what he'd done this morning. "*You're* the one who has some explaining to do." I turned toward the guy in the back. "Don't you think?"

"Me?" Trey said, glancing toward Jake. "I think whatever *he* thinks."

God, what a butt-kisser. Maybe Jake *was* his employer.

"Trey," Jake said. "Headphones."

Without missing a beat, Trey reached into that same black satchel. He pulled out a thick set of headphones and slipped them on over his ears. From somewhere on the floor, he pulled out a sleek-looking notebook computer and opened it up onto his lap. He looked down at the screen and started tapping away.

I turned toward Jake. I mimicked him talking to his so-called assistant. "Trey. Headphones." Then, in my normal voice, I said, "You know, that was really rude, don't you?"

"To who?"

"Trey. Obviously."

"He doesn't mind," Jake said.

"How do *you* know?"

"Because it's in his job description."

"Seriously?" I glanced toward the back seat. "Uh, Trey?" I said.

He ignored me.

"Don't worry," Jake said. "I'm paying him plenty. So go on. Spill it."

This was beyond strange. Jake had come from a poor family, and that was putting it mildly. I glanced around, taking in the exotic car, the designer clothes, and the professional butt-kisser in the back seat. Since when did Jake Bishop have employees? As far as I knew, he'd never even *been* an employee, much less an employer.

Stalling, I snuck another glance at Trey before returning my attention to Jake. I lowered my voice. "Exactly how much are you paying him?" I asked.

"If you want, you can ask *him*," Jake said. "Otherwise, none of your business."

"Oh, so now you're being rude to me?" My gaze narrowed. "In case you forgot, I don't work for you. Remember?"

"So?"

"So as far as taking your crap?" I said. "It's not in *my* job description. Alright?"

Thinking of job-descriptions, I wanted to groan. Until this morning, I *did* have a job. Maybe there'd been a description. Who knows? It's not like I'd asked for one. At least I still had the bartending gig, but that was part-time, nights only. The other job – the one I'd just lost – was full-time.

Sure, the hours could be brutal, and I had to work a few Saturdays, like today for instance. But in sixty days, I might've even gained health insurance. No way I'd be giving up that job without a fight. I reached for my phone and started scrolling through my contacts.

"Calling someone?" Jake asked.

"Yeah. My employer."

"You don't have an employer," he said. "Remember?"

I found the contact and pressed the button. "Shh!"

He gave a slow shake of his head. "Not a good idea."

"Be quiet," I hissed, listening as the phone began to ring on the other end. I glanced out the window, watching as we passed an ornate bank building with marble columns and big double doors. Things were getting nicer with every mile we traveled away from Maddie's. No surprise there.

Finally, Vonnie answered with a curt, "Hello."

"Hey, Vonnie," I said. "It's me. Anna."

She made no response. My hands grew clammy as the silence stretched out. Next to me, Jake gave a low chuckle and said under his breath, "Anna. Right."

I gave him a dirty look. I'd been going by the name Anna for a few weeks now. So far, I liked it. It was a ton better than my given name, anyway. I turned away, huddling against the passenger side door as I spoke into the phone. "About that email," I said.

Her voice was clipped. "What about it?"

"Well, the thing is," I said, "it wasn't real."

She said nothing. I waited until the silence became awkward and then said, "Vonnie? Are you there?"

Her voice was cold. "Uh-huh."

"See, my email was hacked and—"

"Uh-huh."

"And anyway," I continued in a rush. "I didn't *really* quit."

On the other end, I heard a hard, scoffing sound. "And I suppose you didn't *really* call me a whacked-out control freak?"

"Whacked out?" I swallowed. "Control freak?" I whirled toward Jake and gave him a what-the-hell look. Obviously, he hadn't shown me *all* of that email exchange.

He gave me a half shrug and kept on driving.

Desperately, I spoke into the phone. "That wasn't me," I said.

"I don't care if it's out of character—"

"No," I said. "I mean it *literally* wasn't me."

"Right," she said. "A hacker? *That's* your story?"

"It's not a story," I said. "It's the truth."

"Uh-huh. So who was this 'hacker' of yours?"

I opened my mouth and hesitated. Would it be better if Vonnie thought I was hacked by a stranger? Or by someone I knew? Screw it. I took a deep breath and went with the truth. "It was this guy I used to know." I glared over at him. "And I'm pretty sure he's flat-out crazy."

"Right," she said.

"Honest."

"So what is it?" she said. "You want your job back?" She gave a humorous laugh. "What happened? Your other job fell through?"

"Other job? What other job?" I didn't recall seeing anything in that email about another job. "There *is* no other job," I told her. At least, there was no other *daytime* job. The bartending gig was nights, so that didn't count, right?

"Uh-huh."

"You've got to believe me," I said. "I don't even know why the guy did it." I turned to give Jake another long, murderous look. Into the phone, I spoke through clenched teeth. "But trust me, he's gonna be really, *really* sorry when I get ahold of him."

"You know who's sorry?" Vonnie said. "Me."

"What do you mean?"

"I mean," she said, "I took a chance on you. I had a stack of resumes a mile high. But I chose you." She made a sound of disgust. "And you didn't even last a month."

"I did too," I said.

"And then," she continued as if I hadn't spoken, "you wait 'til our biggest event of the year, and you quit. By email. With no notice." Her voice rose. "And you insult me in the bargain."

"But I *didn't* insult you. It wasn't me." My palms were sweaty. "And I didn't quit."

"Yeah?" she said. "Then why aren't you here?"

I glanced around the car. "Uh, that's a really good question…"

"In case you forgot," she said, "we start at eight."

"Well," I stammered, "there was this thing at my apartment." I sucked in a breath. "Never mind. That's not your problem. I get it. Just give me a half-hour. I'll be there. Alright?"

"You know what?" she said. "I don't have time for this. I've got a replacement to train."

"You replaced me?" My heart sank. "Already?"

"Sheldon had a friend."

Damn it. "Vonnie, please."

"And just between us," she said, "I wouldn't be using me as a reference if I were you." And with that, she hung up.

I whirled to Jake. "You jerk!" I said.

"Told you it was a bad idea."

I wanted to throttle him. "Why the hell would you do this to me?"

"For one thing," he said, "that job sucked."

"It did not," I told him.

He turned to give me a look. "So you *wanted* to work as a hotel clerk?"

"I wasn't just a clerk," I said. "It was a foot in the door, you know?" My degree was in hospitality management. When not manning the front desk, I was part of their event-planning team. If all went well, I wouldn't have been manning that front desk forever.

"And they paid you squat," Jake said.

I glared at him. "How would you know?"

"Not hard to figure out."

I gave him a dirty look. "You owe me a job," I said.

"So I'll get you one," he said.

"Yeah, right."

"First things first," he said. "About that text—"

I buried my face in my hands. In my concern for everything I'd just lost – my apartment, my job, my sanity – I'd almost forgotten about that stupid text. Besides, it still didn't make any sense.

Jake made a show of glancing toward the back seat. "The longer you stall," he said, "the longer Trey wears those things."

"Like you care."

"You're right," he said. "I don't. But I figured you might."

I peeked around my seat. In the back, Trey was tapping

away on the computer keys. Working? Or playing? He didn't look *too* miserable. Then again, he *was* being paid. Supposedly.

I looked toward Jake and held out my hand. "First," I said, "let me see your phone."

He glanced at my hand. "Why?"

"That text you showed me, I want to read it again."

Silently, Jake pulled out his phone and handed it over. It was a similar model to my own, and I slid my finger across the smooth screen. I frowned. "It wants a password," I said.

Jake said nothing.

My fingers waited, still poised at the password prompt. "Well?" I said.

He glanced out his window and said, "Luna."

"Yeah? What?"

Looking oddly uncomfortable, Jake cleared his throat. "That's the password."

I gave him a good, long look. His password was my name? "Really?" I said. "Why?"

"Just read the text," he said.

My mind whirling, I tapped in the password. When the screen came to life, that previous text was still showing. Looking down, I felt my eyebrows furrow.

It still didn't make any sense.

CHAPTER 6

I squinted down at the text again. From the driver's seat, Jake said, "Read it out loud."

Unsure, I glanced toward the back seat, where Trey was still tapping on his computer.

"Trey!" Jake said.

The guy didn't even flinch. Either he was used to Jake barking out his name, or those headphones were a lot nicer than anything *I* had ever used. Maybe it was a little of both.

Jake returned his attention to me. "Scroll up," he said. "There's more than what I showed you before."

Reluctantly, I returned my gaze to the phone. I scrolled upward. Starting with the earliest text, I began to read, translating the text shortcuts to actual words. "Looking for a girl from your old neighborhood."

I scrolled down. "And you ask, 'Who?' And they say—" At the next words, heat flooded my face, and I stopped reading.

"What?" Jake said. "You don't wanna read it?"

As if he didn't know. I looked down, reading the words again in my head. *Jenna Moon. Or whatever she's going by. Chick changes her name like once a month.*

"Oh shut up," I said, looking over at Jake. "So they're obviously looking for me. But who is it?"

"You tell me," Jake said.

"Hey, it's *your* phone," I reminded him.

His jaw tightened. "I want to hear it from you."

"Oh come on," I said. "How would *I* know?"

Jake gave me a dubious look.

Okay, so I had a few guesses. But none I'd bet my life on. "Honestly," I said. "I really don't know."

"Then keep reading," he said.

I looked down. "Okay, so *you* ask, 'Why?', and they say—" My stomach clenched. "—to settle a score." I looked up. "What does *that* mean?"

He flicked his gaze to the phone. "Go on."

Again, I scrolled down. "So you ask, 'What score?' And they say, 'She stole something. I need to get it back. ASAP." I looked toward Jake. "But that's a total lie."

"Yeah?"

"Definitely," I said. "I didn't steal anything."

"Uh-huh."

"I didn't," I insisted. "I'm no thief."

He leaned back in his seat. "Now that's funny."

"Funny how?"

At the next stoplight, Jake turned to give me a long look. "You stole from *me*."

At this, I felt my face grow uncomfortably warm. I knew exactly what he meant. "Your motorcycle?" I said. "That doesn't count, and you know it."

"Yeah? Why's that?"

"Because," I said, "I was just messing with you. And besides, you got it back, didn't you?"

That was how long ago? At least seven years. I'd been only sixteen at the time. Back then, Jake had been a twenty-something bad-ass with a terrible reputation. I'd taken that bike on a dare. I bit my lip. Okay, so it wasn't *only* because of the dare.

Mostly, I'd been hoping for a ride.

I'd fantasized about it, actually. In my adolescent dreams, I saw myself riding behind him, feeling the wind in my hair and savoring the tautness of his abs as I wrapped my arms around his waist and held on for dear life.

In my fantasies, I pressed my cheek against his muscular back and squeezed my thighs against his tight hips. And maybe, just maybe, when we stopped, Jake would turn around and kiss me like I'd always wanted him to. And then, somehow, in that impossible moment, he'd realize that I was the girl for him, even if I *was* still in high school.

It never happened.

Now, inside his car, I heard myself sigh. I didn't get that ride. There was no kiss. And I'd almost gotten arrested for grand-theft, well, motorcycle, I guess. Worst of all, Jake had called me a brat, like I was still a chubby-cheeked kid who played with dolls.

That had been the worst part.

Sitting in the passenger's seat, I stiffened my spine. That was a long time ago, and I'd grown up a whole lot since then. I didn't want a ride, and I sure as hell didn't want to be Jake's girlfriend, not that he'd offered.

"So you *didn't* steal the bike?" he said.

"It's not stealing if you return it," I said.

"Uh-huh."

I turned to face him. "Will you *please* stop saying that?"

"Why?"

"Because it's annoying, that's why."

"You know what's 'annoying'?" he said. "Losing your motorcycle to a sixteen-year-old smart-ass."

"Oh quit whining," I said. "That was like a hundred years ago."

"It was seven," he said.

"Close enough," I said. "Besides, it's not like I actually drove it. Remember?" With the help of a couple girlfriends, I'd rolled the thing at least a mile though. Probably, I should have ridden it all by myself. Then I would have gotten at least *some* fun out of the deal.

When I'd been younger, I'd watched as my older sister rode around with Jake's brother, who was practically Jake's twin. Just like everyone else, I'd been shocked as hell when she'd hooked up with a Bishop. To think, she had always been the good girl in the family.

Me, not so much.

Still, the thing with Jake's brother had cost my usually smart sister plenty – a full scholarship and half her sanity. The way I saw it, she'd dodged a huge bullet the day she left that guy.

Bishops were nothing but trouble.

Inside the car, I glanced toward Jake. In profile, he looked just as good, maybe better, than I remembered. My heart gave a little flutter. Damn it. If my own sister had finally wised up, why couldn't I?

From the driver's seat, Jake gestured toward the phone. "Keep reading," he said.

Reluctantly, I returned my attention to his cell phone. Funny, I'd almost completely forgotten about those text messages. That had to be Jake's fault too, right?

See? He *was* trouble.

I resumed reading. "So you ask, 'Stole what?'" I scrolled down. "And they say—"I glanced toward Jake.

"Read it," he said.

I didn't want to. But I did anyway. "A little black book."

Oh crap.

Slowly, I turned toward Jake. "Wait a minute," I said, my mouth feeling way too dry. "You're not taking me to *him*, are you?" I reached toward the door handle and eyed the next red light.

"What are you gonna do?" Jake said. "Jump?"

I bit my lip. "Maybe."

"Well don't," he said.

"Why not?"

"Because," he said, "Rango can kiss my ass."

I swallowed. "He can?"

"Yeah," Jake said. "Because from now on, you're with me."

Something about the way he said it made butterflies dance in my stomach. I didn't know what to say, so I said nothing. When we reached the light, Jake turned to face me. Briefly, his gaze dipped to my lips, and I felt my tongue brush the back of my teeth.

Okay, so the guy had just spent most of the previous night screwing my roommate. I should've been disgusted. Part of me *was* disgusted. But there was another part – the remnant of the girl I used to be – that was more than a little intrigued. What exactly had he been doing to her?

Somehow, I found my voice. "I'm not following."

His dark gaze met mine, and I saw possessiveness in his eyes. If looks could claim, I'd have already been his.

But then, he spoke in a voice cold enough to give me goosebumps – not the good kind, the other kind. "No one," he said, "screws with my family."

I stared over at him. "Huh?"

A few cars behind us, a horn honked. I glanced ahead. The light was green. Jake hit the accelerator, and we roared forward.

Jake glanced in the rear-view mirror. His jaw tightened. A horn honked again.

I refused to be distracted. "What do you mean, family?" I said.

"Not now," Jake said.

"Why not now?" I demanded.

Jake reached back to wave a hand in front of Trey's face. Trey looked up and removed the headphones.

Jake turned to me. "Hang on," he said.

Before I could ask why, he whipped the car onto a narrow side street. I glanced outside my window. There was barely any traffic, but along the sidewalks, I saw a fair number of pedestrians, some in business attire, some in workout clothes.

We weren't speeding, but something about Jake's demeanor was making me uneasy. I glanced behind us, but saw nothing out of the ordinary, just some oversized luxury car, mostly white, except for a big gold grill that took up most of the front end.

I returned my attention to Jake. "So," I said, "you live around here?"

"No."

"Oh fine. I give up." I closed my eyes and leaned back in the seat. Maybe if I were lucky, I'd wake up in my own bed – correction, in Monica's old bed, before she was busted – and before Jake got me fired and kicked out of my sorry excuse for an apartment.

"Luna," Jake said.

I didn't bother to open my eyes. "What?"

"Brace yourself."□

CHAPTER 7

It all happened so fast, I still don't know what startled me more – the crunching of metal, the tightening of my seatbelt, or the whiplashing sensation that rocked my body forward, even as the seatbelt held me tight.

With a shriek, I sat up and looked around. We weren't moving. Not anymore. And neither was anybody else. From the sidewalk, the pedestrians had stopped to gawk at us like spectators at a zoo.

Jake reached for my arm. "You okay?" he asked.

My heart was racing. "I think so." I gave myself a little shake. "Yeah, I'm okay."

Jake's gaze skimmed my body, and he gave a quick nod. "Good," he said. "Now stay in the car, alright?"

"Why?" I asked.

"Just do it."

But what about Trey? I whirled toward the backseat. Trey, apparently unharmed, was grinning like he'd just lost his mind. With a half-crazed chuckle, he reached down to fumble with a small black carry-case.

"What are you so happy about?" I said.

Trey glanced out the car's back window. "Showtime," he said.

"What?" I followed his gaze. Directly behind us, a massive guy in a sports jersey was getting out of that same luxury car that I'd noticed trailing us just moments earlier. The car's massive grill was a crumpled golden mess, along with the rest of the front end.

As for the guy, he looked surprisingly okay, even if he did look mad as hell. When the stranger turned to glare in our direction, I felt myself swallow.

My heart hammering, I turned to Jake. "What going on?" I asked.

"Later," he said.

I frowned.

"Don't worry," Jake said with that same old cocky grin. "I got this." His smile faltered. "Sure you're okay?"

Why was he smiling at all? I didn't see anything to smile about. "No, I'm *not* okay," I said.

His grin disappeared. "You serious?" His gaze dipped to my body before returning to my face. "What's wrong? You hurt?"

"No." I glanced down. "I mean, I don't think so, but—"

Suddenly, a huge, lurking form appeared just outside the driver's side window. It was the man from the white car. "You cocksucker!" he bellowed. "Get out of the car. Now."

Jake spared the guy half a glance. He held up a hand. "Hang on," he told the guy through the glass.

"I'm not gonna hang on," the guy said. He reached for the door handle and gave it a useless tug. "Get out!"

Holy crap. Seeing the guy up close, I realized something. I'd seen him on TV, hawking some popular sports drink. Wasn't he a famous linebacker or something? Desperately, I searched my memories and came up with only one word.

Chainsaw.

That was the guy's nickname. But it couldn't be. Famous football players didn't go around rear-ending people for no good reason.

Did they?

No. They didn't. It had to be someone else.

I lunged for Jake's arm. "Don't go out there," I said.

"Why not?" Jake asked.

"Oh for God's sake," I said, "look at him. The guy's huge. And he's totally ticked off."

Jake was grinning again. "Yeah. I know."

"Why the hell are you smiling?" I scanned his head for injuries. Either he'd suffered one hell of a bump to the head or he'd totally lost it.

I whirled toward the back seat. Trey was holding out a camera, capturing, from what I could tell, Jake and the guy just outside the car. Trey was grinning too.

Obviously, they'd both lost their minds. I gave Trey a pleading look. "Aren't you gonna do something?" I asked.

"Yeah. Totally," Trey said.

"Well?" I said.

"Well what?"

"Well, what are you gonna do?"

"I'm doing it," he said.

I gave him an exasperated look. "Taking pictures?"

"Video," he corrected.

"Oh, come on!" I said. "How is that helpful?"

When he answered with only a shrug, I gave up and turned my attention to the guy outside. He was leaning down, hollering spit-laden obscenities through the glass. His face was red. His fists were clenched. He looked like he'd kill the next person he came across.

Apparently, that person was supposed to be Jake.

In spite of the commotion, Jake looked oddly unconcerned. "Trey, you ready?" Jake asked.

"Yup," Trey said. "Whenever you are."

My heart was pounding. "Ready for what?" I asked.

Neither guy answered.

With an expression of near-boredom, Jake calmly pressed a control-switch on his armrest. Slowly, the driver's side window slid down. Jake looked up at the big guy, who'd grown suddenly quiet, as if he couldn't quite believe that Jake would do something so incredibly stupid.

That made two of us.

"Can I help you?" Jake asked.

The guy found his voice. "Yeah," he said. "Get out of the car, asshole."

Jake looked at him with mild curiosity. "Hey, don't I know you from someplace?"

The guy's eyebrows furrowed. "What the hell's *that* supposed to mean?"

With that same cocky grin, Jake turned toward Trey, who was still holding out the video recorder. Jake said in a loud stage-whisper. "I think somebody's angry."

What the hell? Was he taunting this guy on purpose? I had to stop him. I reached frantically for the armrest, seeking the control-switch to roll up Jake's window. I pressed the first switch I came across, and then stifled a gasp as my own window began to slide slowly down.

"Damn it," I muttered and reached for the next control over. I pressed it. Nothing happened. I pressed it again. Nothing. I looked desperately toward Jake. Suddenly, a giant fist shot through his open window. It caught Jake on the side of his face. Jake's head jerked sideways. I stifled a scream.

Jake made a sound. A laugh? No. It couldn't be.

Could it?

CHAPTER 8

Frozen in shock, I stared dumb-struck at Jake. A thin stream of blood trickled from his nose. He made the sound again. Another laugh. This time, I was sure of it. What the hell was wrong with him?

Again, Jake turned toward Trey. "Yup," Jake said. "He's angry alright."

Still holding out the recorder, Trey gave a quick, happy nod.

"What the hell's wrong with you?" I yelled, not even sure who I was yelling at. Trey? Jake? The maniac outside?

It didn't matter. None of them were paying me the slightest bit of attention. When the guy's fist flew inside the car again, Jake bobbed his head to the side and gave a low chuckle. "Missed me," he said.

With a guttural roar, the guy reached in with two meaty arms. He grabbed Jake's torso, and yanked Jake up upward, like he wanted to rip Jake right out of his seat.

"Stop it!" I screamed. Frantically, I lunged for Jake as he practically flew out the car window and disappeared from sight.

Gasping for breath, I reached for my door handle and pushed. Nothing happened. I pushed harder. I whirled toward Trey. "Why won't it open?" I yelled.

Trey gave a silent shrug.

"What's the matter with you?" I screamed. "Put down that thing and help, will you?"

Trey, video-recorder and all, swiveled in my direction. What the hell? Was he filming *me*?

"That's not helping!" I yelled.

Something thudded against the driver's side door. I whirled to see Jake's back pressed against the driver's side glass. The other guy, obviously crazed, was swinging wildly – sometimes hitting, sometimes missing as Jake dodged to the right and to the left.

The guy pulled Jake off his feet and slammed his body onto the hood of the car. Jake rolled to the side. The other guy dove on top of him. I watched in stunned disbelief as the guy grabbed Jake by the shirt to lift him up for another impact.

But then, Jake bucked upward. He spread his arms wide. Like lightning, Jake slammed his fists into the guy's ears. The guy struggled backwards, and Jake kneed him in the groin. With a sound that wasn't quite human, the guy slid off the hood and disappeared from sight.

I heard a scuffling sound from somewhere in the back seat. I whirled around to see Trey, still holding out that stupid recorder. Carefully, he climbed over the center console and into the driver's seat.

I glared at him. "What are you doing?"

"Better view up here," he said.

"You dipshit!" I said. "Go help him."

The guy snorted. "Like he needs *my* help. Now shush, I'm working, alright?"

"Did you just shush me?"

"Shh!" he said.

"Oh for God's sake." Turning, I craned my head to see what was going on outside. Around us, the small crowd had somehow tripled in size. Again, I tried the door. Again, it didn't budge. I whirled toward Trey. "How come the door won't open?" I asked.

He put a finger to his lips.

"If you shush me—" I said.

"Shh!"

"Damn it," I muttered.

Like some sort of crazed bird-watcher, Trey kept his camera trained toward the front of the vehicle. Why, I had no idea. We couldn't see a darn thing from inside the car.

Still, I knew something *had* to be happening, because the crowd was going absolutely nuts. Some were cheering, some were hollering encouragement, and a few of them were holding out their phones to capture whatever was going on.

Was I the only sane person in the world?

Craning my neck, I hollered toward the crowd just outside my car window. "What's happening?" I called out to no one in particular.

A tall guy near the front said, "Fight."

"No kidding!" I yelled. "Who's winning?"

The guy shrugged.

With a low curse, I tried the door-handle again. Nothing happened. Frantically, I unbuckled my seat belt and pushed myself up to crawl out my car window. I was maybe halfway out when two bodies thudded against the front bumper.

I ducked back inside and watched in open-mouthed horror as Jake and the big guy faced off. Jake's shirt was torn and splattered with red, but the rest of him looked surprisingly unscathed. In contrast, the stranger's face was a bloody mess. The guy was swinging wildly as Jake bobbed and weaved, avoiding blow after blow.

And then, Jake reached out. He grabbed a handful of the guy's shirt and somehow managed to toss the guy forward, sending him sliding, face down, across the hood of the car.

The guy kicked back, catching Jake in the chest. When Jake reeled backward, the guy crawled forward until his face, leaving a trail of blood across the glass, was mashed against the front windshield mere inches in front of me.

"Oh my God," I said, whirling toward Trey. "Do something!"

Holding the camera-phone steady in his right hand, Trey reached out with his left. He hit a switch near the steering wheel. A stream of water squirted across the windshield's glass. A moment later, the wipers started moving back and forth, whacking the guy in the face.

"That's not what I meant!" I screamed.

In front of me, the wipers were still going strong, leaving a trail of soggy blood as the guy sputtered and tried to swat the wipers aside.

From the driver's seat, Trey snickered.

"It's not funny!" I said.

And then, as if my prayers were answered, I saw the flashing of police lights. On the hood, the big guy was still sputtering. Beside me, Trey was still filming. In front of the car, Jake was still standing.

I breathed a sigh of relief. Thank God.

And then, through the blood-smeared glass, Jake's gaze zoomed in on me. When he caught my eye, he gave me that same cocky grin I'd seen a million times in my memories.

Oh yeah. I'd seen that smile before. It did the same thing now as it did back then. God, he was such an ass. But I couldn't help it. There was a part of me that wanted to smile back.

CHAPTER 9

A few minutes later, I was standing outside the car along with Jake, Trey, and the stranger, who was throwing a massive hissy-fit. Two policemen – one about my parent's age, and one not much older than me – were trying to sort through the whole ugly mess.

Around us, the crowd hadn't moved. I could see why.

The big guy was yelling, "Arrest this motherfucker, right now!"

"Sir," the older policeman said in a bored tone, "I'll tell you again. Let's keep it clean, alright?"

"And I'll tell *you* again," the stranger said. "Arrest him now, or you'll be hearing from my lawyer." The stranger turned to Jake. "And *you'll* be hearing from my lawyer too. Got it?"

"Yeah?" Jake said with a look of polite interest. "What does she look like?"

"Who?" the guy said.

"Your lawyer."

"It's not a 'she'," the guy said. "It's a 'he.'"

"Oh," Jake said. "Then forget it."

"God, you are such a pig," I said.

"No law against that," Jake said. He turned to the younger of the two cops. "Is there?"

"No sir," the policeman said.

"Sir?" I said under my breath.

The officer turned to face me. "What's that?" he asked.

I shook my head. "Nothing."

When the older officer went to retrieve something from the police car, the younger officer lowered his voice and said, "I know I shouldn't ask, but can I get your autograph?"

"You arrest him," the stranger said, "and then we'll talk. Maybe get you some good seats too."

"Sir," the officer said, "I wasn't talking to you."

I looked around. Then who was he talking to?

"Got a pen?" Jake asked.

Grinning, the officer pulled out a pen and small notepad. He thrust it in Jake's direction. "Can you make it out to Seth?"

"You got it," Jake said.

As I watched, Jake scribbled something onto the officer's notepad and handed it back.

"This is such bullshit," the stranger said. He pointed back toward his own vehicle. "Look at my car. It's a mess."

I turned to look. It *was* a mess. The front grill was smashed in, and the gold hood ornament was dangling sideways from the crumpled hood. While we'd been talking, Trey had sidled away from Jake and was now circling the stranger's vehicle. Trey stopped near the back of the car and studied the license plate. He grinned.

I returned my gaze to the stranger. His car wasn't the only thing that was a mess. The guy looked like he'd been put through the ringer, literally. His shirt was ripped, his hair was soggy, and his face was swollen and smeared with streaks of blood.

I glanced over at Jake. His bloody shirt looked nearly shredded too, but his face looked fine. It seemed odd, considering he'd taken at least one punch to the face, and probably more. I squinted for a better look. Other than a scrape across his cheek, he looked the same as always.

My gaze traveled from his full lips to his dark eyes. Catching my eye, he gave me a wink. My stomach fluttered, and I felt myself swallow. I gave my head a quick shake. I wasn't a teenager anymore, so there was no need to act like one.

I was done crushing on Jake Bishop, no matter what he was doing to my insides. With an effort, I pulled my gaze from Jake's and zoomed in on Trey, who had just returned from checking out the stranger's car.

Trey cleared his throat and tapped the guy on the shoulder.

The guy whirled on him. "What?" he bellowed.

"Your tags are expired," Trey said.

"Huh?" the guy said.

Trey pointed toward the guy's vehicle. "The license plate. The sticker says last year."

"Blow me, pipsqueak," the guy said.

"Sir," the older cop said, returning from the police car, "for the last time. Let's keep it civil." He glanced toward the guy's car. "And," he said, pulling out a citation book. "Did you know your plates are expired?"

"Told ya," Trey said. "So who's the pipsqueak now?"

"Get bent," the guy muttered.

The older cop finished writing a ticket and handed it over to the big guy, who snatched it out of the officer's hand and said, "I'm still pressing charges."

Across from him, Jake laughed. "For what?"

The guy glared over at him. "Assault, vandalism, reckless driving." His gaze narrowed. "Being a douche."

"Gee, I haven't been called *that* before," Jake said.

"Actually," Trey said, "you have. Just yesterday, in fact."

"Yeah, well." Jake reached up to rub the back of his neck. He turned to the younger officer. "Are we done here?" He turned to flash me a quick grin. "I've got to get my girl back home."

I swallowed. His girl? Home? I knew he was joking, but my stomach did that fluttering thing again just the same.

"Yeah, we're done," the officer told Jake. "Unless you want to press charges?"

"Hey!" the stranger said. "Aren't you listening? *I'm* the one who wants to press charges."

Jake gave a low chuckle. "Is that so?" He flicked his head toward Trey. "Show him," Jake said.

Grinning, Trey held up his video recorder.

The stranger's gaze narrowed. "What the hell is that?"

Now Jake was grinning too. "Guess," he said.

The guy looked heavenward and closed his eyes. "Shit," he said. "Not again."

"Not what again?" I asked.

"I'll show you later," Jake said.

From somewhere in the crowd, a female voice called out, "Jake! Jake! Over here!"

Jake turned to look. So did I. The voice belonged to a buxom blonde in a tight white T-shirt. She was bouncing up and down and waving at him with both arms. "I love you!" she called.

As we all watched, she started tugging at the bottom of her T-shirt. She'd lifted it just above her navel when the guy next to her yanked the fabric down and gave her a murderous glare. Gripping her forearm, he started hustling her off toward a nearby building – some three-story apartment complex called The Meadows.

I sidled closer to Jake. "Who was that girl?"

Jake shrugged. "Got me."

I shook my head, trying to make sense of it all. "Well, she obviously knows *you*," I said. "In fact, almost everyone does.

Why *is* that?"

His gaze held amusement and maybe a hint of something else. Flirtation? "Not everyone," he said.

I felt my tongue brush my suddenly dry lips. "That's no kind of answer," I said. "Seriously, who was she?"

He flicked his gaze to the apartment complex. "You wanna ask her?" he said. "Be my guest."

I glanced toward the building. "You think I won't?" Obviously, Jake didn't know who he was dealing with. I turned to march away.

Jake gripped my arm. "Don't," he said.

I turned to face him. "Why not?"

"Because," he said, "you're staying with me."

"So much for being your guest," I muttered.

"Listen," he said. "You *are* my guest. And you're gonna stay my guest. At least 'til this blows over." He glanced toward the building. "This other stuff, it's nothing."

I crossed my arms and stared up at him. "Nothing?" I said. "That's your story?"

"I'll fill you in when we get home. Alright?"

"Home?"

"My home," he said. "And yours too, until we get a few things worked out."□

CHAPTER 10

A couple minutes later, things were mostly settled. No one was pressing charges. No one was going to jail. And no one was telling me anything. When the police officers returned to their cruiser, the big guy turned and started stalking toward his own vehicle.

Neither Jake, nor Trey, moved. They weren't the only ones. Around us, the crowd was still waiting. For what, I had no idea.

Shivering in the cool morning air, I glanced toward Jake's car. "What are we waiting for?" I asked.

"Maybe nothing," Jake said. "But you never know."

Trey lifted his video recorder and aimed it toward the stranger. As we all watched, the guy reached out to tug on the driver's side door. Nothing happened. With a string of profanity, the guy tugged harder. The door still didn't budge.

The guy pressed his face to the glass and peered inside. "Son-of-a-bitch!" he yelled. He stalked around to the passenger's side door and gave it a tug. Again, nothing happened. Muttering to himself, he circled back to the driver's side. He glanced in our direction. When he saw us looking, he yelled out, "Get the hell out of here!"

Next to me, Jake chuckled. "You couldn't make this stuff up," he said.

I glanced toward the stranger. "What stuff?"

Jake shook his head. "The dumb-ass locked his keys in the car."

The guy tried his door again, and then turned to glare in our direction. When he spotted Trey's video-recorder, he did a double-take. "That thing better not be on!" the guy hollered.

When Trey gave him a big thumbs-up, the guy made a guttural sound low in his throat. He stalked to the front of his vehicle and ripped off the hood ornament. He stalked back to the driver's side window, and with a primal scream, he hauled back his fist, ornament and all, and slammed it into the glass.

The glass shattered. His car alarm blared to life. And on the sidewalk, the crowd gave a rowdy cheer. The guy reached in through the shattered window and yanked out his keys. He hit a button on the remote, and the alarm grew silent. He hit the keyless again, wrenched open the door, and climbed inside.

From his newly claimed spot in the driver's seat, the guy leaned his head out the broken window and called out, "This ain't over!"

Jake chuckled. "I sure as hell hope not."

As we watched, the guy's car squealed into reverse. It did a sloppy U-turn, jumping the curb just before it rejoined traffic. Finally, it disappeared from sight. I turned to Jake. "So who *was* that guy?"

"You didn't recognize him?" Jake asked.

"Well, he sort of looked familiar, but..." I let my words trail off. My best guess sounded so unlikely, I didn't want to say it.

"You a sports fan?" Jake asked.

I shook my head. "Not really."

"That," Trey said, "is Dirk Leonard.

"Dirk?" I said. "Seriously?"

"Yeah," Trey said, "but wanna know what he likes to be called?"

"What?" I asked.

Trey grinned. "The Chainsaw."

Holy crap. It *was* him. "You're kidding," I said.

Next to me, Jake spoke. "Nope."

"Yeah, but the guy's a royal dick," Trey said. "Everyone hates him. Even the fans. It's kind of pathetic, actually. Shitty driver, too."

I glanced toward Jake's car. The spoiler was shattered, and the trunk, which had been all sleek lines earlier, was looking more like a crumpled soda can. I turned to Jake. "So what happened?" I asked. "I mean, was it just a random accident?"

"Not *that* random," Jake said. "Long story."

I turned to zoom in on the rear of the car, bothered by something I couldn't quite place. And then it hit me. "Oh crap," I breathed. "My suitcases."

"What about them?" Jake asked.

With a shaky finger, I reached out and pointed toward the damage. "They're in the trunk."

Trey reached up to stroke his chin. "Well that's not good," he said.

I looked down and covered my face with my hands. In the big scheme of things, it shouldn't have been a big deal. When I considered all the destruction – two vehicles and some guy's face – my two cheap suitcases barely registered on the scale of importance.

But for some reason, they suddenly seemed very important. Within the last couple hours, I'd lost my apartment, my roommate, and the job that was supposed to be my stepping-stone out of crapville. Instead, I was on a joyride to nowhere fast.

No. Not a joyride. Because there was nothing joyful about *this* journey. Why had I even gotten into Jake's car? Sadly, I knew the answer all too well. I had nowhere else to go.

Oh sure, I could slink back to my hometown and crash with one of my parents, but the thought of hearing "I told you so," was more than I could stomach. Everyone had expected me to fail, and I'd be damned if I'd live down to their expectations. Again.

But who was I kidding? I already had.

Desperately, I ran through my options. Maybe I could call my sister. She'd take me in. Probably. Sure, we hadn't talked in a few months. But she *had* been calling me, well, before I changed my phone number, anyway.

I blew out a long, unsteady breath. Damn it. But between both my jobs and the thing with Rango, I'd been avoiding almost everyone and everything. Just until things settled down, I told myself. But somehow, they never had.

"Is she okay?" Trey asked.

"Hey, I'm right here," I muttered into my hands. "I can hear you just fine, you know."

"Are you sure?" Trey said, "because you've been standing there like a zombie for like ten minutes."

Behind me, I heard Jake say, "Lay off her, will ya?" A moment later, I felt strong arms gather me into him. I caught my breath. I'd never been this close to him, but he felt exactly as I'd always imagined – lean and hard and utterly invincible. I turned and buried my face against his chest.

I tried to laugh. "This is all your fault," I said against his shirt.

He stroked my hair. "I know," he said.

I pulled away and gazed up at him with bleary eyes. "Really?"

"No," he said. "But I'll still make it up to you."

This time, I did laugh. I couldn't help it. Reluctantly, I pulled away to look at his car. I winced. "I'm sorry about your car. How bad is it?"

"Eh, it's drivable," he said.

"Yeah, but for how far?" I asked.

"Far enough," Jake said. "Now come on." He flicked his head toward the vehicle. "Let's get out of here."

I studied his shirt, ripped and splattered. "That's blood, isn't it?' Of course, the question was utterly stupid. What else could it be?

Jake tucked his chin to look down. "Well, it's not ketchup. That's for damn sure."

"Is that yours? Or his?" I closed my eyes. "Forget it. I'm not sure I want to know."

When I opened my eyes again, Jake was staring down at my breasts. And frowning.

My face grew warm. Okay, so I wasn't the best endowed girl on the planet, but I didn't have anything to be ashamed of. And besides, talk about rude.

"Hey!" I said, pointing to my face. "I'm up here. Okay?"

From off to the side, Trey said, "Oh man, that's gross."

I whirled on him. "What?"

He pointed toward my breasts. "Your shirt."

I looked down. My white blouse was smeared with ugly red splotches. I bit my lip. "Is that–?

"Yup," Trey said. "Chainsaw blood."

Well, this was just great. Once in my whole life I'm actually held by Jake Bishop, and he sullies me with another man's blood. Talk about a mood-killer.

No way I'd be wearing this shirt for any longer than I had to. I glanced toward the trunk of the car. "I'll need my suitcase," I said.

Trey snorted. "Out of there? Forget it. We'd need a freakin' crowbar."

"How would _you_ know?" I said.

"Well, that's what it took last time," Trey said.

I whirled toward Jake. "There was a last time?"

"You could say that," Jake said.

"How many accidents do you get into, anyway?" I said.

Before Jake could answer, Trey gave a bark of laughter and said, "A lot."

I whirled on him. "I don't see how this is funny."

"Trey," Jake said. "Tone it down, will ya? She's freaked out. Can't you tell?"

I whirled back to Jake. "Of course I'm freaked out!" I said. "You got me kicked me out of my apartment. And fired. And—"

"Technically," he said, "you resigned."

"No," I said, "*You* resigned. On my behalf."

"That job sucked," he said. He lowered his voice. "Baby, you're better than that, and you know it."

I gulped. Baby?

Damn it. He was distracting me again. I reminded myself to focus. Okay, so maybe he was right. The job did kind of suck. But it's not like I'd wanted to quit.

"That's not the point," I told him. "You know how hard it was for me to get that job? I had to go through five interviews."

Jake nodded. "Impressive."

"Are you making fun of me?"

"Nope."

I whirled to Trey. "Is he?"

Trey turned to study Jake. "Nah. I don't think so."

From somewhere above, a female voice rang out, "Jake, over here!" I looked around, and heard it again. "Jake! Jake!"

Finally, I spotted her. It was the same girl as before. She was leaning out an upper-story window of that same apartment complex.

"I love you!" she called. And then, she lifted the hem of her shirt high above her head, revealing a pair of naked, ample breasts. She jiggled them out the open window.

Next to us, Trey was absolutely riveted. "Man, I love this job," he said.

Slowly, I returned my gaze to Jake.

To my infinite surprise, his gaze wasn't on the girl, or her goodies. It was on me. "Get in the car," he said.

Bossy or not, that suddenly seemed like a terrific idea. I stomped toward the car and wrenched open the passenger side door. With obvious reluctance, Trey turned away from the girlie-show and reclaimed his spot in the back. Finally, after a casual wave at his half-naked fan, Jake climbed into the driver's seat and slammed the door shut behind him.

I sank low in my seat, wanting to disappear, or at the very least, roar away at lightning speed. Apparently though, Jake had other ideas. Because he didn't start the car. □

CHAPTER 11

Desperately, I looked toward Jake. From the driver's seat, he reached a hand, palm-up, toward the back seat. "Shirt," he said.

From the back seat, Trey went through the same motions as before, pulling a shirt from who-knows-where and snipping off the tags. But this time, when Trey dropped the shirt into Jake's hand, Jake handed the shirt out toward me.

I looked at it. "What's that?" I asked.

"A new shirt." He glanced down at my blouse. "Go ahead. Put it on. Then pull yours off underneath."

"Here?" I glanced around. "In the car?"

"Don't worry," Jake said. "We won't look." His voice took on a note of warning. "Right, Trey?"

"I guess not," Trey muttered.

I glanced at the shirt Jake was wearing. It was tattered, bloody, and maybe a little bit soggy. Probably from the wipers. "What about you?" I asked. "Wait. Lemme guess. You've got a dozen more shirts in the back? Am I right?"

From behind me, Trey said, "Nope. That's the last one. Funny too, because two's normally enough."

"Normally?" I said.

Jake thrust the shirt in my direction. "Just take it," he said.

Reluctantly, I took the shirt. I glanced out the car window.

The crowd was still there. So were their phones. The last thing I wanted was to become famous for a wardrobe malfunction on a public street. As if reading my thoughts, Jake cranked the engine and hit the accelerator. We roared away, circling back to the main thoroughfare.

As Jake navigated the city traffic, I struggled into the shirt. It wasn't quite as easy as Jake made it sound, but it wasn't half as difficult as I anticipated. On my own smaller body, his shirt was huge, giving me lots of room to tug off my blouse and drop it onto the floor-mat beside my feet.

I heard movement in the back seat and turned to see Trey pull out that same notebook computer. He flipped it open and reached for that same set of headphones.

I returned my gaze to the road and tried not to think about the mess I was in.

Soon, I heard a chuckle from the rear of the car.

Beside me, Jake spoke over his shoulder. "How is it?" he asked Trey.

Trey removed the headphones. "You're gonna love it," he said.

I turned around. "What is it?"

"I'll show you when it's done," Trey said.

I turned to Jake. "Does this have anything to do with what just happened?"

Jake grinned. "Maybe."

"I don't get it." I squinted over at him. "And why did that officer want your autograph?"

From the back seat, Trey said, "Oh come on. Like you don't know."

I whirled around. "I *don't* know."

He gave my face a good, long look. Then he turned to Jake. "She's messing with me, right?"

Jake, navigating the city streets, didn't turn around. A smile played across his amused face. "Yup."

"I am not!" I said.

Trey returned his gaze to the keyboard. "Yeah, right."

I sank down in my seat. "I give up," I said.

Out my car window, I watched as our surroundings changed with virtually every block, sometimes for the worse, sometimes for the better. Soon, we were travelling the outskirts of downtown Detroit.

"Don't tell me we're going to Detroit," I said.

"Yup," Jake said.

"Why there?" I asked.

"Because," he said, "it's where I live."

I didn't know what to say, so I said nothing. From what I'd seen with my own eyes, some parts of the city were on a definite upswing. Others, not so much. Since graduating from college, I'd been mostly living in the suburbs, sometimes one city, sometimes another, but never right downtown.

The nice areas were way too pricey, and the not-so-nice areas made Maddie's apartment look like a slice of heaven.

Before I knew it, we were pulling up to a stately building, maybe twenty stories high. I glanced around. Surprisingly, the area looked pretty nice. Too nice.

"Why are we stopping?" I asked.

"Because this," Jake said, flicking his head toward the nearby building, "is home."

"Really?"

His voice was deadpan. "Don't look so surprised."

We were parked in a circular turnaround near a pair of double-glass doors. In front of those doors stood a uniformed doorman.

Jake pushed open the driver's side door. "Come on," he said.

I glanced at his shirt, still a bloody, torn mess. Sometime during the drive, the blood stains had changed from a vivid red to a dull brown. Was it an improvement? I wasn't sure.

I glanced down at my own clothes. They were clean, but I still looked ridiculous. The shirt was huge, my skirt was tiny, and I was still wearing those stupid high heels. Reluctantly, I pushed open my door and stepped out, shivering in the cool morning air.

Trey climbed out of the back and into the driver's seat.

"Aren't you coming with us?" I asked.

Trey glanced at Jake.

"Nope," Jake said. "He's gonna park the car, and then he's gonna head to the office. Right?"

Trey nodded. "Right."

A moment later, Trey drove off, leaving me and Jake standing alone, except for the doorman, who said, "Welcome home, Mister Bishop."

I turned to Jake. "*Mister* Bishop?"

"I've been called worse," Jake said.

I heard myself laugh. It was true. He *had* been called worse. Recently, in fact.

As the doormen held the door, Jake and I walked past him, entering an ornate lobby with high ceilings and clusters of expensive-looking furniture, artfully arranged into semi-private seating areas.

"What is this place?' I asked.

"I already told you. It's home." He flicked his gaze toward the elevator. "Now come on."

Inside the elevator, Jake pressed the uppermost button and leaned back against the back wall. With growing confusion, I watched the floor-numbers change on the lit display. "We're not really going to the penthouse?" I said.

He glanced down. "We're not? Damn." He looked down at his bloodied shirt. "Because I could really use a shower."

So much for a straight answer. Even though we were alone

in the elevator, something made me lower my voice. "Tell me the truth," I said, "weren't you shocked he didn't say anything?"

"Who?" he asked.

"The doorman," I said. "I mean, look at us. I'm kind of surprised he'd let us in at all."

In fact, not only had he let us in, he'd been surprisingly oblivious to our appearance. Or at least he sure *seemed* oblivious.

"Hell," Jake said, "I've looked a lot worse than this." His gaze slid to me. "As for *you*, there's nothing to complain about there."

I glanced down. I was still wearing Jake's shirt. It fell nearly to my knees, covering my skirt entirely. I could only imagine how I looked – like some hoochie in high heels, wearing her lover's shirt and nothing else.

Just great. The doorman probably thought I was a damn hooker.

With a ding, the elevator doors slid open, revealing a marble entryway leading to a single set of double doors.

"Come on," Jake said.

I gave Jake a dubious look.

"Or," Jake said, "you could stay in the elevator. Ride it up and down a while. Your choice."

When I still didn't move, he claimed my hand and tugged me out of the elevator. At the double doors, he reached into his pants pockets and pulled out a wallet. He removed a key card and slid it into a control pad to the right.

But it wasn't until he pushed open those double doors that I heard myself speak. It was one word, and it was all I had.

"Wow."

CHAPTER 12

When the doors shut behind us, I turned to Jake. "Is this really your place?" Confused, I looked around. "The rent must be insane."

He gave something like a laugh.

"What's so funny?" I asked.

"Rent."

"What about it?"

"I don't pay it," he said.

"Because, uh, you're staying here with a friend?"

"No," he said. "Because I own it."

I stared at him. "You do?"

I glanced around, taking in the sleek, modern décor, the panoramic view of the Detroit River, and the furniture that looked way too expensive to actually sit on. "So, um, did you win the lottery or something?"

"Sorry. I don't gamble."

"Never?"

"Not unless it's a sure thing." He tossed his car keys onto a small marble-top table. "Wanna see your room?"

I crossed my arms. "No."

Actually, I did. But earlier, he had promised me answers, and I was done waiting.

He raised an eyebrow. "So, you wanna see *my* room?"

"Hardly." It was another lie. I did want to see it. For curiosity's sake. That's all. But I didn't want him to *see* me seeing it. Besides, there were so many mixed signals flying around, I could hardly keep track.

What exactly was I to him? A former friend? A potential lover? Some bratty kid from his old neighborhood? I stiffened my spine. I wasn't a kid anymore. And it was long past time he stopped treating me like one.

I pointed to a nearby sofa. "Sit," I said.

"It's my place," he said. "Shouldn't I be ordering *you* around?"

"You already have," I said. "And it's getting old."

"Not to me." Still, in a show of indulging me, he ambled toward the sofa.

"Wait." I pointed to his bloodied shirt. "You should probably take that off first."

"Why?"

Well, not because I wanted to see his rippling abs again, that's for sure.

"Because," I said, "you don't want to ruin your furniture, do you?" I glanced around and spotted a glossy black chair. I pointed to it. "As a matter of fact, sit there instead." I gave it a closer look. "Wait. That *is* leather, isn't it?"

With cool deliberation, Jake sank down onto the original sofa. I winced as he settled into it, relaxing against the pale cushioned surface. He patted the spot beside him. "Now you," he said.

In a show of defiance, I marched to the black leather chair and sat.

"I guess you showed *me*," he said.

"You promised me answers," I reminded him.

His gaze met mine. "That makes two of us."

I looked around. "It seems to me, you've got more to talk about than I do."

"This?" he said, glancing toward the massive windows. "It's nothing."

"You are so full of it," I said.

"Am I?"

I couldn't help it. I just had to ask. "Is all this really yours?" I made a sweeping gesture with my hand. "This place. The car. The furniture. The fancy clothes." I shook my head. "I don't get it."

Frowning, he looked down at his tattered shirt. "Fancy?"

"Fancy. Expensive. Whatever. I saw the tags." Either the guy was living well beyond his means, or he had one hell of a story to tell. I'd get it out of him sooner or later.

Jake looked down. Soon, I heard a low chuckle.

"What's so funny?" I said.

"Most girls kiss my ass."

No surprise there. From the hints that I'd seen, his ass was infinitely kissable. Yet somehow, I didn't think that's what he meant.

"Is that what you really want?" I asked. Sure, I could see the appeal short-term. But wouldn't that get old after a while?

He flashed me a grin that somehow didn't meet his eyes. "Sure. Why not?"

"Oh forget it," I said.

"Done."

Damn it. He wasn't really supposed to forget it. But then, something else jumped to the forefront of my mind. "Wait a minute," I said, recalling an earlier comment. "What'd you mean about no one messing with your family?"

He gave me a good, long look. "You really don't know?"

"I don't know what?" I said. "You and I aren't related." I swallowed. "Are we?" *Oh God, please say no. Or at least be a really distant cousin, like five times removed, whatever that meant.*

"The funny thing is," he said, "we are."

Damn it.

"Or at least," he added, "we *will* be."

"Huh?"

"Get this." He gave a laugh devoid of any real amusement. "My brother? Your sister? Wanna know what they did?"

I shrugged. "What?"

"They went and got engaged."

My jaw dropped. "Really? When?"

"Valentine's Day." His voice grew sarcastic. "Isn't that romantic?"

"Oh my God," I breathed. "That was weeks ago." My heart sank. "And no one told me?"

Okay, so I hadn't exactly been diligent about returning my family's phone calls, but someone could have left me a message at least. I felt myself frown. No. They couldn't have. I had a new phone number that I hadn't been eager to share.

"So," Jake continued, "what do you think of that?" His voice hardened. "Sis."

He *had* to be lying. I reached for my purse. "I'm calling Selena."

"Go ahead," he said. "The story won't change just because your sister's telling it."

I met his gaze, and reality sank in. He was telling the truth. I could see it in his eyes. Slowly, I settled back into my seat. "Oh crap," I breathed.

"You're telling me."

"Wait a minute," I said. "Why are *you* unhappy? It's bad for her, not for him."

"That's one opinion," he said. "Not mine."

I ignored the jab. On too many levels to count, this wasn't good. My sister, supposedly the smart one, was being way too stupid for words. Here, I'd wised up. And what did she do? She got stupider. Looking down, I felt my frown deepen. Was stupider even a word?

Maybe I wasn't as smart as I thought I was.

When I looked up, something in Jake's gaze made me pause. "What is it?" I asked.

His voice was low in the quiet room. "You."

"What about me?"

He looked around, as if cataloguing the luxury surrounding us. "With you here, the place feels different."

I narrowed my gaze. "Different good? Or different bad?"

After way too long, he finally spoke. "Ask me later."

I drew back. "No."

"Suit yourself." And then, as if shaking off some lingering gloom, he flashed me that same old grin. "Either way, you're stuck here a while."

I shook my head, trying to decipher what just happened. I gave up and asked the obvious. "How long?"

"'Til the thing with Rango's settled."

I blew out a long breath. Oh yeah. Rango. And that stupid black book. "Settled how?" I asked.

"I'm working on that," he said. "I'd give it a week. Maybe more."

Was that good news? Or bad news? In truth, I was lucky to have a place to stay at all. Maybe two weeks would be better than one.

And then, I remembered something. "Oh no," I said.

"What?" he said.

"That stupid book. It's still at Maddie's." I jumped from my seat. "We've got to go back."

I recalled the ugly scene from earlier, and my stomach clenched. The last thing I wanted was a repeat performance. Maybe I could go back later tonight, when she was at work. She *was* working tonight, right? I couldn't remember for sure.

I looked down at my lap. "Damn it," I muttered. "I should've grabbed that stupid thing on the way out."

"*This* stupid thing?" Jake said.

I looked up and stifled a gasp. "Where'd you get that?"

He gave the book a little wave. "Guess."

I knew where *I'd* seen it last – tucked under the mattress of my single bed.

He set the book on a side table. "You need to find a better hiding spot," he said.

I gave Jake a hard stare. "You went in my room?" The thought was infinitely unsettling in more ways than one. "When?"

"Last night."

"When I was sleeping?"

"No. Before you got home."

I gave him a look of disgust. "Unbelievable."

"Want to know what's unbelievable?" he said, his voice growing harder now. "That you're hiding from some low-life when you could've called for help."

"From who?" I tried to laugh. "You?"

"Why not?"

"Because," I said, "we've lost touch. Remember?"

"If you wanted to, you could've gotten ahold of me."

"Yeah, right," I said. "And about Rango? I didn't know he was a low-life, okay? I met him at some club. We hit it off. He seemed nice."

"Uh-huh."

"And by the time I figured out he was a jerk, it was too late." I pushed a hand through my hair. "After things got too crazy, I figured a change of scenery would do me good."

"I saw your scenery," he said. "It wasn't *that* good."

"Hey, it wasn't that bad," I lied.

"You're lucky you've been going by a different name," he said.

"Lucky?" I made a scoffing sound. "Try growing up with a name like Luna. See how lucky *you* feel."

His voice softened. "I like your name. You should stop changing it."

I gave him a sarcastic smile. "I'll think about it."

"By the way," he said, "you quit your bartending gig too."

My jaw dropped. "What?"

"Sorry."

He didn't look sorry. I slouched deeper into the chair, feeling utterly overwhelmed.

"So about Rango?" he said.

"What about him?" I said. "We had a bad break-up. End of story."

"The way I heard it, you trashed his Beamer."

"No," I said, considering Rango's once-beautiful car. "He *smashed* his Beamer, and tried to pin the blame on me when the cops came. The idiot didn't even have insurance."

"He didn't have insurance," Jake said, "because it wasn't his car."

I did a double-take. "Really? Whose was it?"

"Someone higher up the chain."

"What chain?"

"A family chain."

I stared at Jake. "And you know this how?"

"I've got friends."

"Yeah, I just bet." My sister claimed that Jake ran with thugs and criminals. Did I believe her? I still didn't know. Maybe I *didn't* want to know how he made his money.

"So then," Jake continued, "you take his little book of passwords and use it for what? To get a rise out of him."

"Yeah, I know," I told him. "That was the whole point."

Stupid Rango. The guy had trashed my furniture, stolen my clothes, and cost me my perfect little apartment. And the sad thing was, I couldn't prove anything. But I just knew it was him. He's lucky *all* I did was post some crazy stuff online.

"You embarrassed him," Jake said.

"So?" I said. "He deserved it, just like I said."

His voice was quiet. "It's dangerous to embarrass guys like that. You know that, don't you?"

"Well, I didn't know it at the time." I lifted my chin. "And even if I did, so what?"

He gave me a dubious look. "So what?"

"Oh c'mon," I said. "You know how bullies are. The more they get away with, the worse they get. It's about time someone did something back to him."

"That someone didn't have to be you," Jake said.

"Oh yeah? Then who?"

He leaned back on the sofa. "Me."

I looked at him a long time. Did he mean it? But I already knew the answer to that. He *did* mean it.

Rango, the ex-boyfriend from hell, was nothing but a bully. And Jake had a special way of dealing with bullies.

I'd seen *that* firsthand a long time ago. □

CHAPTER 13

It was the summer I turned twelve, and I was standing outside the roller-skating rink, waiting for my mom to pick me up. She was late. She was *always* late. I hated that.

The rink had closed a half-hour ago, and I was the only kid left. But I wasn't scared. It wasn't nighttime, and I didn't see any strangers, so I was pretty sure it would be okay.

I looked around. The parking lot was huge and empty. No cars. No trucks. No people at all. I liked it a lot better when the roller rink first closed. Then, there were lots of cars and parents too.

Now, there was just me and a bunch of shopping carts, maybe ten or twenty of them. It was hard to tell for sure, because they weren't lined up or anything. It was kind of weird, because this wasn't even a grocery store.

In a way, I wished this *were* a grocery store. Then, I could go inside and wait by the candy machines, watching shoppers go in and out. It would be a whole lot better than waiting here all by myself.

I bit my lip. Was my mom *ever* coming? I waited some more and tried to think about other things. I counted the shopping carts. There were sixteen. Most were near the back of the parking lot, where nobody ever parked. Four of the carts were standing up, and twelve carts were knocked over.

After counting the shopping carts, I counted the number of parking spots. There were ninety-two. No wonder the lot felt so big. And it was feeling bigger and lonelier every minute.

I tried to think of something else, like Jeremy DeFoe. Today, he'd asked me to skate for a slow song. He was cute and a really good skater, but his hands were clammy. Or maybe *my* hands were clammy. It was kind of hard to tell for sure.

Too bad Jeremy wasn't here now. It would be nice to wait with someone.

I glanced around. There was a party store across the street. It didn't look very nice, but they probably had a phone. Maybe they'd let me use it. I could call my mom and remind her that I was here, waiting.

I had to call her a lot. Sometimes, when she dropped me off places, she forgot completely. Maybe this was one of those times.

If only my sister could drive, she'd come and get me for sure. But she was only fourteen, and besides, she wasn't even home today. She was at a friend's house, working on some big summer project for one of her honors classes.

If she were home, she'd definitely remind my Mom. Selena remembered everything. I tried to smile. Even if my mom forgot, my sister never did.

Maybe I *should* run across the street to the party store. It wasn't that far away. But the street was super-busy. If I ran over there, and my mom came while I was gone, I'd get in big trouble. Or she'd drive away and forget me all over again.

I stuck my hands in the pockets of my jeans and waited some more. She still didn't come.

But suddenly, a bright orange sports car squealed into the parking lot. It wasn't new or anything, but it was super cool. It had big tires and a huge spoiler on the back. The windows were tinted really dark, and loud music blasted from the inside.

The car roared past me, heading to the back of the parking lot, by all those shopping carts. The car squealed to a stop, and the passenger door flew open. Some guy, maybe twenty years old, jumped out. He had long brown hair and bushy eyebrows, and he didn't look very nice.

He wheeled one of the shopping carts to the front of the car. He pushed the cart snug against the car's front bumper, so the car and the shopping cart faced the same direction.

He jumped back inside the car and slammed the door behind him. A second later, the car roared forward, pushing the shopping cart crazy-fast. The car slammed on its brakes, and the shopping cart went flying ahead, rolling fast as anything until it slammed into a dumpster and toppled over on its side.

Over the music, I heard laughter, loud and kind of scary, like they'd gone crazy or something. The car squealed backward to its original spot, and the same guy got out. He did the same thing as before, and another shopping cart went flying, this one straight into the side of the building.

They did this a few more times, sending carts all over the place. Staying close to the bushes, I edged toward them for a closer look.

The long-haired guy got out again and put another cart in front of the car. But this time, the car didn't move for a long time. And when it finally did, it drove the cart forward really slow, toward me.

I stood very still, not knowing what to do. Should I run? I looked around. I was a fast runner, but I couldn't outrun a car. And if I *did* run, would they chase me? I definitely didn't want be chased, at least not by *that* car.

Before I could decide, the car pulled right up next to me and stopped. The shopping cart rolled just a few feet ahead, and then stopped without crashing into anything. The long-haired guy leaned the passenger window and said, "Hey, wanna have some fun?"

He said it all funny, like whatever he was thinking wouldn't be fun at all. I took a step backward. "I can't," I said. "My mom will be here any second." *Please be here any second. Please, please, please...*

"Ooooh," he said in a snotty voice, "so you're waiting for your mommy?"

I glared at him. "I didn't say 'mommy'. I said 'mom.'"

"Well she's not here *now*," the guy said. "Wanna go for a ride?"

By now, my heart was beating so loud that I could almost hear it. I wanted to run. But if they were just teasing, I'd look stupid, like a little kid. I wasn't little. I was in junior high.

Besides, where would I run? I glanced around. The stores on both sides were all boarded up, and the party store was all the way across that busy street.

So instead, I gave the guy a dirty look and said, "Leave me alone, butt-head."

The guy burst into laughter.

"Oh come on," he said. "Just a *little* ride."

"I can't," I said. "Now, go away."

This made him laugh some more. "Aw, why not?" he said.

My hands were sweaty, a lot more sweaty than when I'd been skating with Jeremy. I gave the guy another dirty look. "Because I can't get in a stranger's car. That's why."

"Oh, I'm not talking about the *car*." He gave me a big fake-looking smile. "I'm talking about the *cart*."

I looked toward the shopping cart. If the guy didn't seem so crazy, or if the carts didn't crash, it might have been fun.

I liked things that went fast. It was part of the reason I loved to roller skate. But this was totally different.

I pointed toward the party store. "Uh, I see my mom now,"

I said. "I've gotta go." I turned and started walking toward the road. And then, I couldn't help it. My feet started to run. Behind me, I heard footsteps, and they were getting closer.

CHAPTER 14

Was he getting closer? He *sounded* like he was getting closer. When I started to look back, I tripped. On what, I didn't know. Probably my own feet.

My hands and knees slammed the pavement. Before I could push myself up, the guy grabbed me from behind, and lifted me up into the air. I screamed and kicked, but he didn't put me down. Laughing like a maniac, he tucked me under his arm and started running toward the car.

I was crying now and screaming all kinds of things at him, words I knew I shouldn't be saying. But nothing made him stop. When we reached that one shopping cart, he tossed me into it. I tried to get up, but he shoved me back down. Pressing down on my shoulder, he pushed the cart tight against the car like he'd done with all the other carts.

He turned and gave the driver a thumbs-up. Then, he took a step backwards, out of the way. The engine roared.

I screamed.

And then, something happened.

Something dark and fast slammed into the guy with long hair.

It was another guy, a teenager from the looks of him. He had dark hair, dark clothes, and a dark look on his face, like he was ready to kill someone. He slammed the guy against the hood of the car and punched him hard in the face.

The long-haired guy tried to fight back, but all he did was look stupid, swatting at punches like he was fighting a giant bug or something. He started yelling for help. His voice was different now, all high and whiny. He sounded scared. I was glad.

The car-engine shut off, and the driver got out. He had red hair and lots of freckles, but he still looked at least eighteen, or maybe older. He dove for the guy in black, trying to pull him off his friend.

The guy in black elbowed the redhead in his face and did some crazy kick thing that sent the redhead flying backwards. The redhead landed on in a funny heap and then rolled over on his hands and knees.

"Shit!" the redhead said. "What's your problem, man?"

The guy in black didn't answer. Instead, he turned to me. "You okay?" he asked.

I tried to answer, but I couldn't. He was the most beautiful thing I'd ever seen. And he'd rescued me. Just like in the movies. I wiped at my eyes, hoping they weren't too wet. And then I nodded.

The long-haired guy was still lying across the hood of the car. His mouth was all bloody, and so was his nose. He pushed himself up and said, "Jeez Jake! What'd you freak out for? She's okay. It's not like we *did* anything to her."

Oh wow. So they knew each other?

Slowly, Jake turned to face the long-haired guy. "What?" Jake said.

With a big, dramatic groan, the long-haired guy pushed himself up from the car. He shook his head, and a big chunk of hair stuck to the blood on his face. He looked stupider than before, and I wanted to laugh. But I was afraid to laugh, because then I might start crying again. And I didn't want to cry in front of *him*, that Jake guy.

"Aw c'mon," the long-haired guy said. He shoved the clump of soggy hair aside and tucked it behind his ear. "We were just teasing her." He gave me a big, fake smile. "No big deal. *You* thought it was fun. Right?"

"No," I said. "I thought it sucked."

Jake made a small laughing sound.

The redhead pushed himself up from the pavement. He was cussing, mostly under his breath. But he yelled out, "What the hell is she?" His voice got all snotty. "Your girlfriend or something?"

Still sitting in the shopping cart, I felt myself smile. It would be nice to be Jake's girlfriend. He was really cute. Like a movie star, all dark and handsome, and really strong.

"No," Jake told him. "She's a girl, you asshole."

So he noticed? That was good. My smile got a teeny bit bigger.

"And a kid," Jake continued.

I stopped smiling. Hey, I wasn't a *little* kid or anything. Next year, I'd be a teenager. Then, we'd be practically the same age.

Jake turned toward the long-haired guy and said, "So you're picking on kids now? What the fuck's wrong with you?" He glanced toward me. "Sorry."

Sitting in the cart, I straightened up as tall as possible. "You don't have to be sorry," I told him. "I've heard that word lots of times. And you know what? I said it too." I nodded. "Just a few minutes ago."

Jake smiled at me, and my stomach felt all fluttery. His smile was a lot better than Jeremy DeFoe's. "Good job," Jake said. He held out his arms. "Wanna get out?"

Before I could think about it, I pushed myself up and practically leapt into his arms. He felt really nice and smelled good too. But then, he set me down next to the cart.

He turned back to the two guys. "Alright," Jake said, "which one of you wants to go first?"

The two guys looked at each other. The redhead took a step backward. "What are you talking about?" he said.

Jake pointed to the shopping cart. "Get in," he said.

The redhead took another step backward. "No way."

Jake turned to the long-haired guy, who stood a lot closer. "How about you?" Jake asked.

The long-haired guy swallowed. He shook his head. He glanced toward the car. "Uh, we gotta go," he said.

Jake turned to me. "You wanna see them go for a ride?"

I didn't even have to think about it. I nodded.

Jake started walking toward the long-haired guy, who said in a high, whiny voice, "Seriously, Jake! Quit messin' around!"

"I'm not messing," Jake said. He gripped the guy by his shirt and said in a quiet, but kind of scary voice. "Now get in. Or I'll put you in."

The long-haired guy glanced at the shopping cart, and then, he turned to his friend. He gave a nervous-sounding laugh. "Can you believe this shit?" he asked.

The redhead looked at his car. He looked at Jake. And then, a split-second later, he dove into the car and powered up the engine. The car squealed backwards, turned sideways, and sped out of the parking lot like two seconds later.

The long-haired guy stared after the car. His mouth fell open, and his head tilted sideways. The wet clump of hair flopped over his mouth, giving him a weird fake moustache.

I heard myself giggle.

Jake turned to the give the guy a long look. "We're waiting," Jake said.

The guy's shoulders sagged, and then he started trudging toward the cart. With a huge, overdramatic sigh, he grabbed the edge of the shopping cart and climbed in. He was kind of tall, and his long legs flopped over the sides. He looked really stupid.

Jake turned to me. "You wanna push?" he asked.

I gave it some thought and then nodded.

"Okay," Jake said, "What you gotta do is this. Grab the handle, run as fast as you can toward those bushes." He pointed at the big green bushes that lined the walkway in front of the skating rink. "Then, when you're almost there, let go." He smiled at me. "Okay?"

The guy in the cart gave another big sigh. "This is such bullshit," he said.

Jake turned toward him. "What's that?" he asked.

The guy rolled his eyes. "Nothin'"

"I thought so," Jake said.

Jake gave me another smile. "Whenever you're ready," he said.

I walked toward the shopping cart and grabbed the handle with both hands.

"Don't chicken out on me," Jake said. "Alright?"

Nodding, I gave the cart a little push. It was a lot heavier than I expected, but I wasn't going to let that stop me. I leaned forward and pushed it as hard as I could. It moved faster, and I started to run.

I ran as fast as I could toward the bushes. The guy was holding on to the sides of the cart with both hands, and his long hair was flying behind him. When I got close to the bushes, I let go of the handle. The cart sailed forward, and the guy gave a little girlie scream. A split-second later, it crashed into the bushes and fell over. Muttering stuff under his breath, the guy crawled out and stumbled to his feet.

He looked over toward Jake, who was walking across the parking lot toward us. The long-haired guy put his hands around his mouth and hollered out, "Alright. I did it. You happy now?"

"Ask her if *she's* happy," Jake called back.

With another big sigh, the guy turned toward me. "You happy?" he said.

Well, I was a lot happier than I was a few minutes ago. "I guess so," I said.

"Good. Because I'm outta here." He turned, and stomped away, heading away from the roller-skating rink. When he disappeared around a corner, I turned back around.

Jake was standing behind me now. "I'll tell you a secret," he said.

I looked up at him. "What?"

"Remember the guy with the red hair?"

The driver. Oh yeah. I remembered, alright. I nodded.

Jake grinned. "I know where he hangs out."

"Really?" I said.

"Yeah." Jake leaned down until our heads were nearly at the same level. "And you know what?"

"What?" I asked.

"Tonight, I'm gonna pay him a little visit."

I smiled up at him. "Really?"

"Really," he said. "But you've got to promise me something."

"What?" I said.

"You're not gonna hang out here alone anymore."

"I wasn't *supposed* to be alone," I told him. "My mom's just late. That's all."

He frowned. "Want me to wait with you?"

"Okay." My face was feeling a little hot. "I mean, if you really want to."

He didn't answer, which kind of bummed me out, because it would have been nice to hear that he wanted to stay. But he *did* wait with me, just like he said. He walked toward the building and leaned against it.

He looked really cool. I did the same thing. I probably didn't look as cool as he did, but I still felt cool, hanging out with someone like him.

He didn't say a lot, but he listened to me when I talked. And then, way too soon, now that I was actually had someone to wait with, my mom's car pulled into the parking lot. With a sigh, I turned to tell Jake goodbye.

But I couldn't. He was gone.

It made me sad. I couldn't remember thanking him, but I should have. If I saw him again, I definitely would. And someday, when I was older, maybe I'd even marry him. The idea made me smile.

I was still smiling when my mom rolled down the car window and said, "Sorry I'm late. Can you believe I completely forgot?"

Oh yeah. I definitely believed it. I walked around the car and opened the passenger door. I got inside. That's when I saw that the knees of my jeans were all torn up, probably from when I fell. One of my knees had a big bloody scrape that had leaked blood all over the torn fabric. Funny, I hadn't even noticed.

Even funnier, neither did my mom. Normally, that bothered me. But not today. Just before she drove out of the parking lot, she turned to me and asked, "Did you have fun?"

I gave it some thought and felt a giant smile spread across my face. "Oh yeah," I said. "Best time ever."

And I meant it.

After that, Jake had a funny way of turning up on Saturday afternoons when I was stuck waiting. I never told my mom about him. I never told my sister either. Somehow, I knew she wouldn't like me hanging out with a boy so much older.

Later, when I got a little older, I started running into Jake at other places too – sometimes at the beach, sometimes at other spots around town. Sometimes, he'd let me hang out with him and his friends. Either he liked having me there, or he just didn't know how to make me go away – at least, not until a few years later.

☐

CHAPTER 15

Sitting in Jake's penthouse, I pulled my thoughts to the present. So *Jake* wanted to handle my ex-boyfriend? Why would he do that?

Sitting across from me, he was still waiting for my response.

"Why?" I asked.

"Why what?"

"Why would you want to get involved?" I said. "I mean, you weren't the one who dated him."

"Good thing, since he's not my type."

"Oh, you know what I mean," I said. "He's my mistake. Not yours."

"But I know him," Jake said.

"How?" I asked.

"Friend of a friend." He leaned forward, and his gaze became intense. "Tell me. Did he ever hurt you?"

I drew back. "What? You mean physically? No. Never." I glanced away. "Not really."

Jake's voice was flat. "Not really?"

I pushed a hand through my hair. "Alright," I said, "here's the truth. The last couple times I saw him, yeah, it started to head in that direction. But right after it did, I was out of there. I'm not stupid, you know. I saw the signs."

"Such as?"

This was getting way too personal. "None of your business," I said.

I didn't want to talk about the bruises on my arms, where Rango "accidentally" gripped me too hard. Or the time he showed up in my apartment in the middle of the night, convinced he'd find me with another guy. And I definitely didn't want to mention the time he'd "jokingly" called me a slut when I smiled at some bartender.

Jake was still looking at me. He waited.

"There's nothing worth mentioning," I said. "So don't ask."

"Should I ask *him*?"

I tried to laugh. "First, you'd have to find him."

As for me, I knew where exactly to find Rango. He owned a club in Rochester Hills, a couple of restaurants in Troy, and some title-loan place downtown. Normally, he hung out at his club, especially on weekends.

Rango was a celebrity of sorts, a hotshot D.J. with a big local following. Of course, that knowledge wasn't exactly a secret. If Jake knew anything at all about Rango, he'd know exactly where to find him.

"Or maybe," Jake said, "we'll let Rango find us." He grinned. "Who knows? Might be fun."

Just like it always had, that smile of his was doing funny things to my insides. Watching him, I tried to figure out if the years — or his amazing success, whatever the source — had somehow changed him. I didn't think so. He was still the same larger-than-life guy that I'd fallen for all those years ago, before I knew what love really was.

Who knows. Maybe I *still* didn't know.

"Well?" Jake said. "Ready for some payback?"

"Technically," I said, "I've given him *some* payback already."

"Yeah. I heard," Jake said. "How's that working out for

you?"

From the look on his face, he already knew the answer. My payback attempts were mostly pathetic. Unlike me, Rango hadn't spent the last few weeks looking over his shoulder. *He* hadn't had to find a new place to live, or buy new clothes without any money. And he sure as hell wasn't missing the only car he had ever owned.

Besides, what was Jake's plan? We were a long way from home, and I didn't see any shopping carts.

"What are you planning to do?" I tried to laugh. "Beat him up?"

Jake shrugged.

"Oh come on," I said. "Don't you think we're a little old for that?"

"Never too old for a fight," Jake said.

"Yeah, well, you've already had one today, so let's cross that off the list. Alright?"

He leaned back and crossed his arms. "How about if he hits me first?"

I narrowed my gaze. "Why would he hit you?"

"I dunno. It's just a question."

"Well, I guess," I said. "I mean, if he hit you first, I wouldn't want you to *not* defend yourself, if that's what you're asking."

"Good to know." He glanced at his watch. "By the way, we're going out tonight."

"Out? Where?"

"It's some museum thing," he said.

I stared at him. "A museum thing? You're kidding right?"

"Why?" he said. "You got something against museums?"

"No," I said. "But be serious. They're not exactly your thing." I studied his face. "Are they?"

He left me hanging a few seconds, and then grinned. "No."

"Then why would you go?" I asked.

"You mean, why would *we* go?"

"Either way," I said. "Why?"

"Why not?"

"Well, that clears up everything," I said.

"It'll be fun," he said. "I promise."

I gave him a doubtful look.

"And," he said, "you're going shopping in an hour."

"For what?"

His gaze drifted to my makeshift outfit. "Clothes."

"I don't have time to shop," I said.

It wasn't technically true. The way it looked, I had plenty of time. What I *didn't* have was money.

I bit my lip and tried to figure a way out of this. I considered my suitcases, smashed in Jake's trunk. Even if they were somehow accessible, the clothes I *did* have were pathetic.

Just like everything else today. □

CHAPTER 16

The leggy brunette stared at me with obvious disdain. "But she's a mess," she said.

I felt my cheeks grown warm in the cool penthouse air. "Gee thanks," I said.

"Bianca," Jake said in a warning tone. "You don't wanna do this. Just say so."

As if by magic, her voice morphed from ground glass to warm velvet. "I never said *that*."

Jake pulled out his cell phone. "I'll call someone else. No problem."

"Oh stop," Bianca said, reaching for his arm. She gave him a sultry smile. "You know me. I just *love* to shop." She turned toward me, and her smile became predatory. "Especially with a new friend."

A scoffing sound escaped my lips.

"Pardon?" she said.

I cleared my throat. "Nothing. Sorry."

I snuck a quick glance at Jake. His gaze drifted from me to Bianca and back again. He *had* to know this wasn't a good idea. Then again, he *was* a guy. Even the smartest guys could be surprisingly clueless when it came to stuff like this.

The three of us were standing just inside the door of Jake's penthouse. I'd taken a quick shower and thrown on some clean clothes. Unfortunately, none of those clothes were mine – not my size, and definitely not my style.

Embarrassingly, I was pretty sure that most of them were castoffs from whatever girl – or girls – Jake might've been seeing. I glanced down. Or maybe some hooker was missing half her laundry.

From the corner of my eye, I studied Bianca. She wore a sleek, cream-colored dress with matching heels. *She* didn't look like a hooker. Or at least, she didn't look like a low-rent hooker.

That made one of us.

As I watched, Bianca leaned toward Jake and whispered something flirty in his ear. He pulled away before she finished, leaving her frowning in obvious frustration.

"Remember," he told her. "Dress. Shoes. Extras. Whatever. You've got three hours."

Bianca's lips formed a pout. "Only three hours?"

"Is something wrong?" Jake asked.

"No. Of course not." Bianca hesitated, giving me a long, pointed look. Then, she leaned toward Jake and said in a low whisper that somehow managed to fill the whole room, "except, look at what we're starting with."

"Hey," I said, "I heard that."

"Oh, you did?" She winced. "I'm sorry. It's just that our styles are so different. That's all."

I glanced down. "This isn't *my* style."

Her gaze dipped to my skirt – too tight, too short, and too dangerous, considering I'd refused to wear another girl's underpants. And wearing my own wasn't exactly an option, given the fact that some unseen housekeeper had swooped them up, along with my other dirty clothes while I'd been in the shower.

Bianca gave me a sympathetic look. "Of course it isn't."

My gaze narrowed. "I don't shop at Hookers-Are-Us if that's what you're thinking." I turned to Jake. "You know what? Just get my suitcase, alright? I'm sure I have *something* in there."

He didn't budge. "Not for this thing, you don't."

Damn it. I turned to Bianca. "If you could just point me to the nearest store," I said, "I mean, I'm sure you're busy with, uh..." Actually, I had no idea what she did.

She gave me that same cool smile. "Never too busy for Jake." She turned to Jake and ran a manicured fingernail along his jawline. "Isn't that right?"

Jake gave her a long, cold look. She pulled away and gave me a nervous glance. Jake reached into his back pocket and pulled out his wallet. He peeled off way too many hundreds and handed them over. To me, not her.

Embarrassed, I tucked the money into the pocket of my too-tight skirt and tried not to think about it. Good thing we had never had sex. I'd feel like a hooker for sure, especially in these clothes.

Bianca gave Jake a pretty little pout. "What about me?" she asked.

"Put it on the card," Jake said.

There was a card? Was she on retainer or something?

Before I could give it much thought, Jake's cell phone chirped. He answered with a crisp, "Yeah?" He glanced up and said, "The driver's downstairs."

There was a driver?

That particular question was answered ten minutes later when Bianca and I slid into the backseat of a long, black sedan. Up front, the driver said, "the usual place?"

I glanced at Bianca. How often did she do this? And, did she normally do it alone? Or did she make a habit of shopping with Jake's new, well, whatever I was? When Bianca answered in the affirmative, the driver pulled away, leaving me staring out the car-window as the doorman gave us a professional-looking wave.

Sitting next to me in the back seat, Bianca pulled a cellphone from her designer handbag and started tapping away at the screen. I was dying to ask her about Jake. There were so many questions that I almost didn't know where to start. What exactly did he do for a living? And why did everyone in the world except me seem to know who he was?

I mean, it wasn't like I lived under a rock. I watched TV. I went to the movies. Hey, I even vaguely knew about the Kardashians. So why was Jake such a mystery?

I slid Bianca a sideways glance. She was making an obvious point to ignore me – trying to make me uncomfortable, no doubt. The sad thing was, it was working. She had the upper hand and then some. She knew who Jake was. She knew his driver. She had his credit card, or least some sort of card.

Was she a friend? A girlfriend? Or maybe she was one of those friends with benefits? I bit my lip. Did she work for him? And if she did, what exactly did she do?

I had a few ideas, but none I wanted to dwell on.

The drive passed in absolute silence. I watched out the window as the cityscape changed with every block.

Obviously, the driver knew the city well – a lot better than me, that's for sure. Soon, we were on the interstate. The highway signs told me a lot more than Bianca ever had. We were heading out toward Troy, one of Detroit's most affluent suburbs. Well that solved one mystery at least. Finally, I knew exactly where we were going – to Somerset.

To call it a mall didn't do the place justice. The place was huge with nearly 200 stores. Brand names skittered across my brain – Gucci, Ralph Lauren, Tiffany, and more.

I'd been to Somerset exactly one time, and had vowed never to return. For one thing, looking at luxury goods when you had almost no money was only entertaining in the short-term. In the long term, it just made it that much harder to smile when I paid the bare minimum on my student loans.

In the front pocket of my obscenely short skirt, Jake's money burned against my skin. He'd given me a lot. I didn't know how much, exactly. At the time, I figured it was too much. But now, given our destination, I wasn't so sure.

I wanted to reach into my pocket and pull it out. I wanted to count it so I had some idea of how much I should be spending. Next to me, Bianca was still focused on her phone. And yet, somehow I knew she'd be completely aware – and beyond delighted – if I did something so crass.

Inside the first dressing room, I would definitely be counting it. There was something else I planned on doing – calling my sister. Thinking about it, I pulled out my own phone and tapped out a quick text, telling her it was me and asking if she was available to talk.

Almost immediately, my phone rang. I glanced at the display. It was her. I winced. I wanted to talk, but not this instant, not with Bianca around. Fearful of missing Selena later, I answered anyway. "Hello?"

"Where the hell have you been?" she said. "And what happened with your old number? I keep getting a disconnection notice."

"Oh hey," I said, in my best cheery tone. "It's good to hear from you too. Can I give you a call in a bit?"

"No," she said.

Oh crap. "Why not?"

"Because," she said, "I've been trying to reach you forever. I have some news. And I've been worried sick about you."

"Oh, that's nice," I said.

"What?" Selena said. "No, it's not."

"Sounds good," I chirped. "Talk to you later. Bye."

I disconnected the call and silenced my ringer. Glancing down, I was entirely unsurprised when Selena called back almost immediately, and then five times after that. I couldn't exactly blame her. For girls who liked different things, we were surprisingly close – or at least we *had* been.

But distance and time had taken their toll. She'd moved down South five years earlier, and I'd moved on to guys like Rango, who had a way of consuming all my free time. Suddenly, I missed my sister in the same way I missed summer at the end of a long Michigan winter.

If I were being honest, I'd been missing her for a while, but the news of her engagement was making me heartsick for the relationship we used to have. She'd be planning a wedding soon. Would I even be involved?

With an audible sigh, I tucked my phone back into my purse.

I snuck a sideways glance at Bianca. She was still tapping at her phone. But now, a faint smile played across her full lips. Had she heard more of the conversation than I thought? I decided not to think about it.

After all, I had way too many other things to think about. ☐

CHAPTER 17

Just inside the mall, I hit a casual shoe store, where I purchased the cheapest pair of black tennis shoes I could find and immediately slipped them onto my feet. As I shoved my old high heels into the new shoe box, Bianca made a point of looking at her watch.

"Are you planning to wear those shoes tonight?" she asked.

I looked down at my feet. "No. Why?"

"Because we're wasting time."

"Oh come on," I said. "That took all of five minutes."

"Actually, it took ten."

Somehow, I doubted that, but I didn't argue, because I had one more store to hit before getting down to business. To Bianca's obvious annoyance, that store was Victoria's Secret. Under her scornful gaze, I grabbed a handful of panties off the nearest display.

Standing beside me, she eyed the panties, all silk and satin in various colors. "We're supposed to be shopping for a dress. Remember?"

"And extras." I mimicked the same bossy tone she'd used on me. "Remember?"

Her mouth tightened. "I think he meant accessories."

But I knew something Bianca didn't. If I didn't get my hands on new panties, like now, people on the escalator would be seeing way more of *my* accessories than was legal.

Ignoring her protests, I dashed to the yoga section, where I found long black yoga pants and a soft gray shirt with long sleeves and a V-neck. On my way to the front counter, I grabbed a couple of bras in my size and added them to the mix.

I marched up to the counter and tossed the items onto the smooth surface.

"Aren't you going to try them on?" Bianca asked.

"Nope."

"Why not?" she said.

"Because," I said, "in five minutes, I'll be wearing them."

She eyed the pile of panties. "Those too?" Her gaze fell to my skirt, and her lips formed a sneer. "What are you wearing now?"

Judging from the look on her face, it was pretty obvious she knew the answer to *that* question. Damn it. It wasn't *my* fault I was wearing someone else's clothes – or when it came to undergarments, none at all.

I gave her my sweetest smile. "I'm wearing Jake's."

She drew back, and her face lost a fraction of that cool composure. My satisfaction was short-lived when I considered the long-term ramifications. Why on Earth had I said that? Sooner or later, she'd find out I was lying. And, even if she didn't find out, did I really want people to think I was running around in Jake's underwear?

I felt a reluctant smile tug at my lips. Probably, Jake had nice underwear. I envisioned form-fitting briefs hugging his tight ass. And then, I envisioned his ass without the briefs.

"Will this be all?"

I gave a little jump, and turned to see a teenage sales clerk reaching for my pile of clothes.

"Yup, that's all," I said. "Except, uh, I'm going to be wearing these, so could you please snip off the tags?"

The clerk reached for a pair of panties and stopped in mid-motion. Her eyebrows furrowed. "All of these?" she asked.

"Right," Bianca said. "Like she's going to wear five pairs of panties at once. Just pick one, and cut the tags, will you? We're in a hurry."

The clerk gave a small flinch. "Of course," she said. "Sorry."

I gave Bianca a dirty look and turned back to the clerk. "Don't be sorry," I said. "It's my fault. I should've been more specific." I glanced toward the dressing room area. "Hey, is it okay if I change in the dressing room?"

Bianca rolled her eyes. "That's what it's for, isn't it?"

"Yes," I said, "but not when you've already *bought* the clothes." I looked to the clerk for confirmation. "Right?"

"Um..." Her gaze drifted from me to Bianca.

"Oh forget it," Bianca said. "I'll be waiting outside." With that, she turned away and started stalking toward the store's entrance.

The clerk pulled out a small pair of scissors and started removing tags. I leaned toward her and lowered my voice. "Sorry about that," I said. "The thing is..." I flicked my gaze toward Bianca, "I'm wearing *her* clothes, and she *really* wants them back. Like now."

The clerk studied my decidedly trashy outfit. "No kidding?" she said.

"And," I said, "she's got to be at work in an hour. If someone steals her corner..." I shrugged. "Well, you know how it is."

The clerk's gaze shifted to Bianca, standing just outside the store entrance. As if feeling our combined gazes, Bianca looked up.

I gave her a little wave. "Don't worry!" I called. "I'll be returning them in a minute."

Frowning, Bianca returned her attention to her phone. While the clerk rang up my purchases, I studied Bianca through the glass. Funny, she and I probably *did* wear the same size, even if she was noticeable taller.

I felt myself smile. Maybe I *should* give Bianca the hoochie hand-me-downs, if only to see her reaction. The look on her face would be almost worth it.

Ten minutes later, I was huddled in the changing room, wearing my new shirt and yoga pants, along with – thank God – new undergarments. I shoved the hoochie-wear into the shopping bag and breathed a sigh of relief.

It's not that I minded dressing sexy. What I *did* mind was dressing like a girl who had sex for money, especially in small, grubby bills.

Finally, I pulled out my cell phone and called my sister.

Selena answered with a frantic, "Luna? Why'd you hang up on me?"

Cradling the phone, I said in a hushed tone, "You mean Anna."

"Who?" Selena asked.

"Anna," I repeated. "Me. It's the name I'm going by now."

"Oh for crying out loud," she said, "that's like the tenth name since high school."

"So?" I said. "I'm trying to find one I like. You got the only good one in the family."

That wasn't completely true. My brothers, Steve and Anthony, had normal names. Of course, *they* had been named by my dad, not my flake of a mom, who ran a fortune-telling business of all things.

"Forget that," Selena said. "Is everything okay?"

"Yeah. Why?"

"Because," she said, "you'll never guess who came into mom's shop looking for you."

"Actually," I said, "I bet I can." I glanced at the dressing room door. "But wait. First, I've got a question."

"What?"

I tried to sound casual. "I heard you're getting married. Is that true?"

"Oh crap," she groaned. "Who told you?"

"Thanks a lot," I said. "So it was supposed to be a secret?" My heart sank. "From me?"

"No, it's not like that," she said. "I wanted to tell you myself. That was the whole point."

"Oh." I released a long, unsteady breath. "Really?"

"Yeah," she said. "I had to practically beg everyone to keep it quiet. Not that it did any good. So who told you?" she asked. "Mom?"

"No."

She hesitated. "Dad?"

"No."

"Steve? Anthony? Who?"

"Jake."

"Shut up," she said. "You don't mean Jake Bishop?"

"Your future brother-in-law? Yeah. That's exactly who I mean."

"Oh my God," she said. "He found you?"

"Sort of."

"I knew it," she muttered. "Why was he looking for you anyway? Wait. Are you sure you're okay? He's not with you now, is he?"

"No. Jeez, I'm fine. I'm in a dressing room."

"You're in trouble," she said. "I can tell."

"I am not." Not at the moment anyway. "But I am staying with Jake, so—"

"What!" she said. "You can't be serious."

"Why not?"

"Because," she said, "the guy's a total criminal."

"He is not," I said.

"He is too. He's been in and out of jail for as long as I can remember."

"Yeah, but not for anything big," I pointed out. "Fights mostly. Usually with his dad. Who's a total drunk, by the way."

"So?"

"So no wonder Jake fought with him."

"Wait a minute," she said. "You don't actually know him, do you?"

"I did," I said. "Sort of. Remember?"

"No. I don't remember," she said. "He's like five years older than you. You didn't date him or anything. Did you?"

"God no." Not that he'd asked. "Now seriously, stop worrying. I called because there's something I need to know, like now."

"What?" she asked.

"What exactly does Jake do for a living?"

"Nothing," she said.

"Nothing?"

"Well, nothing legal, I'm guessing."

"So you don't even know?" I made a sound of frustration. "Come on! You're marrying his brother for God's sake. You've *got* to know."

"Why?" she said. "We never talk about him."

"I think he's famous," I said.

"Jake?" She gave a snort. "You mean infamous."

"No," I said. "Famous. People keep asking for his autograph."

"Oh shut up."

"I'm serious," I said.

A hard knock sounded at my dressing room door.

"Sorry!" I called. "I'll be out in a minute."

"You'd better be," Bianca snapped.

Oh crap. It was *her*.

Bianca knocked again, harder this time. "We had three hours," Bianca said, "not three years."

"I've gotta go," I whispered into the phone. "I'll call you later, alright?"

I hung up before she could say anything else – although, as I heard my phone buzz again and again, I was pretty sure my voicemail was getting an earful.

A half-hour later, I stood with Bianca, looking in the full-length mirror. Normally, I liked to shop, but this was less fun than a root canal.

Bianca wasn't helping. Insisting it was part of her job – whatever that meant – she selected every single dress that I tried on, going for an ultra-conservative look that just wasn't my style.

I winced at my reflection. "This *can't* be what he had in mind," I said. □

CHAPTER 18

In the mirrored dressing room, I gave the dress another look. The dress was obscenely expensive, not that you'd know by the looks of it. It was pitch-black with a high ruffled neck and long, flowing sleeves. Its ruffled hem fell nearly to my ankles.

"I look like a schoolmarm," I said.

Bianca gave me a little smirk. "So you'd rather wear something like you had on earlier? From—How'd you put it?—Hookers-Are-Us?"

"That's not what I'm saying." My head was throbbing. I wasn't stupid. I knew Bianca couldn't have my best interests at heart. And I also knew she'd sabotage me if she could. Still, Jake had sent her with me for a reason.

I frowned. What was that reason? Was he that worried about what I might buy on my own? I turned toward Bianca. "You're messing with me," I said. "Aren't you?"

"If you don't like the dress," she said, "just say so."

"I don't like the dress."

She made a sound of annoyance.

"Oh," I said. "So I wasn't *really* supposed to say so?"

"Listen," she said in a tone of forced patience. "I know it's a bit conservative. But you're going to an upscale event. It's at a museum, not a nightclub. I do this for a living. I know what I'm talking about."

I turned to stare at her. "You *shop* for a living?"

"Among other things," she said.

I could only imagine. I snuck another glance in the mirror. "So what's the event?" I said. "A schoolmarm convention?"

"Fine," she said. "It's your call." With both hands, she made a grand sweeping gesture toward the rest of the store. "Go ahead. Pick out something else." She made a show of looking at her watch. "You've got ten minutes."

"What?" I said. "Ten minutes? That's not right. We have at least another hour."

"No," she said. "We don't. Because you can't be late for your manicure."

"I have a manicure appointment?"

"And a hair appointment after that."

I looked down at my nails. I'd never actually had a manicure, but my nails didn't look too bad. I snuck a quick glance at my reflection. About my hair, I wasn't so sure.

"I pulled a lot of strings to get those appointments," Bianca said, "so don't even *think* about cancelling."

With a sigh, I turned to give the dress another look. Maybe with the right hairstyle and shoes, it wouldn't look *so* bad. And it wasn't like *I* was the one paying for it.

Still, five minutes later, as I pulled out the wad of bills and peeled off a sickening number of hundreds, I couldn't help but wonder, would Bianca ever wear such a thing?

She wouldn't. I was sure of it.

"Don't look so glum," she said. "It's not like *your* money's paying for it."

Color flooded my face. It was true. And I'd been thinking exactly the same thing. But hearing Bianca say it out loud, well, it made me more than a little uncomfortable.

Feeling incredibly deflated, I blew out a long, unsteady breath as I tucked the few remaining bills into my purse. This was just my luck. Just once in my whole life, I buy a dress that's obscenely expensive, and all it does is make me feel cheap.

When I looked up, Bianca was staring down at my stomach. And grimacing. "What on Earth was that?" she said.

I looked down. "What?"

Right on cue, my stomach gave a low rumble.

"Is that *you*?" she said.

"Hey," I said, "give me a break. I haven't eaten yet today." Funny, in all the commotion, I hadn't even realized I was hungry. But now that I *had* thought about it, I was utterly starving. "Is there a food court around here?" I asked.

She gave me an annoyed look. "Have you forgotten we're on a schedule?"

"So? I'll grab something to go. No big deal."

Her lip curled. "And eat while your nails are getting done? Tasha will just *love* that."

"Jeez," I said. "What's the big deal?"

With a pained expression, Bianca looked heavenward. "Fine," she said. "*I'll* get the manicure. *You* get a pretzel, or whatever it is that you eat."

"Wait a minute," I said. "I thought I *had* to get a manicure."

"Do you see a gun to your head?" She gave an exaggerated sigh. "Look, you've got one minute. Choose. Manicure? Or food?"

At the mention of food, my stomach gave another rumble.

She stared at me like I'd just farted at the dinner table. "Are you going to be doing that all day?" she asked.

Great. Now I felt cheap *and* disgusting.

Five minutes later, I was standing in the food court, trying to decide between nachos or a cheeseburger. And that's when I heard it – my own voice, screaming out from someone's phone.

CHAPTER 19

I glanced around, and heard it again. It was coming from two college-age types standing near the seating area. More specifically, it was coming from one of their cellphones.

Grinning like idiots, the guys were peering down at the small screen. The one holding the phone, some dark-haired guy in a University of Michigan sweatshirt, was saying, "Wait for it. The best part's coming up."

Suddenly, they both burst out laughing. "Oh man," the other guy said, "he was *so* Jaked."

Jaked?

Almost like in a trance, I moved closer, listening to my own recorded voice carry across the small distance. As if feeling my gaze, the second guy, a tall blond in a hockey jersey, looked up. When he saw me watching, he did a double-take. He elbowed his friend, and said, "Check it out. It's *her.*"

The guy in the sweatshirt was still chuckling. He didn't look up. "Who?" he said.

"Damn it. Hit pause," the blond said. "Like *now.*"

Sweatshirt tapped the screen and looked up. His eyes widened. He looked down at his phone. When he looked up again, his face split into a wide grin. "Holy shit," he said. "It *is* you."

"Me?" I croaked.

"So," the blond guy asked, "are you his girlfriend or something?"

"Nah," the guy in the sweatshirt said. "Jake doesn't do the girlfriend thing. She's gotta be an actress." He turned to me and said, "Am I right?"

"I, uh." I held out a shaky hand toward the phone. "Can I see that?"

He grinned over at me. "Sure," he said, handing over the phone.

Cradling the thing with unsteady hands, I looked down at the small screen. On it, I saw a frozen image of Jake in a bloodstained shirt standing near the hood of an exotic red sports car. I recognized the car. I recognized the shirt. And, a moment later, when I tapped the play button, I recognized myself, screaming, "That's not what I meant!" as windshield wipers whacked that Chainsaw guy in the face.

"Oh my God," I said, scanning the details on the small screen. When I saw the number of page-views, I almost choked. It was over a million. And I knew firsthand, the video was just a few hours old.

"So what's he like?" the guy in the sweatshirt asked.

I gave my head a quick shake. "Who?"

"Jake. Who else?'

I felt myself swallow. "Um, well the thing is…" I glanced around. "Who is he?"

Both guys burst out laughing.

"Good one," the blond said. "But seriously, what's he like?"

An image of Jake flashed across my brain. He was raw and dangerous. He had stormy eyes, dark hair, and an even darker reputation. And yet, for whatever reason, he'd come for me. To rescue me? Or to ruin my life? In one short day, he'd done a little of both.

In front of me, both guys waited.

I considered their question. "First," I said, "tell me what *you* know about him."

The blond gave me a dubious look. "Is this part of some market research or something?"

"Uh, something like that."

Fifteen minutes later, I knew more than I ever imagined.

Apparently, Jake was some sort of internet mogul – a sensation, actually, with twelve million subscribers worldwide and a rabid fan base of frat boys, groupies, and mixed-martial arts fans.

Standing in that crowded food court, I hunkered down with the stranger's phone, watching Jake's greatest hits back-to-back until the phone ran out of juice and I ran out of questions.

Some of the videos were absolutely brutal – with blood-spattered fighting that almost hurt to watch. Some were hilarious, like the one with the Chainsaw and – from what I could tell – quite a few other high-dollar athletes, who tried – and failed – to kick's Jake's ass.

In every single one, Jake looked like a god – a cocky mass of guts and muscle, wrapped in a package that had girls drooling from the sidelines, whether their boyfriends were with them or not.

The way it looked, the whole thing was just a game to him. He took some brutal hits, and yet never seemed to give a crap.

I considered the fight I'd witnessed firsthand. He'd been literally yanked out of his vehicle. Now that I thought about it, he hadn't done a damn thing to stop it.

He had *wanted* that fight to happen. Anything for his fans? Or anything for fun? I felt my eyebrows furrow. Maybe it was something else. Anything for a buck?

A lot of bucks, actually. The numbers the guys threw around were staggering. For someone who'd grown up in a dump, Jake had come a long, long way. Suddenly, the penthouse seemed a modest investment for someone with his financial means.

After the two guys left, I sank down at an empty table and tried to make sense of everything. I was still trying to make sense of it when Bianca's shrill voice sliced into my consciousness. "You were supposed to meet me at the South entrance, remember?"

I glanced up. "What? I was?"

She blew out an irritated breath. "We talked about this. Remember?"

"Oh." Actually, we had. "Yeah. Sorry about that."

Her brow wrinkled. "What's wrong? You're not sick, are you?"

Still dazed, I shook my head.

"Good," she said, "because we need to run, like now. Henry's waiting."

"Who's Henry?" I asked.

She looked heavenward. "The driver. Remember?"

"Oh."

"Are you sure you're not sick?" she said. "Because if you are, you'd better do it here. Not in the car."

"Do what?"

She lowered her voice. "*You* know."

Reluctantly, I stood. "I'm fine," I said.

She gave me a dubious look. "If you say so."□

CHAPTER 20

By the time we reached the hair salon – a twenty-minute drive away – I was absolutely famished. Stupidly, I'd completely forgotten to eat and was starting to feel light-headed. Then again, maybe it had nothing to do with food, and had everything to with Jake.

Sitting in the stylist's chair, I couldn't stop thinking about what I'd learned.

The way it looked, Jake had tapped a gold mine. I never would've pegged him as the entrepreneurial type. He was too brash, too obnoxious, and way too reckless to build a stable anything. And yet, somehow he had.

At least one thing finally made sense. I now realized why he was famous to some people, and not to others. Except for the random viral video here and there, I almost never watched videos on-line. Neither did most of my friends.

I had a sneaking suspicion that I'd be watching a lot more of them from now on.

Carlie, my impromptu stylist, was just finishing up when Bianca appeared over my shoulder. She frowned at me in the mirrored reflection. "That's not what we talked about," Bianca said.

For the last hour, Bianca had been on the far side of the

salon, getting her own hair done. Unsurprisingly, it looked totally gorgeous – gathered in a thick mass high on her head, with long, styled tendrils framing her perfectly made-up face.

I glanced in the mirror at my own hair. It wasn't nearly so elaborate, but it didn't look too bad. Under the stylist's care, my highlights practically shimmered, and my hair fell in soft waves around my face.

Bianca gave my stylist a sour look. "You were supposed to put it in a bun," she said.

Carlie, who'd been setting aside a spray bottle, paused in mid-reach. She said nothing.

So I spoke up. "I know," I told Bianca, "but I wouldn't let her."

Bianca's gaze narrowed. "You wouldn't *let* her?"

It was true. The last thing I needed was a schoolmarm hairstyle to go with my schoolmarm dress. Enough was enough. "If I were going to wear my hair in a bun," I told Bianca, "I could have done that myself."

"Not as well as Carlie could." Bianca glanced toward the stylist. "Of course, that's assuming she can follow simple instructions, which I grant you, is debatable."

In the mirror, Carlie looked from me to Bianca. She opened her mouth, and then stopped short at a low rumbling sound that, embarrassingly, was coming from me.

"What was *that*?" Bianca said.

In unison, we all looked down toward my stomach. I slunk down in the chair and tried to become invisible.

"God, do you *always* sound like that?" Bianca said. "Do you have a medical condition or something?"

My face absolutely flaming, I lifted my chin. "No. I just didn't get the chance to eat. That's all."

"You can't be serious," she said. "What on Earth were you doing in the food court?"

"Nothing."

"Whatever," she said. "Forget it. At this point, I don't even want to know."

I was tired and starving, and yes, a little bit humiliated. "Good," I said, "because it's none of your business."

She drew back. "Excuse me?"

Facing off in the mirrored reflection, I studied Bianca's hair. "And why isn't *your* hair in a bun?" I asked.

"Because," she said, "I have my style. You have yours."

"Right," I said.

"What were you expecting?" she said. "To go as twins?"

"You know what?" I said. "You've been giving me a hard time all day. And honestly, it's getting old."

Behind me, Carlie glanced toward the front register. "I'm going to, uh, check on something," she said, "I'll be back in five minutes, okay?"

"Don't bother," Bianca said. "We're leaving." She gave Carlie a scornful look. "And I hope you realize, you're not getting a tip for this."

I narrowed my gaze. "Yes, she is," I said.

"Really?" Bianca said, meeting my gaze in the mirror. "With whose money?"

I glanced down at my purse, where Jake's money – what little remained – was now folded up in an inside pocket. I opened my mouth, hoping for a snappy comeback. Nothing came out.

"Oh, I'm sorry," Bianca said with an overly sweet smile. "I forgot. You're a charity case." She gave a condescending laugh. "I guess it's easy to be generous when you're not the one actually paying. Isn't it?"

I whirled around and pushed up from the chair. I faced Bianca head-on, trying to control my rapid breathing. I gave her hair a good, long look. "So," I said, "who paid for yours?"

She drew back. "What's *that* supposed to mean?"

Around us, the salon had grown oddly quiet. Carlie looked from me to Bianca. I glanced around, hoping for something, anything to fill the deathly silence. And then, something did – a low, rumbling noise that seemed to fill the whole salon.

My stomach.

I wanted to die of embarrassment.

Silently, Carlie reached past me. She opened a side drawer on her station. She pulled out a granola bar and handed it over. I glanced around. Everyone was staring. At me. I blinked long and hard before turning to Carlie.

"Thanks," I said, "I'll, uh, just eat this in the car."

But I didn't. Sitting in the back seat, food was the last thing on my mind. Between the stress of the day and uncertainty over what I'd find at Jake's place, my stomach was churning with more than hunger. Next to me, Bianca sat in frigid silence, neglecting even her phone as she looked out her car window watching the miles pass.

In front of the glass partition, Henry navigated the streets, apparently oblivious to the tension in the back seat.

About five minutes from Jake's, Bianca turned to face me. "I suppose you're going to tell on me," she said.

"Tell on you?" I said. "Like we're in grade school?"

When she spoke, her voice was very quiet. "If you're smart, you'll stay away from him."

She didn't need to say who she meant. But I made myself say it anyway. "Who? Jake?"

Slowly, she nodded.

"Yeah?" I said. "Why's that?"

"Because," she said, "if you're not careful, he'll destroy you." Her voice hitched. "Just like he's destroyed me."

Caught off guard, I stared at Bianca. Sitting in her perfect clothes, with her perfect hair and perfect nails, she looked anything but destroyed. I shook my head. "I don't get it."

She glanced toward her lap, not meeting my gaze. "You see," she said, "he gives me money. And..." She let the sentence trail off.

"And?" I prompted.

"I do things for him."

My gaze narrowed. "What kind of things?"

She looked up, finally looking me in the eye. "Things *you'll* be doing if you're not careful."

My stomach, already churning, gave another lurch. The implication was obvious. "And he pays you for that?" I said. "I'm finding that hard to believe."

She gave a bitter laugh. "Really? Why's that?"

"Because," I said, "you seem to really like him." I blew out a long breath. "I guess I figured you wouldn't—" How to put this? "—uh, need money for that."

Her voice became brittle. "It's not all fun and games," she said. "Some of the things are—" She looked away, breaking eye-contact. "—unpleasant."

I recalled the sounds that were coming from Maddie's room the previous night. As far as I could tell, nothing remotely unpleasant was going on in *there*. Then again, Jake wasn't paying Maddie for those kinds of services, not that I knew of anyway.

Did Jake expect something extra when money exchanged hands? I shook off the whole idea. Jake didn't pay anyone for sex. I was sure of it.

Or was I?

A horrible recollection hit me. Every once in a while, Maddie *did* get paid for sex – from Julian, and from a few other customers from the strip club. Was Jake one of her customers too?

My queasiness grew.

Next to me, Bianca turned to stare out her car window. Was

she serious? I shook my head. She couldn't be. I knew Jake. He wouldn't pay for it. He was smoking hot. He wouldn't need to pay for it. When we pulled up to Jake's building, I still didn't know what to think.

I opened my door, grabbed my packages, and stumbled out on shaky legs before Henry could even think of getting the door.

From inside the car, Bianca called out, "Luna?"

Relucantly, I turned toward her. "What?"

"If you tell Jake any of this," she said, "I'll be fired. You know that, right?" She fidgeted in her car seat. "I know it doesn't look it, but I do need the money. So please don't. Okay?"

This was way too strange. "I don't know," I said.

"Please believe me," she said. "I *am* sorry. I know I was awful today." She summoned up a weak smile. "But about the dress, you'll look great. Trust me."

I wasn't born yesterday. I didn't trust her one bit. Still, I'd had enough drama for one day. So I did the only smart thing I could. I turned and silently trudged into the building.

But an hour later, as Jake and I faced off in his penthouse, I wasn't feeling terribly smart about that, or anything else for that matter.□

CHAPTER 21

"What the hell is *that*?" Jake asked.

I looked down. "What?"

"That *thing*."

"You mean this?" I grabbed a handful of black fabric and lifted it outward. "The dress?"

We were standing near the balcony doors of his penthouse. I'd just emerged from his guest room, dressed for the museum thing – whatever it was – and eager to get it over with. It was sad too, because I should have been excited. But today, I'd had way too much excitement already.

When I'd returned from shopping, Jake had been gone. I'd let myself in using his extra key card, only to find a note on the entryway table. "Be back soon."

At the time, I'd been relieved. After everything I'd learned, I hadn't been ready to face him. I still wasn't ready to face him. Bianca's words weighed on my mind. Did I believe her? I still wasn't sure. But what did it matter? Whether she was lying or not, I was still dressed like a schoolmarm.

Jake eyed the dress with undisguised loathing. "A dress?" he said. "That's what you're calling it?"

Even though I didn't love the dress either, Jake's reaction still stung. As he eyed me with obvious disgust, I felt my face grow warm. "What would *you* call it?" I said.

His jaw tightened. "Tell me something," he said. "Did *you* pick that thing out?"

As I met his gaze, I felt my own temper rise. Yes, the dress was butt-ugly. But what if I *had* picked it out? Just because he didn't like something, that didn't give him the right to be so nasty about it. I threw back my shoulders and said, "What if I did?"

His mouth opened. No words came out. He reached up to rub the back of his neck. "It's uh, really—" He glanced toward the door. "So you *did* pick it out?"

Unlike me, he looked fabulous, in dark slacks and a dark dress shirt and sports jacket that matched perfectly with his dark hair and dark eyes – and yet somehow managed to accentuate his amazing body.

The fact that he looked so good while I looked so awful only made me more irritated.

"You know what?" I said. "You've been bossing me around since I got here, and I've just about had it." My voice rose. "Do you even realize what you cost me today?"

He leaned back against the wall. "Go ahead," he said, crossing his arms. "Tell me."

"Do I need to spell it out?" I counted off on my fingers. "An apartment. *Two* jobs. And a roommate."

He made a sound of derision. "Your apartment sucked, your jobs paid dick, and your roommate sold you out for some guy she just met."

I stared at him. "Maddie? What are you talking about?"

He smiled without humor. "How do you think I found you?"

"You tell *me*."

"Later," he said. "First, tell me why you're so ticked off."

"I already told you," I said.

"Uh-huh."

"And," I said, "you're being a total pig." I glanced down at my dress, ugly as it was. "The only reason I bought this 'thing' was because *you* made me." I hard sound escaped my lips. "No. In fact, I didn't even buy it. *You* did."

"Do they offer refunds?" he said.

Probably. My gaze narrowed. "No," I said.

"Then take it off," he said. "We'll burn it."

I glanced toward the fireplace, dark and quiet. Was he kidding? He didn't look like he was kidding. "Why are you being such a jerk?" I asked.

He pushed away from the wall and closed the distance between us. Soon, he was towering over me, all coiled muscle and explosive energy. "Because I don't believe for one damn minute that you picked that thing out."

I glared up at him. Bianca's warnings rang in my ear. "So what's the deal?" I said, my tone growing snotty. "It's not sexy enough for you?"

His gaze dipped to the dress. "You think *that's* the problem?"

"Isn't it?"

"Just answer me something." His gaze bored into mine. "Do you really like it?"

"The dress?" Reluctantly, I looked down. "It's not *too* bad."

"Uh-huh," he said. "And I'll ask you again, who picked it out? You? Or Bianca?"

"It was a joint effort."

He gave me a penetrating look. "So Bianca liked it?" His voice grew sarcastic. "She gave it her 'seal of approval'?"

"Well, she thought it would be appropriate for tonight, so…" I shrugged. "Yeah. I guess."

"Good to know." He glanced toward the door. "You ready to leave?"

I drew back, surprised by the sudden change in his demeanor. I glanced down at the dress. "Are you *sure* you're willing to be seen with this 'thing'?"

"We're meeting Bianca downstairs," he said. "So yeah. I'm sure."

I wanted to groan. "She's going with us?"

"Yeah," he said. "Didn't she tell you?"

"No," I said. "And why should *she* have to tell me? *You* could've mentioned it, you know."

Childish or not, I wanted to run back into the guest bedroom, rip off that ugly dress, and dive under the covers. And then, I wanted to sleep for twelve hours straight and magically wake up in my old apartment – before Rango, before Bianca, and now, before Jake.

I looked down, blinking long and hard. When I looked up, something in Jake's expression had softened.

"You're right," he said. "I should've mentioned it. I'm sorry."

My jaw dropped. "You are?"

"Yeah," he said. "But you need remember something."

"What?"

"Tonight, *you're* my guest. Not Bianca."

"Then why is she going?" I asked.

"Because I'm paying her to be there," he said.

Recalling Bianca's earlier words, I felt myself swallow. I still didn't believe what Bianca had implied. Or maybe I just didn't want to believe it.

I heard myself sigh. I'd had more than enough of Bianca for one day. And somehow, I just knew that *she'd* look like a million bucks. My stomach twisted. Maybe she was being *paid* to look like a million bucks.

Maybe later, she'd be paid to wear nothing at all.

Across from me, Jake reached for my hand. It felt big and strong as it closed around mine. It should've made things better.

But somehow, it just made everything worse.

And then he spoke. "Luna?"

"What?"

"You look beautiful."

I made a scoffing sound. "Don't bother lying. You already told me what you think."

"I told you what I thought of the dress, not what I thought of you."

I stared at him, pummeled by my own conflicting emotions. There was something in his voice that I'd never heard before. And he had just called me beautiful.

I should have been thrilled. At the very least, I should have thanked him. It would've been the polite thing to do. Except I wasn't feeling polite. So instead, I withdrew my hand and starting trudging in my high heels toward the entryway.

Inside the elevator, neither one of us spoke. There were so many things I wanted to ask him, but what was the point? Now wasn't the time, and it definitely wasn't the place. In just a couple minutes, we'd be a threesome. Me. Jake. And Bianca.

A bitter sound escaped my lips.

A threesome.

Bianca had mentioned doing things for Jake. Sexual things – or at least that was the implication. Was a threesome one of those things?

One by one, other sex acts drifted through my mind. Starring Jake. I slid another sideways glance in his direction. He stood, facing the elevator doors, with his hands loose, but his jaw set. I'd seen that stance before, countless times – usually before a fight.

He was itching for one. I could tell.

Outside the building, the car was waiting. Henry, who'd been standing at the ready, opened the rear door with a smooth, practiced motion. Inside the back seat, Bianca was waiting, all long legs and high heels.

She leaned across the seat to give Jake a dazzling smile, along with a barely decent view of her cleavage.

"There you are," she gushed. "I was almost getting worried."

Jake didn't return the smile. "Bianca," he said in a cold, flat voice.

Looking at Bianca, my stomach sank. Just as I'd feared, she looked amazing in a little black dress that somehow managed to look sophisticated *and* sexy. As for me, I looked neither. Jake turned to me. "Want the window seat?" he asked.

I shrugged. "Sure. I guess." If nothing else, it might come in handy if I decided to throw myself into traffic. Jake lowered his head and climbed into the back seat, claiming the spot beside Bianca, who reached out to give his knee a friendly squeeze.

I climbed in behind him and pretended to be invisible. When Henry pulled away from the curb, Bianca turned to give Jake a sunny smile. "Isn't this exciting?" she said.

"What?" Jake said.

"Oh come on," she said. "Don't be coy. You're fabulous at this sort of thing." She leaned toward him. "So, how do I look?"

Jake's voice was flat. "Nice dress."

"Oh come on," she said with a sultry pout. "It's more than nice."

"You're right," he said. "Now take it off." □

CHAPTER 22

Inside the car, Jake's words lingered. Huddled against my car door, I remained very still, wishing I were anyplace but here.

Bianca made a sound – a half sigh, half purr. "Why should I do *that*?" she said.

"Because," Jake said, "you're giving it to Luna."

"What?" she sputtered.

"You heard me," Jake said.

She gave a nervous little laugh. "You're not serious?"

"Wanna bet?" he said.

"But," Bianca said, "she has her own dress."

"I know," he said. "And in five minutes, *you'll* be wearing it."

I heard a sharp intake of breath, Bianca's. A moment later, she leaned around Jake and gave me a pleading look. "Luna?" she said. "What's this about?"

I looked down at my dress. Ugly as it was, it *was* mine. I guess. And then there was the ick factor. "Don't worry," I told her. "I don't want your dress."

Jake gave me a hard look. "It's not *her* dress," he said. "It's mine." He turned to Bianca. "Isn't that right?"

Bianca gave a few rapid blinks. "What are you saying?"

"I'm saying, I paid for it," Jake said. "You didn't. That makes it mine. Now take it off."

Even though Jake's words weren't directed at me, they still stung. Remnants of Bianca's earlier words echoed in my brain. *He makes me do things. Unpleasant things.*

"But," she said, "it was a gift."

"No," he said, "it was a business expense. I'm paying you by the hour. And right now, I'm paying you to take off that dress and hand it over."

My heart was hammering. "Just stop it!" I said. "I don't *want* her dress. Okay?"

"Luna," he said in a low, warning tone. "This is between me and Bianca. You don't need to worry about it."

"Oh come on!" I said. "You're asking your paid escort to give me her clothes. How does that not involve me?"

Bianca gave a little gasp. "*What* did you say?"

"I'm sorry," I said, "but let's all stop pretending that we don't know exactly what's going on here."

Bianca's gaze narrowed. "What precisely do you think is going on?"

I slid my gaze to Jake. He raised an eyebrow as if inviting me to continue.

Across the seat, Bianca's voice became shrill. "Just *what* do you think I am?"

I looked from Bianca to Jake. Her face was a mask of civilized outrage. On his face, I saw shades of amusement that hadn't been there a moment earlier.

Screw it. Whatever game they were playing, I wanted no part of it. Better to get everything out in the open than wade through some minefield of their making. I turned to Bianca and said, "I think you're his call-girl."

"What?" she shrieked. She turned to Jake. "Are you hearing this?"

I took a deep, steadying breath. "Look," I said, "it's not that I'm judging you–"

"You?" she said. "Judge me?"

"Jeez," I said. "I already said I'm *not* judging you. Okay?"

Her voice was practically a hiss. "I'm his event-planner, you twit."

I stared at her. "What?"

"That's right," she said. "I organize his calendar. I plan his events." Her gaze narrowed. "And sometimes, I take his little 'friends' shopping for things they don't understand."

I glanced down at my dress. And suddenly, I understood way more than I ever wanted to. I glared across the seat. "Well, I guess you did a nice job on *me*," I said.

Bianca put on her innocent-face. "I have no idea what you mean." She whirled toward Jake. "And aren't you going to defend me from this attack?"

Before he could answer, I jumped in to ask, "And what was all that crap about him 'destroying' you?"

Bianca gave a little sniff. "I don't know what you're talking about."

"You told me," I continued, "that he makes you do 'things'." My voice rose. "Unpleasant things."

She gave me a smirk. "Like carting *you* around?"

Between us, Jake said nothing. I whirled toward him. "And why are *you* so quiet all of a sudden?"

"Because," he said, "I figure if she pisses you off good enough, you'll see things my way." He turned to Bianca. "Go ahead," he told her. "Keep talking. Looks like you're almost there."

"You know what?" she said. "I didn't sign on for this."

"Yeah?" Jake said. "So quit."

She drew back. "What?"

"Or lose the dress," he said. "Your choice."

I gazed at Jake with narrowed eyes. "So you *did* pay her to shop with me? What's the problem? You think I can't buy a simple dress on my own? What is it? You're worried I'll embarrass you?"

"No," he said. "I thought you looked stressed out. I *thought* I was doing you a favor."

"Some favor," I said. "And just for the record, I don't want her dress."

"See?" Bianca said. "She doesn't want it." She gave a little laugh. "Like it would fit her anyway."

"What's *that* supposed to mean?" I said.

Bianca let her gaze travel from my head to my toes. "Well, you're not exactly the willowy type, are you?"

Okay, so I wasn't "willowy", whatever that meant. But I wasn't a freak of nature. I was a normal girl. What was the big deal?

"And," she said, "the dress you already have is fine. I don't know why you're complaining. It's perfectly lovely. Just because *you* can't pull it off…"

"Oh, and I suppose *you* could," I said.

"It's not like it's hard," she said. "That style? It's all the rage in New York. Trust me. You'll be thanking me later."

"Yeah, right," I said.

Between us, Jake rapped on the glass that separated us from the driver. "Stop the car," he called.

Henry eased the car off to the side of the road, and we came to a rolling stop. Jake turned to Bianca. "Get out," he said.

Her jaw dropped. "What? But I'm working tonight."

"So I'll pay you," he said. "Now get out."

She glanced around. "I'm not sure this neighborhood's safe."

"So," he said, "we'll wait for a cab."

Her voice became pleading. "Jake, come on!"

Slowly, he leaned toward her. "What'd you think?" he said in a low voice I barely recognized. "That I wouldn't call you on it?"

She drew back. "I, I don't know what you mean."

"Cut the crap," he said. "I gave you the chance to make it right. You blew it. So get the hell out."

Stunned by the venom of his words, I reached for Jake's arm.

"Luna," he said, not turning to face me, "for the last time, stay out of this."

"Well that's rich," I said. "You're kicking her out because of me? And I don't have the right to say anything?"

"Not if you're gonna stick up for her, you don't."

"I wasn't going to," I said. Probably not anyway.

Finally, he turned to face me. "Oh yeah? What *were* you gonna do?"

"Actually," I admitted, "I'm not sure. But this whole thing, it's freaking me out."

"Don't let it." His voice softened. "I've got this. You don't need to worry."

As I gazed into his eyes, I almost believed it. The moment seemed to go on forever, and then I heard a noise, one I instantly recognized – the sound of a long zipper sliding down.

Reluctantly, I peered around Jake, only to see Bianca yanking that little black dress over her head, revealing black panties and a lacy bra. A moment later, she flung the dress in my direction, saying, "Go ahead. Take it. If it's soooo important to you." ☐

CHAPTER 23

Twenty minutes later, we pulled up to the museum entrance. I still felt beyond awkward in Bianca's dress, even if it did fit like a charm.

I hadn't wanted it. I'd refused to take it. I'd argued with both of them, not that it did any good. In the end, Bianca herself had practically begged me to wear it, no doubt in some twisted effort to earn back Jake's trust, or affection, or whatever it was they had between them.

As for me, I almost felt sorry for her. And, I still couldn't figure out why she'd degrade herself in that way, whether it was for a job, or a guy, or just to prove she could rock the schoolmarm look. Either way, it didn't make me feel any better, even if I did look a whole lot better.

Sitting in the darkened back seat, I had reluctantly shimmied out of my original dress after making Jake turn his back to me. Unfortunately, this meant he was facing Bianca straight-on as she sat half-naked, like some lingerie model, within arm's reach.

I bet she just hated that.

As for Henry, I'm sure he got an eyeful of both of us. But since the car didn't crash along the way, I liked to think he did a pretty good job of keeping his eyes on the road.

But now, idling in front of the museum, my heart was

hammering. Outside the car, I saw a long line of people waiting to get into the place. Most of them looked close to my age, and all of them were dressed to kill.

I turned to Jake. "Are you sure this is a museum?" Of course, the question was beyond stupid. It said "museum" right on the front of the building, a massive stone structure with tall columns and ornate architecture.

He grinned over at me. "I'm sure," he said. "But it's a fundraiser, so it's not the normal crowd." He leaned his head toward mine. "Remember, tonight you're my girl, so act the part. Alright?"

"What do you mean?" I said. "How?"

"I dunno," he said, giving me a wicked grin. "Improvise."

Oh sure, like *that* was a good idea. At one time, I had a wild reputation. Most of it was earned. Some of it wasn't. But these days, I was determined to play it safe. Although I'd never admit in a million years, the thing with Rango had shaken me to the core.

From now on, I was on the straight and narrow.

Before I could ask Jake for more details, a burly guy in a sports jacket opened our car door. Immediately, we were hustled past the crowd and down a long red carpet. I swear, I heard murmurs of Jake's name, but Jake paid no attention. So neither did I. Or at least I tried not to.

Jake had me on one side and Bianca on the other. But it was me he draped a protective arm over as we made our way toward the entryway. I gave Bianca a sideways glance. She used the extra space to her advantage, strutting down the carpet like a runway model at a high-end fashion show.

I had to give her credit. For someone wearing the ugliest dress of the century, she was working it like a pro. I started to wonder. Maybe it *was* the thing they were wearing in New York.

When she stepped ahead of us, struck a pose, and then

called out to some lady holding a clipboard, I gave the schoolmarm dress a good long look. I couldn't help but wince. No way in hell they'd wear that thing anywhere and call it stylish, no matter how fiercely Bianca tried to pretend otherwise.

Pulling my gaze from Bianca, I let Jake lead me through the tall entryway and into a massive hall with a high domed ceiling. Dance-music pulsed from some unseen source, and the hall's center had been turned into a dance floor of sorts, with tables all around and flashing lights from somewhere above.

The dance floor was packed shoulder to shoulder with bodies – some dancing, some standing with drinks, and others weaving their way through the crowd in search of who-knows-what.

Given the time and place, the sight was utterly surreal. It was barely past the dinner hour. Even the busiest nightclubs didn't really get going until ten o'clock. As we strolled through the commotion, I couldn't help but smile as I looked around. "This is crazy," I said. "What kind of fundraiser is this?"

"It's some 'rave the art' thing," Jake said. "Bianca talked me into a sponsorship."

At the mention of Bianca's name, my smile faded. "I'm sorry for thinking she was your, um, paid companion."

He gave me a sideways glance. "Is that what they're calling it?"

"Actually," I admitted, "it was the nicest name I could think of."

"Eh, forget it," he said. "If I know Bianca, she *wanted* you to think that."

"Wow, how'd you know?"

"She's been with me a while," he said. "I know her tricks."

I could only imagine. For all I knew, she was double-jointed. I tried to keep my tone casual. "So she works for you? Like

Trey?"

"No. I'm her client, not her boss."

"Oh. That's good."

"Yeah?" he said. "Why?"

"Oh come on, *you* know." I lowered my voice. "Because you two were intimate." I cleared my throat. "Um, recently, I'm guessing?"

He stopped walking. So did I. Around us, the crowd swarmed past.

He turned to face me. "That was months ago," he said.

"Oh." For some reason, that was a huge relief. "But if she's not your employee, why would she give up the dress?"

"Because she was busted, and she knew it."

"Busted? For what?"

"Not doing her job."

I shook my head. "And what was her job, exactly?"

He gave a hard laugh. "Well, it sure as hell wasn't to stick you in a fugly dress and make you think I pay for sex."

I tried to laugh too. "I didn't really think you paid for it."

"Good to know."

"So she's your event planner?" I said, eager to change the conversation. "What does that involve?"

"P.R. mostly."

"As in public relations?" This time, I did laugh. "Since when do *you* care about that sort of thing?"

"I don't." He leaned close and lowered his voice. Our lips almost brushed, and I had to remind myself that this wasn't really a date. "But," he said, "it helps to spread the money around."

"To who?" I asked.

"The city. Cops. Whoever."

"But why?" I asked.

"Why else?" he said with that cocky grin I loved so well. "To keep my sorry ass out of jail."

From what I'd seen, his ass was anything but sorry. In fact, it was pretty darn fine, just like the rest of him. As he smiled down at me, I caught my breath.

I was so doomed. □

CHAPTER 24

I wanted to kiss him. Earlier, he suggested I improvise. Kissing would be improvising, right? Before that foolish thought became foolish action, Jake turned his head away. His gaze scanned the crowd as if searching for someone. The spell broken, I tried to do the same.

Beside him, I blew out a long breath. These temptations were piling up. I reminded myself that he wasn't my date. And he wasn't my boyfriend. And later on, we wouldn't be doing the naked pretzel, not that he'd offered.

A waiter walked by with a tray of champagne glasses. Jake snagged two glasses. He handed me one. I took a sip. I'd never been a fan of champagne, but whatever this stuff was, it was heavenly. I drank it way too fast and handed off the glass to the next passing waiter.

Across the crowd, I spotted Bianca talking to an attractive man in a business suit. She reached out and gave him a playful slap on the forearm. The guy laughed long and hard at whatever she was saying. When she turned away to reach for a champagne glass, the guy looked down to study her dress. His eyebrows furrowed. A second later, he turned and disappeared into the crowd.

When Bianca turned back, the guy was gone. She froze,

looking at the spot where he'd been standing. And then, as if feeling my gaze, she turned her head in my direction. Our gazes locked, and I felt my face grow warm.

Busted.

Trying for a recovery, I gave her a little wave. She didn't wave back.

Next to me, Jake chuckled.

Eager to break eye contact, I turned toward him. "What's so funny?" I asked.

"Nothing. Just imagining what she'll be telling you next."

"How can you laugh about it?" I said. "That whole scene in the car was awful by the way."

"Eh, I've seen worse," he said.

"I just bet," I said. "And you do know you were pretty hard on her."

"Hell yeah, I was."

"And she's okay with that?"

"I don't know," he said. "And I don't care."

The coldness in his voice surprised me. "So, did you two have a bad breakup or something?"

"No."

"Because…?" I prompted.

"Because she wasn't my girlfriend. No breakup needed."

I gave Bianca a quick glance. She was looking daggers in my direction. "Does *she* know that?" I asked.

"She's smart," Jake said. "So yeah, she knows."

Desperate to look elsewhere, I shifted my body so I was facing a different direction. But when I did, something else caught my eye. A few feet away, a young guy was holding out his cell phone like a camera. The phone was aimed at Jake. A light flashed, and the guy pulled back the phone to study the image. He grinned.

And then, the guy turned his back to us. He raised the

phone toward himself and took another picture – a selfie with Jake in the background.

Next to me, Jake was utterly oblivious. Or maybe he was used to it?

"I think someone just took a picture of you," I said.

He turned to face me. "How do you know they weren't taking a picture of *you*?"

I rolled my eyes. "Oh please."

He grinned down at me. "If I had a camera, that's what I'd do."

As I looked up at him, the noise surrounding us faded to oblivion. Everything else disappeared until we were the only two in the world. No matter how hard I tried, I couldn't seem to pull my gaze away. He lowered his head. I raised mine.

And then, Bianca's shrill voice shattered the spell. "Here," she said, thrusting a gold-embossed certificate between us.

Startled, I shook off the trance and tried to look like I didn't feel like strangling her.

Frowning, Jake looked down at the certificate. He didn't take it. "What the hell is that?" he asked.

She nudged her way between us and looked up at him. "A sponsor award."

His eyebrows furrowed. "From who?"

"The museum."

"You keep it," he said.

"But it's important," she said. "Look." She pointed to a scribbled signature at the bottom. "It's signed by the governor."

"So?" Jake said. "I didn't vote for the guy."

With an irritated sigh, she looked down at the certificate. "Should I get it framed or what?"

"Hell if I care," he said.

"Is that a 'no'?" she said. "Or a 'yes'?"

"It's a 'get that thing out of my face before I wipe my ass

with it,'" Jake said.

She pursed her lips. "You don't have to be so crude about it."

He looked at her with stony expression. "But I *am* crude," he said. "Get over it."

"Alright, fine." She made a "whatever" motion with her free hand. "I'll handle it. As usual." She turned and flounced away.

Watching her go, I heard myself laugh. Sometime in the last minute, the anger had evaporated. Probably, Bianca's interruption had saved me from making a fool of myself. I turned to meet Jake's gaze. I froze. *He* wasn't laughing.

"You wanna share the joke?" he asked.

"Oh come on," I said. "It's funny."

"That's one opinion."

"Seriously," I said, "you don't think they'd really give you a certificate without the frame?" I looked around. "For an event like this? Trust me, somewhere in this building, there's a nice frame with your name on it." I leaned toward him and said in a low, dramatic whisper. "Shall we search for it?"

He didn't crack a smile. "Screw the frame," he said.

"Oh come on," I said. "Aren't you curious where it is?"

"No. She interrupted us."

And it was a good thing too. I'd been almost ready to throw myself at him. Probably, I owed Bianca a framed certificate of her own. What I needed now was a distraction. I gazed out over crowded museum. "Do you want to look around?" I asked.

"Is that what *you* want?" he asked.

Well, it was either that or pounce on him. I felt myself nod. "Yup," I said. "Definitely."

Wordlessly, he took my arm and led me through the crowd. I'd never been an art-lover. And from the looks of it, neither was Jake. Still, as we strolled, I found myself getting lost in the experience. Together, we stopped to gaze at paintings, sculptures, and pottery from civilizations I'd never even heard of.

The music, the crowd, the energy, it all should've been distracting. But somehow, it wasn't. In a way, all of the surrounding commotion just made it easier to get lost with him, to enjoy the scenery without feeling conspicuous.

When we stopped in an alcove surrounded by colorful paintings behind glass partitions, it suddenly occurred to me that for once, I had Jake all to myself. If I squeezed just a little bit closer to him, we'd have a surprising amount of privacy.

To talk. That's all.

Still, as I gazed over at him, I couldn't help but wonder what it would be like to do more than talk. Last night, I'd heard the sounds from Maddie's room. Whatever he was doing in there, she'd obviously enjoyed it, and that was an understatement.

What would that be like? To be that close to him? For as long as I could remember, Jake had been my ultimate fantasy. In fact, he'd been my *first* fantasy, back when sex had seemed more of an abstract idea than a solid reality.

I moved my head close to his and said, "You never told me why we're here."

In a surprisingly intimate gesture, he leaned his forehead against mine. "Is that a complaint?" he asked.

Our lips were achingly close. If I tilted my head a little to the right, they'd be closer still. Kissing distance. My tongue darted between my teeth. It brushed the inside of my lips, and my eyelids threatened to drift shut.

With a mental slap to my forehead, I pulled away. "Heck yeah it's a complaint," I said. "If we're here because of me, I should probably know why."

"I'll tell you later," he said.

"Why not now?" I demanded.

"Because," he said, "in like thirty seconds, someone's gonna try to kick my ass."

I wanted to groan.

Again? ☐

CHAPTER 25

I glanced around. Sure enough, a good-looking blond guy in expensive-looking clothes was stalking toward us.

I glanced toward Jake. Draping a protective arm over my shoulder, he pulled me close. "Don't worry," he said into my ear, "the guy's a pussy."

I snuck another glance in the guy's direction. He didn't look like a pussy. Okay, so maybe he didn't have Jake's powerful build, but still, he didn't look like a wimp either. And from the expression on his face, I had the distinct impression that he'd like nothing better than to beat Jake with a nearby sculpture until there was nothing left – of the sculpture *or* Jake.

When the guy reached the alcove where we stood, he barreled up to Jake and said, "You asshole!"

Around us, a few people turned to look.

Jake looked at him with a faintly amused expression. "Yeah?"

Although Jake's demeanor was easy, I could feel his hard muscles tensing at my side. If the guy wanted a fight, he'd probably get it, and then some.

The guy leaned in close. "Do you know how much money you cost me today?"

Earlier today, I'd asked Jake an eerily similar question. It boggled the mind. How much damage could one guy do in twenty-four hours?

Jake grinned over at him. "How much?" he asked.

"Half a million. You cocksucker."

"Cocksucker?" Jake frowned. "Wait, I thought I was an asshole."

"Stop messing around," the guy said. "That video of yours, it just cost Dirk one hell of an endorsement deal."

I repeated the name in my head. Dirk. As in Dirk Leonard? The Chainsaw?

"Yeah?" Jake said. "Which deal?"

The guy practically spat the answer. "Power Shot."

"Eh, their product sucks," Jake said. "I did the guy a favor."

"A favor?" the guy said. "You cost *him* ten million." His jaw clenched. "And you made him look like an asshole."

Jake's reached up to scratch his chin. "Wait. I thought *I* was the asshole."

"Go ahead," he told Jake. "Keep goading me. You think I'm gonna lose my cool? You think I'm gonna yank you out of some car? Start a fight? Make myself a laughingstock?"

Jake looked at him with mild interest. "You're not?"

"No." The guy's voice ground to a low menace. "That's not the way I work. But let me tell you something, when *I* hit you, it won't be with my car, and it won't be with my fist. But it'll hurt like a son-of-a-bitch just the same. So you remember that the next time you mess with me or one of my people."

With that, the guy turned and stalked away, jostling his way through the crowd until he disappeared from sight.

I was still staring after him when I heard Jake's voice, low in my ear. "Want another drink?" he asked.

I whirled toward him. "What?"

He flicked his gaze to my empty glass. "You're out of champagne. Want me to get you a refill?"

"Forget that," I said. "Who was that guy?"

"Who?"

"Cut the crap," I said. "The guy who just left."

Jake grinned. "That," he said, "is Vince Hammond." His voice became sarcastic. "Agent to the stars."

I shook my head. "Movie stars?"

"Nah. Sports stars. You might say he's not my biggest fan."

"Really?" I rolled my eyes. "I had no idea." I lowered my voice. "Did you really cost him half a million dollars?"

Jake gave it some thought. "Five percent? His cut of ten mil? Yeah. Sounds about right."

"How can you be so casual about it?" I said. "I mean, that's a lot of money."

"Not my money," he said.

I bit my lip and gave it some thought.

"Don't worry," Jake said, "the guy can afford it."

"I dunno…" I said.

"Trust me," Jake said, "he had it coming."

I couldn't help but wince. "Still…" And then I remembered something. "By the way, I saw that video."

"Yeah? Where?"

"At the mall. On some guy's cell phone. Thanks a lot for telling me about it."

"You didn't like the surprise?" he said.

"Oh yeah," I said, "I just *love* surprises like that. Do you know, someone actually asked me if I was your girlfriend?"

"Yeah?" His gaze drifted to my lips. "So what'd you tell 'em?"

Instantly, heat flooded my face. "Nothing. Which was easy, since I'm apparently the most clueless person on the planet." I gave him an exasperated look. "Seriously Jake, why didn't you tell me?"

"About the fight?" he said. "You were there, remember?"

"You know what I mean," I said. "You're like this big deal or something."

"I'm not so big."

"How can you say that?" I said, thinking of everything – his fans, his penthouse, his car. Or should I say cars, in the plural? "It's changed your whole life."

He moved away to lean against the alcove wall. "Has it?"

"Sure," I said. "You're rich. You're famous." I forced out a laugh. "You've got girls flashing you on the street for God's sake."

"And yet," he said, "a certain girl won't let me buy her a drink."

I looked around. "I bet any girl here would jump at the chance."

"But I didn't ask *any* girl," he said. "I asked you."

I leaned toward him and lowered my voice. "Is this about acting like I'm 'your girl'?"

"How do you know you're not?" He reached for my hand. "Now come on."

As he guided me through the crowd, his words rang in my ear. Was this all part of some act? Or was he really flirting with me?

Instantly, I scratched out *that* possibility. He couldn't be. Maybe his words meant something else entirely. Maybe I was his so-called girl because I was going to be his kid sister by marriage.

And yet, he hadn't been treating me like a sister. Or a kid for that matter.

The next time we stopped, he wrapped an arm around my waist, pulling me to his side. His body felt hard and warm. I wondered what it would be like if I *were* his girl. A wistful sigh escaped my lips. That was like wishing for snow on the Fourth of July. Barring a miracle, it was never going to happen.

Still, the fantasy was nice, and I vowed to enjoy it. Against all my expectations, I was having a terrific time. Together, we snaked our way through the crowd, talking and laughing as went.

As the minutes passed, and the champagne glasses came and went, I found it a whole lot easier to improvise. I felt his hand on my back and heard his voice in my ear. Maybe this wasn't a date, but it sure as heck felt like it.

The next time we stopped, I gave up trying to figure it out. Instead, I leaned into him, no longer caring if this was all part of an act or my own crazy imagination.

Soon, I heard his voice, low in my ear.

"Luna?

"Hmmm," I said.

"Kiss me." □

CHAPTER 26

I turned to stare up at him. "Huh?"

Around us, the crowd was still milling, music was still playing, and the Earth, as far as I knew, was still spinning. But for me, everything stood eerily still as I gazed up at him, watching as he looked down on me with a blazing intensity that sent a bolt of heat straight to my core.

He moved his head a fraction toward mine. "Don't think," he said. "Just do it."

And so I did. I stood on the toes of my high-heels and pressed my lips to his. His arms closed tight around me, gathering me close as our lips finally touched. Slowly, my lips moved against his, and his moved against mine, even as our bodies remained nearly motionless amidst the surrounding commotion.

When I flicked the tip of my tongue into his mouth, he gave an audible groan that made my heart race and my knees go weak. My eyes were shut, my pulse was hammering, and my head was spinning – right up until the moment I heard a male voice say, "Jenna? What the hell?"

Jenna? Oh crap. He meant *me*. And that voice was all too familiar. Scary familiar.

Pushing away from Jake, I whirled around, and there he was

— Rango, the ex-boyfriend from hell. His dark spiky hair was styled in a fashionable disarray, and he wore the same kind of expensive, designer clothes he always wore. Beside him, stood Bianca, who looked like she'd give anything for a stick to beat me with.

Jake stepped forward to wrap an arm around my waist. He looked toward Rango and said, "Is there a problem?"

Rango's jaw tightened. He gave me a hard look.

"Hey," Jake said. "I asked the question, not her."

Glancing from Jake to Rango, I felt my temper rise. Was that kiss merely a setup? A sham? Was Jake marking me as his territory or something?

Had I just been metaphorically peed on?

Even amidst all the chaos, one question echoed louder in my brain than the rest. Had Jake known Rango was there? Was that the reason for that kiss? Earlier, Jake had claimed that tonight was for me. Was this what he meant?

My stomach, dancing with butterflies just a few seconds ago, was sinking like a stone.

In front of me, Rango remained silent, but the look on his face was all too familiar. It was the same look I'd seen at the last party we'd attended as a couple. Throughout the night, he'd mostly kept his cool, until we'd gotten into his car anyway.

A half hour later, his Beamer was smashed, and I was hiding out in the back of an all-night coffee house, calling for a cab.

In front of me, Bianca's gaze narrowed. "I thought your name was Luna," she said.

"It is," I said. "Sort of. It's complicated."

She rolled her eyes. "If you say so."

Bianca was the least of my concerns. I looked from Rango to Jake as they sized each other up. The way it looked, my name wasn't the only thing complicated around here.

Jake was giving Rango a hard look. "You got something to

say?" Jake asked.

Rango's gaze shifted to me. "So you're with *him* now?" he said.

Oh God, this was so embarrassing. Not that I cared one bit what Rango thought, but something about this whole scene was way too primitive, like I was a piece of meat being tossed from one guy to the next. And here, I wasn't really with either one of them.

"No," I told Rango in my calmest voice, "I'm not with anyone. But that doesn't mean I want to be with you."

He made a hard scoffing sound. "Like I asked."

Color flooded my face. Talk about humiliating.

Jake looked down at me. "Baby," he said, "you don't need to be nice to him." He turned to Rango. "What Luna's *trying* to say is 'piss off.'"

Rango's face froze.

I pushed away from Jake. "That's *not* what I'm trying to say." Oh sure, the sentiment fit, but the last thing I needed was more trouble.

"Sorry," Jake said. "My mistake." He turned to Rango. "What I *meant* to say was that *I* think you should piss off."

I glared up at Jake. "That's *not* what I meant."

Rango still hadn't moved. I snuck a quick glance in his direction. That vein in his forehead was pulsing in a way I knew all too well.

But when he spoke, his voice was a lot calmer than I'd have ever anticipated. "I don't know what you've heard," he told Jake, "but I don't *want* your girl." His gaze shifted to me. "I've moved on, Jenna. Get over it."

Next to him, Bianca gave a half-laugh, half-snort. "Jenna."

"Oh shut up," I told her.

I returned my gaze to Rango. Had he really moved on to someone new? If I was lucky, he was telling the truth. But that didn't make anything less humiliating when he added, "And stop calling me, alright? My girlfriend doesn't like it."

"Me?" I said. "Call you?" I'd literally changed my phone number to get rid of this guy. I'd had to move out of my apartment. I'd had to replace most of my stuff. Correction – I still *had* to replace my stuff, someday, when I wasn't broke and semi-homeless.

Jake, which his free hand, reached up to stroke his chin. He looked at Rango. "You know what you need?" Jake said.

Rango's answer was a clipped, "What?"

Jake pointed to Rango's shirt. "A new tailor."

Rango's shirts were hand-made, a distinction he was overly proud of. Rango looked down. "What the hell is that supposed to mean?"

"Nothing," Jake said, "I just figured you'd want to know."

Rango gave Jake the squinty-eye. "Are you messing with me?"

"I don't know," Jake said. "Am I?"

Rango looked around. After a long moment, he gave a shaky smile. "I know who you are." He forced out a laugh. "Alright, you got me. Where's the camera?"

"I dunno," Jake said. "Have you checked your mom's room?"

Rango's smile faded. "What the hell's your problem?"

"No problem here," Jake said, before adding under his breath, "Dipshit."

Rango's gaze narrowed to slits. "What'd you just call me?"

Jake's brow wrinkled. "What'd it sound like?"

"It *sounded* like you called me a dipshit."

"Did it?" Jake said. "No kidding?"

Rango gave another shaky laugh. "Yeah."

Jake nodded. "Good hearing."

I grabbed Jake's elbow. "You know what?" I said. "I think

there's some painting or something we wanted to see." I gave the elbow a tug. "Right?"

Jake grinned over at me. "But we're not done talking to Ringo."

Rango's vein gave a special little jump. "It's Rango," he said.

Jake looked at him. "Dingo?"

"No," Rango said through clenched teeth. "Rango."

Jake was nodding. "Wasn't there some movie about a slug named Rango?" He turned to me. "It was a cartoon or something, right?"

I knew what movie he meant, some animated thing from a while back. "I think it was a lizard," I said. "Now come on, let's go."

"Oh for God's sake," Bianca said, "it was a chameleon."

Jake and I turned look.

"I saw it with my nieces," she said. "Jeez."

"Well, there you have it," Jake said. He held out a hand toward Rango. "Nice meeting you, Dongo."

Rango's face was red, and that vein looked in danger of exploding. He looked down at the hand. He didn't move.

"Aw come on, man," Jake said. "Don't leave me hangin' here."

Rango still didn't move. Neither did Jake. I gave another tug on Jake's elbow. He didn't budge. Finally, with obvious reluctance, Rango reached out a hand. But just when it almost reached Jake's, Jake pulled back his own hand and said, "Gotcha." He shook his head. "Man, I can't believe you fell for that." Jake laughed. "Dumbass."

I gave the elbow another tug. "Yeah. Ha ha. Let's go." I gave him a pleading look. "Please?"

Jake hesitated. And then he grinned down on me. "Whatever you say, *Jenna*." □

CHAPTER 27

Rango said nothing as I practically dragged Jake away from the alcove. I was fuming and confused, and desperate to get the two guys away from each other. Just before Jake and I disappeared into a mass of people, I gave one final look over my shoulder.

Bianca and Rango were still there, watching us with twin expressions of malice. If looks could kill, we'd have been dead twice over. Was it because of that kiss? It had to be.

A sickening thought drifted to the forefront of my brain. Was I kept clueless to make the seduction look real? Kiss me, Jake had said.

I hadn't required much convincing, had I?

Turns out, I was just like all the other girls – eager for whatever he offered and too stupid to realize I was the only one being swept away. Probably, Jake was trying to do me a favor. I should feel grateful. I *was* grateful. But I was something else too – disappointed.

When Jake and I ducked into a side hall, I whirled to face him. "What the hell was that about?" I said.

He looked down at me. "What?"

"Oh come on," I said. "Don't play dumb. You *knew* Rango would be here tonight. Didn't you?"

He shrugged. "Maybe."

"How?"

"Rumor was he had an invitation." Jake grinned. "V.I.P. too."

My gaze narrowed. "Did *you* invite him?"

"You mean did I call him up, and say, 'Hey Dingo, you wanna party?'"

"You know what I mean," I said.

"Okay." His voice lost any trace of humor. "Yeah, I made sure he had an invitation."

"So he was here because of you?"

"No," Jake said. "He was here because of *you*."

I glared up at him. "Meaning?"

"Meaning," Jake said, "he knew you'd be here."

"How?" I asked.

Jake reached up to rub the back of his neck. "Bianca might've mentioned it."

My gaze narrowed. "At your request?"

"Maybe."

I made a sound of disgust. "Unbelievable. Why on Earth would you do that?"

"Look," Jake said, his voice softening, "you're gonna run into him sooner or later. You know that, right?"

"So?"

"So better with me than alone."

"And what was your plan?" I said. "To let him think wer're a couple? And hope he just goes away?"

I wanted to laugh. And cry. Me and Jake? A couple? It was an adolescent girl's fantasy. Supposedly, I'd grown up. Apparently not enough.

At the memory of that kiss, my stomach clenched. It had felt so real. To me, it *had* been real. Achingly real. But apparently, it had been real only to me. How pathetic was that?

"No," Jake said. "The plan was to piss him off."

"Why?" I asked.

"Why else? So he'd swing at me."

I squinted up at him. "Why?'

Jake shrugged. "So I could kick his ass."

"You can't be serious."

"Why not?" he asked. "You said you were cool with it, as long as Rango swung first. Remember?"

"No, I don't remember. And if even I did say that, it's not what I meant."

"Eh, close enough," Jake said.

"No, it's not," I said. "That's insane."

He said nothing.

"Well?" I said.

"Well what?" he asked.

I looked around. "So all of this? The dress? The champagne?" I swallowed. "That kiss? It was all about Rango?" I looked toward the entryway. Somehow, I summoned up a hollow laugh. "Well, I guess that's done. Time to head out, huh?"

All along, I had known tonight wasn't real. But somehow, I'd been telling myself I could enjoy this little game of make-believe and walk away when the story ended. God, I'd been such a fool.

His voice softened. "Luna, what's wrong?"

"Nothing," I said. "It's just time to go, right?"

"You wanna go?" he said. "We'll go. But we don't have to."

"Look," I said, "I know you were trying to do me a favor, and I appreciate it. Honestly." I sighed. "But, I dunno, I guess it's been a long day."

When disappointment darkened his face, I realized something incredibly stupid. He didn't *want* to leave, and I couldn't exactly blame him. I looked around. Music was still playing, the crowd was still pulsing, and if I wasn't mistaken, those two scantily clad girls near the archway were just waiting to make their move.

"Oh. Sorry," I said. "You're probably not ready to leave, are you?" I summoned up what I hoped was a cheery smile. "That's okay." I glanced around. "I'll just, uh, call a cab or something."

"You think I'm gonna let you leave by yourself?"

"Sure. Why not?" I bit my lip. Except, where would I go? Did Jake *really* want me hanging around his place when he wasn't there? Or worse, what if later on, he brought home one of those girls? Or *both* of those girls?

Last night, I'd listened to him with Maddie. That had been bad enough. If I had known it was Jake eliciting those sounds, it would have been a million times worse.

And what about tonight? How awful would that be? When I had just kissed him? When I'd felt his lips pressed to mine? When I'd felt him hold me tight? When I'd allowed myself to believe he was actually kissing me back?

Suddenly, my lips felt cold and dry, just like my thoughts. Again, I glanced toward the entrance.

"You okay?" Jake said.

"Sure, I'm fine."

His eyebrows furrowed. He pulled out his phone and started tapping at the screen.

"What are you doing?" I asked.

"Texting Henry," he said. "Now come on." He took my arm. "Let's get you back."

I almost wanted to argue. The night was young, and part of me wished I had the stamina, or whatever, to stick around. But I hadn't been lying. It *had* been a long day. And somehow, I just didn't have the energy to pretend anymore.

The fairytale was over. Closed. The End.

What I needed now was a moment to regroup, before I lost

it right here in the crowd. "I need to hit the ladies room," I said. "Can I meet you out front?"

"No."

"No?" I gave a hollow laugh. "So you're denying me bathroom privileges? Is that it?"

"No. I'm not letting you walk there alone."

"Why not?"

"Because Rango's still around someplace."

"I can handle Rango," I said.

"Uh-huh." Jake took my arm. "Now come on."

I couldn't decide if I was flattered or annoyed. Probably, I was both. This whole evening was turning into a mind-boggling mix of contradictions. It was enough to make me crazy.

Near the rest room entrance, I turned to Jake and said, "I'll be out in a few minutes."

"If you're not," he said, "I'm coming in after you."

I stared up at him. "You wouldn't."

"Wanna bet?"

Actually, I didn't. So I turned around and headed into the ladies room.

Of course, the place was packed, with a long line of girls waiting for stalls, and a handful of others clustered around the wide mirror. If Jake weren't waiting just outside the door, I'd probably turn around and head right back out. But at this point, I'd only look stupid.

Reluctantly, I made my way to the sink, waited for an opening, and then pretended to wash my hands. As the warm water ran over my fingertips, I looked up, catching my reflection in the mirror. Who was I, anyway? A pretend-date in a borrowed dress?

I was so lost in my own thoughts that it took me a moment to realize something. Just over my shoulder, another face had appeared in the reflection. It was the face of Bianca.

And the way it looked, she was griping up a storm. ☐

CHAPTER 28

I stared at Bianca in the mirror. She was still talking to me. But over the sound of the automatic hand-dryer, just a couple feet away, I could hardly hear a thing.

I turned around to face her. "Excuse me?" I said.

She raised her voice. "I was saying," she said in a voice of overblown patience, "that if you're going to be so sulky, you might as well give me back my dress."

"Hey, you were the one who begged me to take it," I said. "Remember?"

She lifted her chin. "That was then. This is now."

I glanced down at the dress I'd borrowed. "You want it back?" I said. "Fine by me." At this point, I hardly cared. Besides, I was leaving anyway.

She wrinkled her nose. "Not after you've *sweated* in it."

I rolled my eyes. "Yeah. That's me. Sweaty."

"You said it. Not me."

I gave her a hard look. "So what are you being paid to do, exactly?" I said. "Other than hassle me, I mean."

"You wouldn't understand."

"Oh yeah? Try me."

Earlier, she'd called herself an event planner. If we were on friendlier terms, I would have loved to hear more about her career. Did she, like me, have a degree in hospitality management? Or had she come up the ranks a different way?

"Well, tonight," she said, "I'm apparently being paid to wear your hand-me-downs and suck up to your ex-boyfriend." She made a sound of disgust. "I can't believe I went to college for this."

"Why are you so hostile to me?" I said. "I never did anything to you."

She made a point of looking down at her – correction, *my* – schoolmarm dress. "Are you sure about that?" she asked.

"Hey, that wasn't *my* doing," I said.

She gave me a dubious look. "Right."

"And besides," I said, "you're the one who picked that thing out."

I didn't even know why I was bothering. She'd sabotaged me. She'd lied to me. She'd probably do worse if I ever let down my guard.

Stepping back, she cocked her head to give me a good, long look. Suddenly, her face lit up with a smile that looked almost genuine. "Oh my God," she said. "I just figured out what your problem is."

"Oh yeah?" I said in a bored tone. "What's that?"

She gave a little laugh. "You thought that kiss was real. Didn't you?"

Before the question died on her lips, my face was already warm. Still, I made myself say, "What kiss?"

"Awww, that's so cute," she said. "You did." She pursed her lips. "Jake's gonna *love* that."

I almost wanted to slap her. But instead, I stepped toward her and said, "Did you come in here for a reason? Or just to give me a hard time?"

"Actually," she said, glancing toward a stall. "I was in here already." She smiled. "Your lucky day, huh?"

On the nearby wall, the automatic dryer suddenly stopped, leaving the restroom a whole lot quieter. Slowly, I realized that no one else was speaking. I glanced around. So did Bianca. One girl – a cute blonde in a blue micro-dress – was staring openly in our direction. But she wasn't staring at me. She was staring at Bianca.

Bianca gave her an annoyed look. "What are *you* looking at?" Bianca said.

The girl glanced down at Bianca's dress. "Your costume," she said. "Are you like, part of the show or something?"

Bianca's gaze narrowed. "What show?"

"I dunno. Isn't there some historical reenactment or something? I mean, it *is* a museum, right? Are you like playing a prairie lady?"

Bianca glared at her. "Do I *look* like a prairie lady?"

"Yeah. Kind of," the girl said.

"Well I'm not!" Bianca said.

"Jeez, you don't have to be all snippy about it," the girl said, "I was just asking."

I couldn't help it. I snickered.

Bianca whirled toward me. "What are you laughing about?" she said. "It's *your* dress."

"Not anymore." I gave an exaggerated eye-roll. "Not after you've *sweated* in it."

Through clenched teeth, Bianca said, "I am not sweaty."

I leaned forward and gave a little sniff. "Are you sure?"

"Oh grow up," she muttered, turning toward the door. "That's it. I'm outta here."

She'd gotten just a few feet before whirling back around toward me. "And just for the record," she said, "this dress sucks! There! Are you happy now? If you wore this thing in New York, they'd mug you for the fun of it. And you'd deserve it. When I get home tonight, I'm gonna burn it." Her voice rose.

"And send Jake the bill!"

She turned away and wrenched open the ladies room door.

"Don't bother!" I called out. "He *already* paid for it! Remember?"

After she disappeared, I glanced around the rest room. Everyone was staring. Now, with Bianca gone, the only person actually being stared at was me. "Um, sorry about that," I muttered. Without bothering to dry my hands, I dashed toward the door and plunged through it.

Outside, Jake was waiting where I'd left him. He must have seen Bianca leaving, but he didn't say a word, and neither did I.

Besides, what was there to say?

He took my soggy hand in his and started leading me toward the main entrance. By the time we snaked our way through the crowd and out of the building, the car was already waiting.

Jake opened the rear passenger side door and motioned for me to climb in. I settled myself into the center spot and waited for him to push the door shut and send me on my way.

He didn't. Instead, he climbed inside and settled himself beside me.

"What are you doing?" I asked.

He gave me a curious look. "Getting into the car."

I glanced toward the museum. "But don't you want to stay?"

He pulled the car door with a decisive thud. "No."

"Why not?"

"Because," he said, "*you're* not staying."

"Oh," I said. "Is it because you don't want me at your place? You know, without you there to keep an eye on things?"

"I don't know," he said. "Are you planning to rob the place?"

I glanced again toward the museum. "But what about Bianca?"

"Last I heard, she's calling a cab."

"Really? When did you hear that?"

"Five minutes ago."

I winced. "Sorry about that."

He gave a soft chuckle. "Don't be. I'm paying for it."

"Oh. Well, um, sorry about that too."

As we pulled away from the curb, I watched through the car window as the museum slid out of view. It should have been an amazing night. In truth, it *had* been an amazing night, right up until the moment it wasn't.

Inside the car, I leaned my head back and closed my eyes. I didn't feel like making small talk, and I sure as hell didn't feel like discussing anything of importance. The motion of the car, all that champagne, the pure exhaustion, it was all taking its toll.

I hadn't even danced with him. I should have danced with him. But stupidly, I'd thought there was plenty of time. I'd been wrong.

And now, I'd probably never get to dance with him. Too bad too, because I'd been dreaming of that since I'd been seventeen. Tired of thinking about the present – or heaven forbid, my uncertain future – I settled back to think about the past. □

CHAPTER 29

It was the summer I turned seventeen.

"You're not actually gonna do it?" Lizzie said.

"Oh yeah?" I said. "Just watch me."

We were standing on the darkened alley behind Razer's, a hometown pub that had dancing on Saturday nights. Jake was inside. I was sure of it. I'd seen his motorcycle outside, along with the bikes of two of his closest friends.

Lizzie looked up toward the small window. "How do you know it goes to the rest room?" she asked.

"Selena told me," I said.

"Your sister?" Lizzie said. "But she's not twenty-one either."

It was true. Selena was nineteen, two years older than me, but still two years away from the legal drinking age. Yet somehow, she'd gotten a fake ID, probably courtesy of her boyfriend, Jake's brother, who had some interesting connections that Selena rarely discussed.

Looking at the window, I wondered if I'd be able to fit through it. From down here, the window looked tiny – just a thick, horizontal slab of hazy glass, propped open by some unseen mechanism.

Too bad I didn't look more like my sister. I'd have simply borrowed her ID and gone straight through the front door. But

I didn't. So instead, I was standing underneath that foggy window and wishing I knew for sure what exactly was on the other side.

Supposedly, Lizzie and I were spending the night above my mom's coffee shop, just a few blocks away. In reality, I was making good on a dare. That was the official reason. Unofficially, I was determined to dance with Jake Bishop, just like I'd always wanted to.

"He probably doesn't even dance," Lizzie said.

That's where she was wrong. I knew him. He was the kind of guy who was up for anything.

Most of the guys that I knew hated to dance. Probably, they were afraid of looking stupid. But Jake, he never cared what anyone thought. And no matter what he did, he *never* looked stupid.

"He will if I ask him," I said, sounding a lot more confident than I felt. Every once in a while, he'd let me hang on the fringes with him and his friends. Sometimes, I felt like their mascot or something, like a kitten or a puppy, too eager to please and too inexperienced to fully fit in, no matter how hard I tried.

Funny too, because I tried like crazy.

Maybe I amused them. Or maybe I got a pass for being Selena's sister, not that *she* ever hung with that crowd. But as for me, I loved almost all of them, especially Jake. He was a twenty-two-year-old bad-ass with a terrible reputation. Until now, I'd been the kid who adored him. But I wasn't a kid anymore, and it was time for him to see that with his own two eyes.

I looked down at my skimpy black top and short black skirt. "How do I look?" I asked.

Lizzie grinned. "Slutty."

"Hey!"

"It was a compliment," she said. "Honest."

"Oh. Then, uh thanks."

Near the delivery doors, we'd found a rickety old ladder, along with a few empty crates. I'd skipped the crates and gone straight for the ladder, dragging it underneath the window, where it now stood waiting.

I reached into the tiny pocket of my skirt and handed Lizzie the key to my mom's coffee shop. My heart was hammering, but I couldn't help but smile. "See you later on," I said.

"Wait," she said. "After you go in, should I move the ladder? Or leave it?"

I gave it some thought. If things worked out tonight, I'd definitely be needing that ladder again in the future. No need to give the pub-owners a heads-up. "Can you put it back where we found it?" I asked.

She nodded, and then paused. "But if the ladder's gone, how will you get out?"

"Easy," I said. "I'm gonna walk out the front door."

And if I was really lucky, Jake would be joining me. For once, *I* could be the girl on his arm. As long as I'd known him, he'd never had a serious girlfriend. But he had girls. Lots of girls. And I heard things too.

One of these girls, Roxie Claymore, who was like five years older than me, claimed he was the best lay in the tri-city area. Even if she hadn't said it straight to me, that didn't mean I wasn't listening. Jake didn't know it, but I'd been saving myself for a reason. Someday, I vowed, Jake Bishop would be my first.

Lizzie took the key and stuffed it into the pocket of her jeans. "Remember," she said, "you promised to tell me everything." Her voice lowered. "And I mean *everything*."

After a quick nod, I started climbing. Lizzie moved forward and gripped the base of the ladder, holding it steady as I climbed. When I reached the top, I peeked through the hazy glass. I saw the outlines of a single bathroom stall, along with one lone sink. I gave the glass a tentative push and peered down through the slim opening.

The tile floor was a long way down, but just underneath the window was a sturdy-looking metal cabinet. It wasn't *that* far down. I wriggled forward until the upper half of my body was firmly inside the rest room.

I was halfway there.

Sure, my clothes might be getting grimy, but I'd worn black on purpose, just in case. Besides, lots of Jake's girls dressed in black, so he must really like it, right? I felt myself smile.

My smile faded when I noticed something else – urinals on the side wall. Oh crap. This was the *men's* restroom? My gaze darted from wall to wall. Should I jump inside fast? Or leave while I still had the chance?

In front of me, the restroom door opened.

I heard the hum of music and rowdy voices. I tensed, holding myself motionless, half in the window, and half out. A moment later, the door opened wide. Someone walked through it and stopped short at the sight of me.

My heart skipped a beat, and my hands grew clammy.

It was Jake. □

CHAPTER 30

Standing just inside the restroom door, Jake studied me with an expression I could only describe as perplexed. My lips parted, but no words came out.

Embarrassment wasn't the only reason for my silence. It was the sight of Jake. He looked utterly amazing in dark jeans and a thin dark T-shirt. The cotton fabric clung to the lines of his lean, muscular physique, making me almost forget where I was or what I was doing.

Under any normal circumstance, I would have stopped to watch him. But this situation was anything but normal. If I were still a kid, I swear, I'd have closed my eyes and pretended to be invisible.

But I wasn't a kid, and I refused to look away. Our gazes locked. His dark gaze probed mine with a look so penetrating, I swear, it pierced my soul.

The silence stretched out until one corner of Jake's mouth turned upward. "How's it going?" he said.

"Uh, good." I snuck a quick glance over my shoulder, toward the half-open window. If I crawled out now, was there any chance he'd forget this had ever happened?

I studied his face. Nope. I was making an impression alright. It just wasn't the one I'd been going for.

My feet were still touching the ladder's upper rung, but it was the metal window frame that held most of my weight. The frame dug into my hips, and I wriggled forward just a fraction, hoping to ease some of the pressure.

I glanced at Jake. Shouldn't he be helping or something?

I envisioned him rushing forward, easing me out of the window and gathering me into his strong arms. He'd kiss my forehead, tenderly at first. And then, his lips would trail downward until they met mine in a long, loving kiss.

That's all it would take. He'd realize that I was finally all grown up. Nothing else would matter – not our age differences, not the fact my sister had warned me to stay away from him, and certainly not the fact that a hundred other girls would kill to take my place.

I gave him a pleading look.

Any minute now.

He didn't move.

A sigh of frustration escaped my lips. "Wanna help me down?" I asked.

The question had barely died on my lips when the door behind Jake started to swing open. My heart jumped, and my body tensed. With barely half a glance, Jake rammed his foot backward, slamming the door shut with a loud thud.

"Hey!" a guy yelled from the other side. "What the hell?"

"Out of order," Jake said.

"But I've gotta go. C'mon!"

"Then use the girl's room," Jake said.

"No way!" the guy said. "There's girls in there."

"Yeah? So deal with it," Jake said.

When the door started to swing inward again, Jake turned around. He opened the door just a crack and stared out at whoever was on the other side. After a long moment, I heard the same guy's voice again. "Uh, I'll come back in a few. Sorry, man."

Wordlessly, Jake slammed the door shut yet again. Slowly, he turned to face me. His face had lost any trace of good-humor. "Time for you to go," he said.

I stared down at him. "What?" I said. "No way. I'm not going anywhere."

Silently, he looked up at me, his expression stony.

The ridiculousness of my statement slowly caught up with me. I cleared my throat. "Well, I'm not staying *here* in the window. Obviously. I mean I'm coming inside. You know." My voice cracked. "With you."

Something about his demeanor was making me feel younger by the minute. I didn't like it. I wasn't a kid anymore. Why couldn't he see that?

His gaze dipped briefly to my tank-top before returning to my face. "You know what kind of people hang out in this place?" he said.

"Uh, well, *you* hang out here so—"

"Yeah," Jake said. "And guys like me."

I stuck out my chin. "There's girls too."

That stupid window frame was killing my hips. I wriggled forward another fraction and gave him another pleading look.

Jake's jaw tightened. He looked away.

From somewhere near my feet, I heard Lizzie's voice call out, "Hey, Luna! Why'd you stop?"

I stifled a groan. Why was she still here? Oh, that's right. The ladder. Damn it. I reached back and gave her a small shooing motion.

Either she didn't see my hand, or she totally misunderstood, because the next thing I knew, she was calling out in a loud sing-song voice. "Go on, lovergirl. Don't keep Jakeepoo waiting."

My face burst into flames, and I started to sweat. A trickle of perspiration inched down my back. Below me, the ladder started to shake. Oh crap. Was she seriously climbing up after me?

Soon, I heard Lizzie's voice, closer now. "Nice thong," she said, "Do you know, I can totally see your ass?"

"So?" I turned my head and gritted out over my shoulder. "Then don't look."

"Why?" she said in that same teasing tone. "Worried Jakeepoo will get jealous?"

I turned around as far as I dared. "Seriously," I hissed, "shut up!" I returned my attention to Jake, who was eyeing me with that same stony expression. "She's just kidding," I told him.

Almost losing my balance, I turned again to call over my shoulder. "Seriously Lizzie. Just go away. Okay?"

From inside the restroom, Jake spoke. "You too," he said.

I turned to stare at him. "Huh?"

Behind him, the door started to swing inward again. With the sole of one foot, Jake kicked it backward, slamming it against the door-jamb.

"What the hell?" a male voice yelled. I recognized the voice. It belonged to one of Jake's friends – a guy called Loke, short, apparently for Loco, if any of the stories were true.

"It's out of service," Jake said.

"Jake, you dick," the guy said. "Let me in."

"In a minute," Jake said.

"I don't got a minute," Loke yelled. "I've got a new meat-sleeve waiting." He laughed long and hard. "Drunk off her ass too. Ten bucks she goes ass-to-mouth."

I felt my brow wrinkle. What did *that* mean?

Jake turned his gaze on me. "Get out," he told me.

"But—"

His muscles tensed, and his voice grew harder. "And don't come back."

I blinked hard, embarrassed to realize my eyes were tearing up. I squeezed my eyes shut and tried to think of something to say.

I heard a couple of loud knocks, followed by Jake's voice. "What's the matter with you?"

I glanced up, expecting him to be looking at the door. But he wasn't. He was looking at me.

I bit my lip, choking off a sob before it escaped. Desperate to leave before I totally lost it, I started scrambling backward.

"Watch it!" Lizzie called from below. "You almost kicked me."

"Then move it!" I yelled.

Soon, the ladder shook with her movements. My feet found the next-lowest ladder rung, and then the one right below. I stopped. My head remained the only thing inside the building. I raised it to give Jake one last look.

He stood, with his arms crossed and his back against the door. He wasn't even looking at me. He was looking down at his shoes. He was shaking his head.

I waited.

He still didn't look.

So I found the next ladder-rung and kept on going.

After that, I was never welcome anywhere near him or his friends. For a while, I hated him. He'd been the guy of my dreams, and he'd made me feel young and stupid, just when I'd been ready to become a woman.

And I never did get that dance. ☐

CHAPTER 31

His voice was soft. "Luna."

"Shhhhh…" I said. "Just five more minutes. Okay?"

"Want me to carry you?" he asked.

"No," I mumbled. "Just hit the snooze button, alright?"

A soft chuckle sounded in my ear. "Snooze button. Got it."

Awareness hit me like a sack of potatoes, and I bolted up in my seat. Oh crap. I wasn't in bed. I was in the back of Jake's car. I glanced outside. We were idling outside Jake's building.

How long had I slept? Had I snored? Drooled? I reached a hand up to my chin. It was dry. Thank goodness. "So, I guess I fell asleep, huh?" As if I didn't know.

"Yeah, but I could still carry you."

I gave him a dubious look. "What? Over your shoulder?"

He grinned over at me. "If that's what you want."

"I'll walk. Thanks."

"My loss," he said, pushing open the car door. He held it open while I got out on legs that still felt way too wobbly, just like my thoughts. The elevator ride was short and silent. Either Jake was giving me time to wake up, or he had nothing to say. That was good, because my thoughts were far too jumbled to discuss anything of any importance.

Once inside his penthouse, I stood, feeling foolish, while he flicked on some lights. It wasn't even midnight, on a Saturday no less. The night was still young. I was dressed up. So was he. Was he sorry that I'd pulled him away from all the action?

"Are you sure you don't want to go back?" I asked.

Across the room, he turned to face me. "To the museum?" He raised an eyebrow. "Do *you*?"

"Not particularly."

"Good."

"Are you positive?" I gave a weak laugh. "I mean, you could hang out with Bianca."

His voice was hard. "Or Rango."

"Don't you mean 'Dingo'?" I muttered.

Jake leaned against the far wall and gave me a penetrating look. "What the hell did you see in that guy?"

"Rango?"

"Rango. Dongo. Whatever," Jake said. "He's a dick. Why would you go out with him?"

"You're one to talk," I said. "Tonight, you were way more dicky than he was."

"Is that so?"

"To Rango," I clarified. "Not to me." I shook my head. "I still can't believe he didn't take a swing at you."

"He would have," Jake said, "if someone hadn't dragged me off."

I did a mental eye-roll. Sure, like Jake could be dragged anywhere he didn't want to go. And yet, he did have a point. He *had* let *me* drag him away. Why was that?

"So I interfered with your plans?" I said. "Is that what you're saying?"

"Pretty much."

"Well maybe," I said, "I'd have been more helpful if you had told me what was going on."

"Why?" he said. "So you could spend half the night looking

over your shoulder? Now answer the question. What'd you see in that guy?"

I didn't want to discuss it. "Maybe you're not the only one with questions around here," I told him.

"Fair enough." He crossed his arms. "Answer mine, and I'll answer one of yours."

"Anything?" I said.

"Anything."

"Deal," I said.

I knew exactly what I was going to ask him, too, and it wasn't going to be a simple yes or no thing. This was going to be a full essay question, something that required multiple pages. I smiled. And footnotes. Jake had no idea what he was getting himself into.

Sucker.

"What are you smiling about?" he asked.

"Nothing." Just that in a few short minutes, he'd be telling me everything he'd been doing since I'd seen him last.

"I'm waiting," Jake said. "About Rango?"

"Oh alright," I said. "Fine. I'll go first."

I made my way to the nearest sofa and sank onto it. Jake pushed away from the wall and claimed the love seat opposite me. He stretched out his long legs and made a forwarding motion with his hand.

"Okay," I said. "I guess he was fun. At first." I cleared my throat. "And hot."

"Hot." Jake gave me a dubious look. "Rango?"

"Well, I don't think that anymore," I said. "Now that I know he's a jackass."

"That's one word for him."

I rolled my eyes. "I know. He's a dick. I got that." I leaned forward. "Now, it's my turn, right?"

"No."

I sank backwards. "Why not?"

"Because you need to hear something."

"What?"

"Guys like that? They're not for you."

"Guys like what?"

"Guys who come on strong and have more flash than brains. Guys who think that just because they're somebody, they can treat nice girls like dirt." His voice hardened. "Guys who'd make a girl like you afraid and get their rocks off doing it."

"Get real," I said. "I wasn't afraid of Rango."

"Yeah?" he said. "Is that why you were living in some dump with a low-life skank?"

My jaw dropped. Well, that was rich. Before I could stop myself, words I never planned on saying flew out of my mouth. "You mean the lowlife you screwed last night?" □

CHAPTER 32

Across from me, Jake's face lost any trace of emotion. The words lingered in the quiet room. Did I regret saying them? I still wasn't sure.

When he spoke, his voice was cold and flat. "Yeah, I did. What of it?"

"Sorry, it's just that, you know, I heard you two last night, and it seemed like you were getting along pretty well."

"You didn't hear *me*," he said.

Now that I thought about it, it was true. I *hadn't* heard him. Okay, so maybe I'd heard the muffled sounds of a male voice, but as far as sounds of passion, they were all female.

"Fine," I said. "So I heard Maddie."

"And?"

"And now you're calling her a low-life. So excuse me for being confused."

"If you've got a question," he said, "come out and ask it."

"Okay." I tried to choose my words carefully. "Well, what exactly was she to you?"

"Nothing."

"Nothing at all?" I said.

"Nothing but your roommate."

"So you used her?"

"Did it sound like she was complaining?"

Actually, it sounded like she was screwing a hockey team, and loving every minute of it.

He leaned back, and his voice became harder, colder, the voice of a stranger. "Yeah. I screwed her. And I'd do it again. Come to think of it, I *did* do it again. And a couple more times after that. And you wanna know why?"

Images of Jake and Maddie skittered across my brain. I tried to shut them out, but they kept on coming. I mumbled, "Not really."

"Too bad," he said. "Because here's the truth. I wanted her good and tired." He gave me a smile that looked devoid of any real happiness. "And if she couldn't walk, even better."

"You know what?" I said. "That's disgusting."

"You think?" His voice grew sarcastic. "But hey, anything for a friend."

"Oh, please," I said. "You're saying you did it for me? How noble of you."

"I'm a lot of things, Luna," he said, "but not noble."

"Yeah. And you're not my friend either. Are you?"

"Meaning?"

"Meaning," I said, "back in Riverside, I thought we were friends, and then—" I looked away. "—one little thing happened, and you totally ditched me."

"Yeah. I did," he said.

Okay, maybe to call us friends was a bit of an exaggeration. But I worshipped him. And for whatever reason, he'd let me hang out with him and his friends. Maybe I'd been like a puppy to him. And once I grew up, and tried to be something more, he took me back to the pound.

Jake laughed without humor. "So you wanna know why I stopped letting you hang around?"

I felt myself nod.

"Alright," he said. "It's because you grew up."

Something inside me twisted. "I knew it," I muttered.

"You don't know as much as you think."

"What do you mean?"

He was quiet a long moment, and then said, "You remember Loke?"

I *did* remember. Loke wasn't his real name, but it was the name everyone called him. The guy was crazy, and not in a good way.

"Yeah," I said. "What about him?"

"He was the first one to notice."

"Notice what?"

"That you weren't a little kid anymore."

"So?"

"So you wanna know what kind of shit came out of his mouth?" Jake's expression darkened. "Forget it. Don't ask, because I'm not gonna repeat it."

Knowing Loke, I could only imagine.

Jake glanced toward the windows, and his voice ground to a low menace. "But the stuff he says, it gets the rest of the guys talking."

"About me?" I asked.

"Yeah. About you. And you're like a kid sister to me."

"Oh." That was nice. Sort of.

"But you're *not* my sister," he continued. "So yeah, I could kick Loke's ass. But then what? What happens when the next guy steps up, wanting a piece of you?"

I tried to laugh. "You could've kicked *all* their asses."

His gaze returned to mine. "Yeah. I could've. But then what? What happens when I'm not there? What happens when one of them takes a shot at you for real? And what happens when you say yes?"

With some of Jake's friends, it might not have been an

entirely bad thing. They were wild and dangerous, just like him. But there were others – I tried not to think about it. Loke in particular, he was bad news. "About Loke," I said. "Whatever happened to him?"

"He's upstate," Jake said. "Serving ten to twenty."

"For what?" I asked.

"You don't want to know."

He was right. I didn't want to know. Besides, I didn't care about Loke. I cared about Jake.

"But the Maddie thing," I persisted. "I don't get it. How could you have sex with her if you didn't even like her? I mean, that's pretty cold."

"Want to know what's cold?" he said. "Some girl who sells out her roommate for a guy she just met."

"You mentioned that before," I said, "but I still don't know what you mean."

"It's how I found you," he said.

"Through Maddie? But how?"

"You know the strip club she works at?"

"Yeah. What about it?"

"Maybe a week ago, you called your sister from there. Right?"

I tried to think. Oh yeah. I had. I'd dashed into the club for only a minute, after giving Maddie a ride to work, in *her* car no less. At the time, I'd been between cell phones, thanks to Rango. We didn't have a landline at the apartment, and Maddie's cell phone had been shut off for non-payment, so I'd been a little desperate at the time.

Okay, a lot desperate.

It was the first and only time I'd set foot in that club. But I still didn't understand what Jake was getting at. That night, I didn't even talk to my sister. All I got was her voicemail. I hadn't even left a message.

I shook my head. "But how would you know I called her?"

"I got a look at Selena's phone, checked her incoming calls."

My gaze narrowed. "How? Through your brother?"

"Yeah, right," he said. "Like he'd let me within five feet of your precious sister."

Jake was right, so I didn't bother to deny it. There had always been a lot of tension among them, but for the life of me, I couldn't understand what caused it. "Why *is* that?" I asked.

Jake gave a hard laugh. "For one thing, because he's mainstreaming."

"What do you mean?"

"Pretending to be a good boy." Jake's voice grew sarcastic. "An upstanding, law-abiding citizen. Just like your sister wants."

"Oh please," I said. "Selena knows exactly what he is."

"Sure she does," Jake said.

"Forget that," I said. "How'd you get a look at her phone?"

He shrugged. "I borrowed it."

"Oh." I didn't bother to hide my sarcasm. "Like I 'borrowed' Rango's little book of passwords?"

"No," he said. "You got caught. I didn't."

"Goodie for you."

"And just for the record," he said, "the book's not his."

"Oh shut up," I said. "It is, too."

"Wanna bet?"

I waved away the distraction. "Forget the book. Finish your story."

Jake gave me a long look, and then continued. "So I go to the strip club–"

Ugly images flashed in my mind. Not of the girls. Of Jake. Well, Jake *and* the girls. Together. Damn it. "I bet you just hated *that*," I said.

"And," Jake continued as if I hadn't spoken, "I start asking around, throw some money here and there…"

"Don't you mean *tuck* some money here and there?"

He gave me another look. This one stretched out so long, I started to squirm. "Sorry," I mumbled. "So you throw around money, and...?"

After a long moment, he continued, "And I hear that Maddie's got a roommate that fits your description. Different name though. So I start asking Maddie about you. At first, she's all tight-lipped, thinking I'm an ex of yours looking to track you down."

"So, she was protecting me?" I asked.

"No. She was worried about competition."

"Oh come on. How do you know?"

"I know," he said, "because as soon as I mentioned settling a score, she gets real chatty about you."

"Chatty, how? What'd she say?"

"Nothing you wanna hear."

"Oh come on," I said. "Yes, I do."

"Alright," Jake said. "She said you were a deadbeat."

"Me?" Well, that was rich, considering she still owed me fifty bucks and a security deposit.

"And a thief," Jake said.

"What?" I sputtered. "I am not." Well, not in the technical sense anyway.

"And," Jake continued, "she said you got busted last month for hooking."

My blood pressure shot through the roof. "Oh come on!" I said. "That was her other roommate. Not me."

"That wasn't the story she told."

Flabbergasted, I sank back against the sofa. "I knew she wasn't the nicest person in the world, but..." I shook my head. "Wow."

"Yeah," Jake said. "So the next time you stick up for her, remember something."

"What?"

"She thought I was there to hurt you, and she didn't give two shits one way or another."

"And yet," I reminded him, "you had sex with her."

"Yeah. So?"

"So, aren't you seeing the disconnect there? I mean, you just proved she's not a nice person, but you still got intimate with her."

"Intimate?" He gave a hard laugh. "No. As you said, I 'screwed' her. Big difference."

"Oh come on," I said. "It's the same thing."

"No," he said. "I don't screw nice girls."

I almost didn't know what to say. "So, uh, what *do* you do with them?"

"Nothing."

I felt my brow wrinkle. "So you don't have sex with nice girls? Is that what you're saying?"

"Pretty much."

"But what happens if you're on a date, and, well, you know?"

"I don't date 'em," he said.

I shook my head. "I don't get it."

"Want me to spell it out?"

Actually, I wasn't sure. I felt myself nod anyway.

"Alright," he said. "I don't date them. I don't 'screw' them. I don't 'have sex' with them. I'm not 'intimate' with them. I don't kiss them. I don't hold them. And I sure as hell don't lie to them."

"Lie to them? How?"

"By claiming to be anything but a bastard."

I stared at him. "You are *not* a bastard."

"Right," he said.

"I still don't get it," I said. "Why would you think that way?"

"Because," he said, "I'm not a nice person. What am I gonna

do with a nice girl?"

I could think of lots of things. Was *I* a nice girl? I always thought I was. I was a lot nicer than Maddie, that's for sure. But the truth was, tonight, I'd been exactly the opposite. Ever since that stupid kiss, I'd felt foolish and disappointed, and I'd been taking it out on Jake.

I was still trying to process everything when his voice broke into my thoughts. "You think I'm gonna involve some nice girl in my shit?" he said. "You think I'm gonna drag her into the gutter and call it okay? You think I'm gonna let her hang with my friends when I'll have to watch them every damn minute?"

"Watch them?" I said. "Why?"

He gave a hard laugh. "To make sure they don't hassle her. Or worse."

Worse?

His voice rose. "You think I'm gonna let someone like Loke try something when I'm not there to protect her?"

"Wait a minute," I said. "Loke's in prison. So who exactly are we talking about?"

Jake got to his feet. "No one." He turned away and strode toward the door.

"You're not leaving?" I said.

Wordlessly, he kept on going.

"Wait," I said. "I need to tell you something."

With obvious impatience, he stopped and turned around. "What?"

"I'm sorry," I said.

I didn't know what, exactly, I was sorry for. But I *was* really sorry to see him like this, especially if I'd somehow triggered it.

"Forget it," he said. "No big deal."

He was lying. I could see it all over his face. Maybe I shouldn't have pried. But his reaction was a total surprise. During all the years I'd known him, I'd never seen him lose his cool, not once – not during any fights, not with any of his girlfriends, not even the time I'd seen him arrested for mouthing off to some cop.

He had plenty of attitude, but nothing got under Jake's skin. Ever.

"Jake," I said. "Seriously. Don't go. Okay?"

He glanced toward the kitchen. "If you want anything, help yourself. That's what it's there for."

I stared after him. "But where are you going?"

"To kick the shit out of someone."

I stood. "You're kidding, right?"

He stopped near the door and turned around. "Yeah. I'm kidding. See you later."

"You don't look like you're kidding." Desperately, I racked my brain for a way to make him stay. "But wait," I said. "I never got to ask my question."

"You asked plenty."

He was right. I'd practically driven him out of his own home. "Seriously Jake, hang on. Alright?"

He shook his head. "See you later," he said. And with that, he opened the door and strode through it. □

CHAPTER 33

The instant Jake walked out the door, the place felt utterly empty. For a long time, I sat silently on the sofa, hoping he'd come right back. But he didn't.

As one minute dragged on after another, the more miserable I felt. Tonight, he'd been trying to do me a favor, and how had I repaid him? By driving him away from his own place.

Earlier, he'd mentioned having me stay here for a week, maybe more. Somehow, I didn't see that happening. Tomorrow morning, I'd need to leave – if not for my sake, then definitely for his.

But where would I go?

I looked around my temporary home, feeling like a giant intruder. I looked down at Bianca's stylish little dress and heard myself scoff. I was an imposter too. I didn't bother going into the kitchen, because although I had eaten nearly nothing all day, food was the last thing on my mind.

I didn't have his cell phone number, so I couldn't even call him. Instead, I tried my sister. There was no answer. I gave up and just sat there on the sofa, putting off everything – a shower, changing clothes, eating, sleeping.

When my cell phone rang, I dove for it and checked the display. The number was unfamiliar, but at this point, I didn't care. I answered anyway with a breathless "Hello?"

"Hey babe," he said.

With a mental groan, I sagged back against the sofa. It wasn't Jake. It was Rango. And he sounded way too friendly, given everything that had happened between us.

"How'd you get this number?" I demanded.

"Friend of a friend."

The number was practically brand new. Only a few people had it. I gritted my teeth. "Bianca. Right?"

"Sorry, but I'm sworn to secrecy."

At this little statement, I did some swearing of my own.

Rango laughed. "Aren't you the dirty girl."

Ick. I mean, okay, the guy *had* been my boyfriend, but the creepy stalker routine had definitely taken its toll.

I didn't bother to hide my annoyance. "Is there a reason you called?" I asked.

"Aw, don't be that way," he said. "Did I mention you looked smokin' hot tonight?"

In the phone's background, I heard dance music and the buzz of voices. "Where *are* you?" I asked.

"I'm still at the rave," he said. "It's really slamming. You should come back, check it out."

"Sorry," I said in my snottiest voice. "I'm busy."

"With who?" He laughed. "Your 'boyfriend'?"

"What's so funny?" I asked.

"You. Trying to make me jealous."

I made a sound of disgust. "You really are full of yourself, aren't you?"

"Aw c'mon," he said. "It was cute. You almost had me there too."

So he *knew* it was all just an act? Thanks to Bianca, no doubt. God, how humiliating. Rango was the last person in the world I wanted to impress, but I hated looking pathetic in front of anyone, especially someone who had cost me so much already.

"I don't know what you mean," I said.

He gave a soft chuckle. "Sure you don't. Now admit it. You miss me."

"Yeah," I said, "like a hole in my head."

"You wanna mouth off?" he said. "Come on back. Do it in person."

I wanted to tell him that if I did come back, I wouldn't be coming alone. But of course, it would be a lie. I didn't even know where Jake was. And even if I did, I wouldn't be dragging him any further into my problems. The way it sounded, he was fighting plenty of his own demons.

"Forget it," I said. "I'm not going anywhere."

"Fine," Rango said. "I'll come to you."

"Oh yeah? What about your girlfriend?"

"Aw lighten up," he said. "You were kidding. I was kidding. Let's get together, talk it out, alright?"

He was up to something. I just knew it. "Is this about that book?" I asked.

"Don't worry," he said. "We'll get to that."

"I heard it's not even yours."

"Well, you know what they say about possession," he said. "Nine-tenths of the law, babe."

"If that's your logic," I said, "then the book's more mine than yours. Right?" In truth, I didn't even want the thing. But I couldn't resist goading him at least a little more after everything he'd done.

"We'll see about that," he said. "And before you get any funny ideas, I've changed all my passwords, so your little joke-fest is over."

"Like I didn't know *that* already." It was kind of a bummer too, because I'd come with some great new ideas for his personal Web page.

"Shit," Rango muttered, "what's *he* doing here?"

"Who?" I asked.

"I've gotta go." A split-second later, he ended the call without so much as a goodbye.

I stared at my phone, wondering what the hell had just happened. I was still wondering when I heard the telltale sound of a key card in the entryway.

Jake?

I looked toward the door just in time to see it fly open. I jumped to my feet. My heart sank. It wasn't Jake. It was Bianca in all her schoolmarm glory. And she wasn't alone. □

CHAPTER 34

Standing behind Bianca was Vince Hammond, the sports agent who'd confronted Jake at the museum. Talk about double the fun – someone who hated me and someone who hated Jake.

I gave Bianca an annoyed look. "What are you doing here?" I asked.

She strode through the front door like she owned the place. "I came to get my things."

I turned to Vince. "And what about you?" I asked.

He flicked his head toward Bianca. "I'm her ride."

"He's more than my ride," Bianca said. "He's my newest client."

From the look in her eye, he'd probably be more than a client before the night was through. I could see the appeal. The guy was rich, successful, and if I were being honest, good-looking in that classic sort of way.

Without another word, Bianca started heading toward the back hallway. I strode forward to block her path.

"Jake's not here," I said, "so you'll have to come back later."

She gave her key card a little wave. "In case you haven't noticed, I have a key. That means I don't need your permission."

"But you still need Jake's," I said. "And as I already

mentioned, he's not here."

"Ooooh, what happened?" she said in a voice of mock concern. "Did he ditch you? So soon? Poor baby."

"It's not like that," I said.

"Sure it isn't." She glanced down at my torso. "And I'll be needing my dress back now."

I did my best Bianca impression. "Oooooh, are you sure?" I made a show of fanning myself. "Because I've been sweating buckets in this thing."

"Oh grow up," she said. "I'm not planning to actually *wear* it. I just don't want *you* to have it."

"Gee, who was being childish now?" Still, two could play at this game. "In that case," I said, "I'll be needing *my* dress back too."

She pursed her lips. "Why?"

Actually, I didn't have a clue why. The dress was butt-ugly and had Bianca cooties all over it. Still, I heard myself blurt out, "Jake thinks it's sexy."

"Don't be ridiculous," she said. "He does not."

"Well, maybe not on *you*," I said. "I mean, you're not exactly the 'willowy' type, are you?"

"Hey! I'm more willowy than you are."

"If you say so…"

Her gaze narrowed. "Are you returning my dress or not?"

Before giving the dress to anyone, I'd need to change out of it. And there was no way I'd be leaving Bianca unattended, especially with Vince in tow. It was no secret the guy wanted to do Jake harm. I'd be a fool to turn my back on him for even a minute.

"If you want the dress," I told Bianca, "you'll have to come back tomorrow."

She made a sound of annoyance. "Why tomorrow?"

I smiled. "Because I'm not done sweating in it yet."

Bianca whirled toward Vince. "You see what I've been putting up with?"

Vince gave a noncommittal shrug.

Bianca frowned. "Is that all you have to say?"

He held up a hand. "Hey, I'm just the guy with the car keys."

Again, Bianca made a move toward the hall. Again, I blocked her path.

She glared at me. "Will you stop that?"

"Sorry, but I can't let you go back there. Not without Jake's permission."

"Who *are* you?" she said. "Suzy Hall-Monitor?"

"Who are *you*?" I said, glancing down at that ugly dress. "Petunia Prairie Lady?"

Her jaw clenched. "Petunia? Really?"

I smiled. "Don't forget the prairie part."

With a long-suffering sigh, she threw up her hands. "Fine. I'll call him."

She reached into her little purse and pulled out her cell phone. She tapped away at the screen and put the phone to her ear. Standing just a couple feet away, I could hear the phone ring once, and then twice.

On the third ring, I heard Jake, loud and clear, say, "Yeah?"

At the sound of his voice, my heart ached. I wanted to yank that phone out of Bianca's bony clutches and beg Jake to come back home.

I gave Bianca a speculative look. She was taller. And mean as hell. She wouldn't give up her phone easily. But if it came to a catfight, I could probably take her.

Bianca cupped a hand around her phone and gave me an annoyed look. "Do you mind?" she said.

I blinked over at her. "Mind what?"

"Oh for heaven's sake." She turned and started stalking toward the balcony. I didn't bother trying to stop her. If she wanted to freeze her butt off, that was *her* business, not mine. Besides, there was nothing to steal out there, unless she wanted to lug off some patio furniture. And in that case, more power to her.

After she strode out through the French doors and shut them behind her, I turned to Vince, who was still standing in the entryway.

"How about you?" I asked.

"Me?" he said. "I'm not talking to the guy."

I gave him a no-nonsense look. "Good."

"But there *is* another reason I'm here," he said.

Just great. Was this where he tried to trash the place? Threatened to sue? Went for the good silverware? I frowned. Did Jake even have good silverware? Honestly, he didn't seem the type.

Under Vince's gaze, I put my hands on my hips. "And what reason is that?" I asked.

"To apologize."

My mouth fell open. "Excuse me?"

"Earlier, I was a jackass. And I'm sorry for that."

I glanced around. "So, uh, you want me to relay that to Jake?"

"Hell no," he said. "The apology wasn't for him. It was for you."

I shook my head. "I'm not following."

"Bianca mentioned you'd be here tonight, so…" He gave a shrug. "I figured I'd kill two birds with one stone – give her a ride and tell you that I'm sorry. I shouldn't have blown up like that."

I couldn't help it. I just had to ask. "Did Jake really cost you half a million?" □

CHAPTER 35

Inside the penthouse, Vince gave a humorless laugh. "At least."

I let out a long breath. "Wow."

"Yeah," he said. "It really ticked me off too."

"Really?" I said. "I didn't notice."

He gave me a sheepish grin. "Right. Well, the thing is, I worked my ass off to get that deal. And here, it's gone–" He gave a quick snap of his fingers. "–just like that. I'm not one to lose my cool, but, eh, what can I say? It happens."

In spite of myself, I felt a tiny tug of sympathy. "So there's no chance of working it out?" I asked. "I mean, you probably had an official contract or something, right?"

"Not yet," Vince said. "We were set to sign next week."

"Oh," I said. "I'm sorry to hear that." And for some reason, I meant it too. If someone cost *me* that much money, I'd definitely go for the silverware. And maybe the patio furniture too.

I glanced toward the balcony. Through the glass doors, I saw Bianca talking into her phone, looking anything but happy. Still, something made me lower my voice when I turned back to Vince and asked, "So, have you known Jake long?"

"You could say that," Vince said. "We used to be friends."

I laughed. "Yeah, right."

"I'm not kidding," he said.

My laugher trailed off as I studied his face. "Really?" I said.

He gave a half-shrug. "Friendly enough, anyway."

"But you're not anymore?"

"Hard to be friends with someone who costs you that much money."

I winced. I could see his point. "So you were friends until today?"

"Nah. Not today. A few months ago, we had a falling out."

"Over what?" I asked.

"The truth?" he said, looking slightly embarrassed. "A girl."

For some reason, this wasn't the answer I wanted to hear. "Oh."

"But forget that," he said. "So, about my apology." He grinned. "Do you accept? Or do I have to beg?"

I looked over at him. Somehow, he didn't look the begging type. "Would you?" I asked.

"Wanna try me?"

I couldn't help but return his smile. "I almost feel like it would be rude not to."

"Good," he said, "because I'll tell you a secret." He motioned me closer. When I moved forward only a fraction, he said in a low, oddly intoxicating voice, "because I hate to beg."

I glanced down at my empty hands. Suddenly, I wished I had a drink or something, anything to take the edge off. I thought about Jake. Would he be gone all night? And when he returned, would he be alone? Or with a guest?

"So," Vince asked, "are you and Jake friends, or…" He met my gaze. "—something more?"

The question hung in the air. What was I to Jake? That kiss had felt so achingly real. But the whole thing had been a sham, a ruse, a lie. I was an idiot, and Jake was, well Jake.

I heard myself say, "I guess you'd call us old friends."

Vince gave a slow nod. "Good to know."

Behind me, I heard the balcony doors open. I turned to see Bianca stalk back inside. She looked at Vince and said, "Come on. Let's get out of here."

"What about your things?" he asked.

She turned to give me a dirty look. "I *guess* I'll have to come back tomorrow."

I couldn't help it. I felt myself smile.

"You don't have to look so smug," she said.

"Oh come on," I said. "You had to know he wouldn't want you rummaging around here when he's gone. I mean, it doesn't take a rocket scientist to figure *that* out."

"I wasn't going to 'rummage' anything of his," she said. "I was going to rummage mine."

I couldn't help but wonder, what kind of stuff did she mean? Visions of lingerie and sex toys popped into my brain. Maybe their relationship had been more serious than Jake had implied.

Against my better judgment, I asked, "When you talked to Jake, did he say when he'd be back?"

Her lips curved into a slow smile. "So you don't know?"

"Never mind," I said. "Forget I asked."

"Oh, I wouldn't *dream* of it," she said. "Let's put it this way. He wasn't alone. So I wouldn't wait up if I were you."

Something in my stomach twisted. I'd feared as much. But then again, this was Bianca. She was lying. She had to be. But what if she wasn't?

Somehow, I managed to suck it up and say, "It doesn't matter, because Jake and I are just friends."

Long after they left, that's what I kept repeating to myself over and over again. We were just friends. That's it. I had no claim on him.

I'm not sure what time it was when I crawled, half-asleep into the guest bed, but I knew it was late. Jake still hadn't returned, and after a certain point, it became pretty obvious he wasn't going to.

Sometime in the middle of the night, I woke, feeling parched and anxious. I sat up in bed and looked around. Moonlight was streaming in through the open blinds, and I tried to get my bearings as I pushed aside the covers.

I was still missing most of my clothes, so I had slept in panties and an oversized T-shirt that I'd found in the spare closet. Quietly, I crept out of bed and cracked open the bedroom door. I peeked around the corner and into the hall. The place looked dark and quiet, just like I'd left it.

Disappointment coursed through me. Either Jake had returned and gone straight to bed, or he was still gone. I tried to count my blessings. The silence might be unnerving, but it was a whole lot better than listening to more female screams of passion.

Unwilling to take any chances, I tiptoed toward the kitchen in search of a cold drink of water. I was just passing through the main living area when something caught my eye, a shadowed figure sitting on the sofa.

I stifled a gasp. "Jake?"

"Yeah," he said. "It's me."

I squinted into the darkness. "Why are you sitting there in the dark? Is, uh, anyone else here?"

"No."

Relief flooded through me. "So what are you doing?" I asked.

"Thinking."

"About what?"

His voice was soft in the quiet room. "You." □

CHAPTER 36

I stared into the darkness. "Me?" My thirst forgotten, I moved toward him. "Why?"

"You want the truth?" he asked.

Wordlessly, I walked through the shadows. Soon, I was standing barefoot beside the sofa where he sat. I was so close, I could have reached out to stroke the side of his face. But I didn't. Jake and I were just friends, and I needed to remember that.

"I always want the truth," I said. "Don't you?"

"No."

"Why not?" I asked.

"Because it's ugly."

I felt myself stiffen. "So you're about to tell me an ugly truth? Is that what you're saying?"

"Pretty much."

I stood, stupidly, beside the sofa, waiting for him to say more, and dreading what it might be.

Unlike me, Jake wasn't dressed for bed. From what I could tell, he was wearing the same clothes as earlier. But now, his shoes were off, and his shirt was open, leaving his chest and stomach nearly bare. Determined not to stare, I lifted my gaze to his face, hoping for a hint of what he might say.

Into the darkness, he finally spoke. "I knew you were there."

"Where?" I asked.

"In that sorry-ass apartment. Last night."

"Oh." I sank down onto the sofa beside him. "When you were with Maddie, you mean?"

Through the darkness, I saw him nod. I stared at his profile, still cast in shadows. "Is there a reason you're telling me this?" I asked.

"Yeah," he said. "But not a good one."

"What do you mean?"

He turned toward me. "You're important to me. You know that. Right?"

Funny, I never knew I was important to him. Still, I felt myself nod. "You're important to me too," I said. And I meant it. Okay, so I hadn't seen him much lately, but he was such a fixture in my memories, it was almost like he had never left.

"Are you ready for that truth?" he asked.

The ugly one? No. I wasn't ready. But I squared my shoulders anyway and made myself say, "Sure. Go ahead."

"Alright, here it is," he said. "I didn't *want* you interested in me."

Heat flooded my face. I couldn't say it was a surprise. For as long as I could remember, I'd had that stupid crush on him. In my fantasies, Jake someday felt the same about me. But life wasn't a fantasy, and the idea of him crushing on *me* was too far-fetched to consider. Somehow, I'd always known that. But it still hurt to hear the words said out loud.

"Wow," I said, getting to my feet. "Thanks for sharing that. I guess." I turned to go.

"Luna," he said.

"What?"

"Wait."

I heard myself sigh. "For what?"

"The rest of it. Sit back down. Alright?"

Oh God, there was more? Well, it's not like it could get any worse, right? Wordlessly, I sank back down and tried to ignore the sudden ache in my heart.

"I *wanted* to scare you," he said, "to show you what a bastard I was, to let you see for yourself how I treat the girls I'm with."

From the sounds that *I'd* overheard, he treated those girls pretty darn good. But somehow, I didn't think he meant in the bedroom. "What do you mean?" I asked. "How do you treat them?"

He made a hard sound deep in his throat. "Like garbage," he said. "I use them a time or two. And when I'm done? I just throw them away."

The more he talked, the uglier this truth was sounding. "Why are you telling me this?" I asked.

"Because," he said, "there's a messed-up part of me that wishes you never saw that side."

"Only a part of you?" I said.

"Yeah. Because there's another part, maybe a bigger part, that's glad you did."

I shook my head. "I'm not following."

"The thing is," he said, "girls like Maddie. I've had my share."

Probably, he had more than his share. "So?" I said.

"So it's what I'm used to. I never wanted anything else. I never wanted to want anything else."

"What are you saying?" I asked. "That you want something else *now*?"

The question hung in the air, and the longer he went without answering, the more I regretted asking it.

But then he *did* answer. "Yeah," he said. "I shouldn't. But I do."

Fearful of embarrassing myself, I tried to keep my tone

casual. "What is it that you want?"

"I dunno." He shoved a hand through his hair. "It's all messed up. That's why if you're smart, you'll go back to bed and forget you saw me here."

I gave a little shake of my head. "Why?"

"You *know* why," he said. "Because, the girl who's got me thinking, you *know* who it is."

I held my breath, wondering if he'd actually come out and say it. And then I wondered if this was just a stupid dream. Maybe I was still in bed and just didn't know it.

But then he spoke in a voice filled with such longing that it took my breath away. "It's you." □

CHAPTER 37

I caught my breath. Jake's words hung in the air. Obviously, it was my turn to say something, but for the life of me, I couldn't seem to form a coherent sentence.

The silence loomed large between us. Bits of our conversation drifted across my brain. I knew what *I'd* always wanted, but his signals were decidedly mixed. The way it sounded, he might be a whole lot happier in the long run if I ran to the guest room and locked the door behind me.

I didn't want to do that. But more than anything, I didn't want to be just another girl who couldn't take a hint. Somehow, I found my voice. "Are you saying you *want* to be alone?" I asked.

"Yeah."

My heart sank.

And then, he leaned toward me. His voice grew raw, like the words were being wrenched out of him against his will. "For your sake, not mine."

He was so close now. I could kiss him if I wanted. I *did* want to. Quietly, I spoke into the darkness. "What if I don't want to leave?"

He didn't move, but he did speak. "Then you're even dumber than I am."

"I'm not dumb." My heart was hammering. I moved my head a fraction toward his. "And neither are you."

Suddenly, a cold splash of reality hit me in the face. I stopped short. A few hours earlier, Bianca had talked to Jake on the phone. She'd been standing in this very same room. Her words, a taunt really, echoed in my brain.

He wasn't alone.

What if it was true?

That was hours ago. Jake had just returned. From where? I stomach twisted. From who?

I wanted him so bad. And the way it sounded, he might want me too. I had wanted him for so very long. And now, more than anything, I wanted to bury the questions that were begging to be asked. *Where were you? Who were you with?*

If I asked those questions, and received the answers I feared, what then? Would I have the self-respect to pull away? A smart girl *would* pull away, if only to regroup. There was always tomorrow. Right?

"What is it?" Jake asked.

I looked out toward the balcony. I didn't want to ask, because part of me didn't really want to know. But somehow, the words slipped out anyway. "Earlier tonight," I said, "where were you?"

I half expected him to be angry, or maybe refuse to answer, to tell me it was none of my business. After all, I wasn't his girlfriend. And even if I were, I couldn't imagine him answering to anybody.

But surprisingly, he did answer. And his voice was so devoid of anger that it took me by surprise. "I went back to the museum," he said.

"Why?" I asked. "I mean, was it to see anyone in particular?" Like those two girls who had been molesting Jake with their eyes?

"Yeah," he said. "It was."

"Really?" I tried to keep my tone casual. "Who?"

"Rango."

I squinted at him through the darkness. "Rango? Why Rango?"

"You don't wanna know."

"Actually, I do."

"Okay," he said. "I was looking for a fight."

From what I'd seen, he never had to look very far if that's all he wanted.

"And," he continued, "this time, I didn't give a rat's ass who swung first, or if I landed my ass back in jail."

"Don't say that."

"Why?" he said. "It's the truth."

"So, did you see him?"

"Yeah, I saw him. He was talking on his damn cell phone. But as soon as he saw *me*, he was outta there."

"What do you mean?"

"The place was packed," Jake said, "with maybe double the people as when we left. My guess? He was hiding out in in the crowd and slipped out a side door." Jake made a sound of disgust. "The coward."

"I don't get it," I said. "What made you go back there? I mean, if all you wanted was a fight..." I reached for Jake's arm. "You know what? Forget it. I'm glad Rango left. And I'm glad you didn't find him."

"Yeah?" An edge crept into his voice. "Why's that?"

"Because," I said, "if you *had* found him, you wouldn't be here with me now." Desperately, I wanted to kiss him. I wanted to do more than kiss him. But first, there was something I had to know. "Jake? Can I ask you a question?"

His voice was softer now. "Yeah?"

"Earlier, at the museum, why'd you kiss me?" ☐

CHAPTER 38

He leaned toward me, and our lips almost brushed. When he spoke, his voice was a quiet caress. "You gotta ask?"

In spite of all my longings, I forced myself to pull back. "Yes. I do." I swallowed. "I mean, was it all for Rango's benefit?"

With a soft chuckle, Jake turned and leaned back against the sofa. "No. It was for *my* benefit."

"But..." I struggled to find the right words. "Did you know Rango was standing there?"

"Yeah. I knew." Through the shadows, I saw him turn again to face me. "And yeah, I wanted him to see. I wanted him to get good and pissed off. And I wanted him to know that you weren't *his* anymore."

He leaned close. "But you know what I wanted more than all that?"

"What?"

"I wanted *you*." He moved a fraction closer. "And I wanted more than a kiss."

My head was swimming. "I want more than a kiss right now," I confessed.

Soon, his lips were on mine. I melted into his embrace. His arms closed around me and pulled me tight against him. His body felt warm and hard, just like I'd always imagined. He moved his head lower and nibbled on my bottom lip.

My pulse jumped, and a soft moan escaped my lips. I was wearing next to nothing, just that oversized shirt and black lacy panties. But what I *wanted* to be wearing was nothing at all. And I wanted *him* to be wearing nothing too.

His lips trailed lower. They zeroed in on my neck, teasing, tantalizing. Unable to resist, I leaned my head back, exposing more of my neck and praying that he wouldn't stop. His tongue caressed my jumping pulse, making heat surge from my head to my toes and everyplace in between.

The room, so cool just a few minutes earlier, was feeling nearly tropical. His hand slid up to cradle the back of my neck, and his lips drifted to that sensitive spot just between my neck and shoulder. With his mouth, he pushed aside the thin cotton fabric of the borrowed T-shirt.

His teeth grazed my skin, and I caught my breath. If he was driving me to distraction now, when we were still mostly clothed, what might happen if things kept going?

They *had* to keep going. No matter what, I'd make sure of it. I crept forward to straddle his lap. I pressed my knees to either side of his hips and laced my fingers behind his neck. When I pressed myself against him, his hardness pulsed against me.

"Luna." He drew a ragged breath. "If you were smart, you'd run."

Liar. If I was smart, I'd do exactly what I was doing. His words might say one thing, but his body said another. When I ground against him, he made a sound of frustration that made me smile.

I pressed myself tighter against him. "Are you *sure* you want me to run?"

"No." He slid his hands up the back of my T-shirt. "But you should."

His hands felt big and strong, but his touch was soft, a sweet caress that left me aching for more. His hands drifted lower, finding the waist of my panties. If I was lucky, he'd tear them off and take me right now.

"Run?" I said. "Why would I do that?"

"Because you're way too sweet for the likes of me." His hands dipped lower. "I ruin everything." His hands dipped lower still. "And I sure as hell don't want to ruin this." His fingers skimmed my ass-cheeks, and his voice became raw. "I don't want to ruin you."

Under my fingertips, his neck muscles were tense, straining, as if his control might suddenly break. I wanted it to break. With both hands, I trailed my fingers over his broad shoulders and then down over his chest. It felt every bit as good as it looked, a perfected mass of smooth skin and hard muscle.

I moved my hands lower until I reached his flat stomach, with its washboard ridges and hard valleys. The muscles contracted, tensing as if preparing for battle, whether with me or with himself.

If the battle was for self-control, he wasn't going to win, not if I could help it.

I leaned against him and whispered in his ear. "I'm not *that* sweet."

I heard his sharp intake of breath. "You're sweeter than I deserve."

"Wanna bet?" I ran my fingertips lower. When my fingers brushed over his hardness, he surged against me. I made my tone light, playful even. "I don't want to run, but if you insist…"

"Now you've done it," he said.

"What?" I asked.

"This."

Somehow – I still don't quite know how he did it – I was

suddenly on my back, lying across his sofa. He loomed large over me, a shadowed silhouette of muscle-bound splendor. He reached out to brush the backs of his fingertips across my cheek. "You're so beautiful it hurts," he said.

I leaned into his caress. "How would you know?" I teased. "It's awful dark in here. I mean, I could be a goblin for all you know."

He ran a fingertip down my neck. "No," he said. "You're not. And you know what?"

My voice was breathless. "What?"

"If you were, I'd never see it."

"Liar," I teased.

"I'm a lot of things," he said, "but a liar isn't one of them." He moved his hand behind my neck, cupping it with hint of possession that made me quiver in all the right places. He lowered his face toward mine. I felt my lips part and my breathing grow ragged.

And then, his mouth sealed mine with a kiss of such intensity that I forgot what I'd been planning to say next. It was our third kiss. Yes, I *was* counting, because each one was better than the last, more fierce and more tender. Whatever happened later on, I wanted to remember every single one of them, always.

Too soon, he pulled away. With a whimper, I reached for his waist. With both hands, I tried to pull him toward me.

He didn't budge. "Last chance," he said.

"For what?"

His voice might have been playful, except for the primal edge that made turned my insides to jelly. "To run."

Right. Like *that* was going to happen. Leveraging my hands around his waist, I yanked my torso upward until our faces were just inches apart. "No way," I said.

Slowly, deliberately, he reached out and gripped the neckline of my borrowed T-shirt. His voice was raw, possessive. "Good," he said. And then, with one forceful motion, he grabbed a handful of fabric in each hand and gave it a hard yank in opposite directions.

I heard the tear of fabric and his soft inhalation of breath. Cool air drifted across my bare nipples as the torn cotton fell aside, exposing my bare breasts to whatever he planned to do next.

His hands found my breasts, tracing the outlines with his smooth fingers. I felt his powerful hands cup either side of them, pressing them together as if savoring their shape and feel.

There was something raw and wonderful about his touch, something I'd never before experienced, but something I wanted to feel over and over again.

When he lowered his face, and I felt his warm mouth on my hard nipple, I moaned into the darkness. His tongue flicked the sensitive peak, and I arched upward into him, wanting more, so much more. I raised my trembling hands to the back of his head and felt thick hair dancing between my fingertips.

Soon, I felt his hand on my other nipple. He worried it between his fingertips, playing and lightly pinching, coaxing sounds out of me that shouldn't have been possible, given the fact we were still mostly clothed.

Clothes – there were too many of them. Especially on him.

I moved my hands lower, trailing them downward until I reached the waistband of his pants. I found a button and tugged frantically against it. When the button finally came loose, I moved to the zipper. I pulled it downward. Then, I reached along the sides of his hips to give his pants a frantic tug.

His mouth and fingers were still at my breasts, coaxing new sensations from who-knows-where. By now, I was nearly panting. I was so wet and so hungry for him, I felt like I'd fade into nothingness if I didn't have him right now.

Years – that's how long I'd been waiting for him. Another minute felt way too long.

When I reached out to grip his length, he moaned against my breast and whispered my name. With my right palm, I encircled his hot hardness, giving it a slow and steady squeeze as I marveled at the size and feel of him.

I spoke into the darkness. "Jake?"

His mouth vibrated against my skin. "Hmm..."

"I want you," I said. "I don't want to run. And I don't want to wait anymore."

Slowly, he pulled away, leaving my nipple warm and wet in the cool darkness. In my grip, he was pulsing hard and huge, and I was dying to know how he'd feel inside me.

"But you *are* gonna wait," he said.

"What?" My voice was breathless. "Why?"

He lowered his mouth to my ear and teased my earlobe with his tongue. "Because I say so." □

CHAPTER 39

Before I could argue, he moved to seal my lips with a kiss – our fourth one now – that left me breathless and aching for another. When he pulled away, I leaned up toward him, desperate to feel his lips on mine again and again.

Between us, I gave his length another long, smooth stroke. His words might say wait, but body was good and ready. And mine was more than ready.

An aching heat flooded my core, making me slick with yearning. I wanted him now. I wanted that fullness, that closeness. I wanted to feel his skin against my skin and to feel him pulse deep inside me like he was pulsing in my hand.

And then, my hand was maddeningly empty. With a moan of frustration, I realized he had pulled away. Didn't he know I was dying for him?

I wanted to protest, to drag him back against me, or to beg, if that's what it took. But then, something made me stop. It was the barest whisper of fingers brushing against my thigh. They crept upward with a maddening deliberation that made my knees tremble with wild anticipation.

I clamped my lips shut to keep from begging aloud. Soon, I felt a finger brush the center of my panties, rubbing that aching knob through the thin lacy fabric.

It was bliss and madness wrapped up in one. The touch was light, more a promise than an actual act. I lifted my hips in a silent plea. I wanted more. But more never came. Instead, the teasing continued, a butterfly touch that made me squirm with longing and melt from the inside out.

Just when I thought I'd die of the yearning, he reached around with both hands. He gripped my panties and yanked them downward. I heard a ripping sound as the thin fabric gave way. I couldn't help it. I gave an audible moan and lifted my hips higher.

"That's my girl," he said, brushing something – maybe a thumb, maybe a finger – across that singular spot until I squirmed harder against him. My legs trembled, and my breath caught. When I felt a finger slide lower and slip slowly inside me, I gave a soft moan and reached for him yet again.

This time, he didn't pull away. I gripped him in a hungry hand, savoring the feel of him as I stroked his length and heard the sweetest sound of my name on his lips.

Still, I wanted more. With his shirt open and his pants mostly on, he was wearing way too many clothes. Trying to sit up, I said, "My turn to undress you."

"Not yet." With aching slowness, he slid another finger inside me. On the outside, he moved his thumb a fraction faster. I tried to protest, to tell him that I wanted him naked too, that I wanted *him* to feel the wonderful things that I was feeling.

And yet, in the darkness, I heard his breath and felt his desire. Somehow, I knew I wasn't the only one loving this.

Gazing at his silhouette poised above me, it felt like a dream, a wonderful dream, a fantasy that by some miracle, had actually come true. His hands were magic, and so was he. Soon, words were impossible, and I let myself fall into the dream as he teased and tantalized me to utter distraction.

When my body began to convulse with those impossible waves, I didn't fight them. Instead, I let myself get lost in those sensations, not caring what sounds I made or what Jake might think of me in the morning.

As my hips rose and fell, he rode the waves with me, stroking me inside and out, coaxing out more bliss than I ever dreamed possible. When my trembling reached a fevered pitch, he leaned his head down to mine and said in a low, possessive voice. "I've been thinking of you, of this, all night."

My breath caught. I found those words hard to believe. But I wanted to believe, so I shut off the logical part of my brain and let myself get carried away with his motions and his words, trying not to care whether he meant them or not.

When my trembling subsided and something like sanity returned, I surged upward and wrapped my arms around his back. I was naked. But he still wasn't. I pushed him back against the arm of the sofa and shimmied backwards.

I reached down and gripped the hem of his pants with both hands. I gave the fabric a hard tug, dragging his pants downward until his body was finally free of them.

I longed for more light. I wanted to look at him, to drink in the sight of him. I wanted to remember this forever and to make sure that he remembered it too. In the back of my mind, a little voice whispered that to me, this was a big deal. But to him, it all might be forgotten the moment I left.

I told that voice to be quiet and moved forward to straddle his hips. I pressed myself against him and felt his hardness pulsing against me. Catching my breath, I pressed my palms flat against his chest. I trailed my fingers downward. I pushed aside his shirt and ran my hands first along his sides and then up toward his broad shoulders.

When I leaned my face close to his, he whispered my name, a plea, a caress. "Luna?"

I raised my hips and reached down with one hand. I positioned the head of his massive erection at my opening. "Hmmm?"

His voice was ragged. "Don't go."

Slowly, I lowered my hips, welcoming his body into mine, not a lot, but enough to get his attention. "Don't go where?" I whispered, lowering my hips another fraction.

He gave a low groan. "Anywhere," he said. "Don't go anywhere."

He had no idea what he was saying. He was my drug, my hero, my fantasy. At this point, nothing could drag me away. What tomorrow brought, well, that was another matter. Tonight, he was mine, and I intended to show him just how much.

Before our hips met, I pulled back, wanting him to want me as much as I wanted him. I felt his body tense, and his breath hitch. When he was nearly in danger of sliding free of me, I lowered my hips down tight against his, taking all of his fullness deep inside.

I let out a long, unsteady breath, intoxicated by the nearness of him, savoring the fullness that grew as my hips continued their downward motion.

And then, I couldn't make either of us wait any more. I gave in to the movements of my hips, letting them carry me away, and him along with me. I arched upward and rocked back down, over and over, taking him into me again and again.

I kissed his lips and let my tongue dance along his neck. I felt his hands on my hips, and heard his voice in my ear, sometimes a moan, sometimes a murmur. My name fell from his lips as often as his fell from mine.

It was so blissful I wanted to cry, and I wanted to laugh. In real life, the reality never lived up to the fantasy. But this time, it did. Jake was everything I'd ever dreamed of and more. And he was mine, if only for tonight.

When he shuddered against me, and cradled me hard against him, I gave up any semblance of control and joined him in riding the waves of a climax so intense I couldn't stop myself from crying out. My sounds mingled with his, and soon, I sagged against him, almost embarrassed, but not nearly enough to regret it.

When he spoke, it was with a tenderness that took me by surprise. "You should've run." He pressed his forehead against mine. "But I'm so damn glad you didn't." □

CHAPTER 40

I woke to the sounds of angry voices. Slowly, I opened my eyes. In my peripheral vision, I saw the palest hint of morning light filtering in through large double windows. Blinking, I sat up in bed. Oh my God. The bed. It was Jake's. I looked around. I was in Jake's bedroom.

And I was naked.

Memories of the previous night came flooding back to me. Our encounter on the sofa had been just the beginning. We'd gone from the sofa to the floor and finally to his king-size bed, where the night had ended with me falling asleep, utterly sated, in his arms.

But now, he was gone, not too far it seemed. From somewhere outside the bedroom, I heard his voice, along with another voice that I instantly recognized. The second voice belonged to his brother – technically my future brother-in-law, since he'd soon be marrying my sister.

His name was Jim, but like everyone else, my sister always called him by his last name, Bishop. Funny too, because that was Jake's last name too. I couldn't help but wonder why one brother went by his last name, while the other went by his first. Weird.

Before I could dwell on it further, their voices rose to a new level.

"Where the hell is she?" Bishop said.

Jake's response was chilly, but calm. "None of your business."

"You think it's not?"

"I *know* it's not," Jake said.

I heard receding footsteps, followed by the sound of someone opening and slamming an interior door, and then another. Oh crap. Was Bishop searching the place? For me? God, how humiliating.

I looked around, wondering if I should try to hide someplace or just brazen it out. I glanced toward the closed bedroom door. It had a lock. Thank God.

I crept out of bed, dragging the nearest blanket around me as I tiptoed across the smooth tile floor. As quietly as I could, I twisted the lock in place and then, turned to lean my back against the thick oak door.

Why on Earth was I creeping around? Honestly, I had no idea. I wasn't a kid anymore. I was twenty-three, for crying out loud. And Jake? He was even older than I was. This whole thing was beyond ridiculous.

And besides, Jake was a full year older than his brother. If anything, shouldn't Jake be searching Bishop's place for wayward naked girls?

No, I realized. He shouldn't. The only thing Jake would find would be my sister, and I definitely didn't want him to see *her* naked. Come to think of it, I didn't like the idea of Jake seeing any girl naked, well, except for me. But not with Bishop here.

I heard another door slam, and again, those footsteps grew louder. Soon, they were dangerously close. A moment later, I heard Jake's voice on just the other side of the door. "You touch that doorknob, and you're gonna get your ass kicked."

I tensed, afraid to move, and half-afraid to breathe. Stupid or not, I didn't want to be caught in Jake's bedroom. I didn't want an ugly scene. I didn't want to explain myself to anyone. And I sure as hell didn't want to jump in the middle of whatever was going on between them, especially since I was wearing nothing but a blanket.

Bishop gave a muttered curse. "Don't tell me…" he said.

"I'm not telling you shit," Jake said, "because, as I already said, it's none of your business."

"Your ass," Bishop said. "It *is* my business. I'm here to bring her home."

"She *is* home," Jake said. "So stay out of it."

I caught my breath. This wasn't my home. I didn't live here. Best case scenario, I was a temporary guest. How temporary, I still wasn't sure.

"Cut the crap," Bishop said. "I'm taking her to Selena's."

"That's what *you* think," Jake said.

To that, Bishop made no response, or at least none I could hear. When the silence stretched out, I turned my head and pressed my ear to the door. Holding my breath, I listened. I waited. I heard nothing.

Why not?

And then, I heard footsteps again. But this time, they were receding.

Crap.

Had they known I was listening? I wanted to scream in frustration. If they were still discussing me, I refused to remain a silent bystander while they decided when or where I'd be going, and with whom.

I should march out there and confront both of them. There was just one teeny problem. I was standing buck-naked under a rumpled blanket that probably reeked of sin and sex. At the thought of the previous night, I felt my toes grow warm and my insides flutter.

Damn it, Luna. Focus.

I glanced around Jake's bedroom. Desperately, I wished for some of my own clothes. Or hell, I'd even settle for some of Jake's, as long as they could pass for mine.

Yeah, right.

Compared to me, Jake was massive. And a guy. Any idiot would know the difference. And whatever else Bishop was, the guy wasn't stupid. Still, my gaze scanned the room, looking for Jake's closet. I didn't see one. But I *did* see the wide door to the master bath.

I recalled using it the night before. From what I remembered, it was huge and magnificent, just like Jake's... I bit my lip. *Damn it. Not helpful.*

From somewhere in the penthouse, I heard muffled male voices. Eager to catch them before things got worse, I hurried toward the bathroom, flung open the door, and peered inside. On the far wall, I spotted another door – a closet, it had to be. I hustled toward the door and threw it open.

Jackpot.

The closet was larger than my last two bedrooms combined. In it, I saw an expanse of men's clothing, hung in rows around the perimeter. On shelves near the center, I spotted stacks of casual clothes folded in nice, neat piles. In the middle of the space was a low wooden bench with random clothes draped across it.

I dove for the nearest stack of T-shirts and rifled through them. I picked the smallest shirt available and yanked it on over my head. I reached to a lower shelf and found a pair of black workout shorts with a string-tie waist. Ignoring my lack of panties, I jumped into the shorts, tugged them up, and tied the waist as tight as it would go.

I was turning to leave the closet when something made me stop short. It was the sound of voices, quieter than before, but surprisingly clear. Where on Earth were they coming from?

And then it hit *me*. Jake's study was the next room over. Were they talking in there? More to the point, were they still talking about me? I couldn't help it. I was dying to know.

I wish I could say I tried to resist. But that would be a lie. Besides, I told myself, before I marched off to make a fool of myself, I should have *some* idea of what I was jumping into.

Right?

CHAPTER 41

Skirting the low wooden bench, I edged closer to the far wall. As quietly as I could, I pushed aside some sturdy metal clothes-hangers and nestled myself in the narrow gap that I'd just made.

Through the closet wall, I heard Bishop's voice, low and dangerous. "Don't tell me you screwed her."

Instantly, heat flooded my face. Like this was any of *his* concern.

"For the last time," Jake said, "it's none of your business."

I felt myself nod. Exactly.

"Yeah?" Bishop said. "What's your story *this* time? Wait. Lemme guess. She fell just happened to fall naked into your bed?" His voice rose. "Like Debbie?"

I stiffened. Debbie? Who was that?

"She's no Debbie," Jake said. "And keep it down, will ya? She's still asleep."

"I wouldn't count on that," Bishop said.

"Trust me," Jake said. "If she slept through some asshole pounding on the door at dawn, she can sleep through anything."

"Let me get this straight," Bishop said. "You screw *my* girl's little sister, and *I'm* the asshole?"

I rolled my eyes. *Little* sister? Oh please. I wasn't twelve. I was twenty-three. Why couldn't anyone remember that?

"Yeah," Jake said. "You *are* the asshole. Because one – in case you didn't notice, she's all grown up now." His voice softened. "And two – I didn't 'screw' her." He paused. "It was something different."

I felt myself smile.

"Like what?" Bishop said. "Another blow-job under the bleachers?"

What?

For a long moment, no one said anything. Finally, Jake broke the silence. "Get out," he said.

"You wanna make me?" Bishop asked.

"No," Jake said in an oddly controlled voice, "not with her in the next room. But I *am* asking you, politely."

"You?" Bishop said. "Polite? That'll be the day."

"Look who's talking," Jake said.

"Listen," Bishop said, "I'm not trying to be a dick about it."

"Too late for that."

"But," Bishop continued, "she's not your type. I know it. You know it. So if you're just messing around…"

"So I have a type now?" Jake said. "Wanna tell me what it is?"

"You *know* what type it is." Bishop said. "Come on, be reasonable. Selena's worried about her."

"You are such a pussy," Jake said.

The sentiment was so silly, I stifled a laugh. Bishop was a pussy the way cats were motorcycles.

"So what's the deal?" Jake continued. "Your fiancée says jump, and you say 'how high?' She says, 'fetch my sister,' and you say, 'yes ma'am.'"

"If you're trying to piss me off," Bishop said, "give it up. I'm not here to fight with you."

"Could've fooled me," Jake said.

"And," Bishop said, "just for the record, Selena doesn't know I'm here."

"So," Jake said, "you're back to the secretive shit. She'll just *love* that, won't she?"

"What she'll love," Bishop said, "is finding out that her sister's okay."

"And away from *me*," Jake said. "Am I right?" He gave a humorless laugh. "Too bad. Because Luna's not going anywhere."

"Shouldn't we get *her* opinion?" Bishop said.

"No."

"Why not?"

"Because," Jake said, "I don't want you bothering her."

After a long pause, Bishop asked. "What's up with you, anyway?"

"Nothing."

"Bull," Bishop said. "Shouldn't you be glad to be rid of her?"

"Why's that?"

"Because you already screwed her," Bishop said. "Why keep her around, right?"

My jaw dropped. What a total dick. Or, as Jake had said, what an asshole. But then again, I'd always known that.

Whatever my sister saw in the guy, I had no idea. Well, except for the fact that he looked almost exactly like Jake. And he was a bad-ass. And, if my sister's implications were true, he was obscenely good in bed.

Come to think of it, Jake and Bishop weren't that different. Oh crap. Maybe my sister and I were both stupid.

Through the wall, I heard a thud. I tensed. What was that? A chair falling?

And then Bishop laughed. "What are you gonna do? Kick my ass?"

A long silence followed. What was going on in there?

Finally, when Jake spoke again, his voice was scarily calm, almost casual. "Hey, I've got an idea," Jake said. "Let's head back to your place. We'll talk trash about your girl." He gave a low laugh. "About you screwing her, or not screwing her—"

"Shut up," Bishop said.

"Oh, am I getting too personal?" Sarcasm oozed through the wall. "Sorry."

"Keep it up, and you will be."

"We'll see about that," Jake said.

"Just do me a favor," Bishop said. "Wake her up. Let me talk to her."

"Not a chance."

"Fine," Bishop said. "I'll wait."

"The hell you will."

Damn it. I didn't want Bishop to wait either. And really, what the hell was I doing? Hunkering down in some closet? Eavesdropping on a conversation that was supposed to be private? Had I no shame at all?

Apparently not.

Still, I'd hidden out here long enough. It was time to confront this head-on. I pushed away from the closet wall. But when I turned, my head bumped into those stupid metal hangers. They clattered, first against each other, and then onto the tile floor.

The metallic noise sounded way too huge in the small space. My heart thudded, and I held myself absolutely still. I tried to listen. I heard nothing from the neighboring room – no voices, no footsteps. Desperate to be out of there, I scrambled forward, forgetting to watch where I was going.

Suddenly, something hard smacked me in the face. The floor. I was lying face-first across it. Near my feet, that stupid bench was lying on its side. Damn it.

I had barely begun to push myself up when I heard footsteps. They stopped just outside the master bedroom door. Recalling the lock, I breathed a ragged sigh of relief.

"Luna?" Jake called. The doorknob rattled. "Shit," he muttered. A moment later, he called out, "You okay?"

Oh God, how embarrassing. Before I could answer, he called out again. "Luna? Baby? Say something, alright?"

I groaned, not in pain, but in humiliation. "Um, yeah," I called. "I'm okay. I just, uh, I tripped. That's all."

The doorknob rattled again. "Sure you're okay?" he called. "Let me in, alright?"

Soon, I heard Bishop's voice. "Here. Lemme get it."

Oh God. *He* was out there too? Muttering, I pushed myself off the closet-floor and stood on shaky legs. Aside from my dignity, I wasn't hurt, or at least I didn't think so. I'd barely gotten to my feet when I heard the doorknob rattle and give a small click.

Crap.

A split-second later, I heard the bedroom door fly open and slam against the doorstop or whatever. Before I could react, Jake burst into the bathroom, wearing long black running pants and no shirt. He stopped short and looked around. Finally, he spotted me standing in his closet.

He plunged toward me. "Baby, are you okay?"

"Uh, yeah," I said, giving him a shaky smile. "Just, uh, borrowing your clothes." With an unsteady laugh, I flicked my hand toward the bench. "I think that bench jumped out in front of me."

"You say the word," he said. "I'll burn it."

I couldn't help but laugh, for real this time. It was the second time in twenty-four hours that he'd mentioned burning something because of me. "First the dress," I said, "now this? What are you a pyro or something?"

From somewhere in the hall, I heard Bishop's voice, loud and clear. "Hey Jake," he called. "Know what you should do?"

Jake made a sound of annoyance. He turned and called out through clenched teeth, "What?"

"Ask how long she was listening to us."

Damn it. □

CHAPTER 42

Five minutes later, I was sitting beside Jake on the living room sofa, with Bishop sitting across from us.

"For your information," I told Bishop, "I was in the closet getting dressed. That's all."

"Right." Bishop glanced down at my makeshift outfit. "Nice clothes."

"Jeez, they're not *mine*," I said. But that did remind me of my two suitcases, smashed in Jake's trunk. I turned to Jake. "Hey, where *is* my stuff, by the way?" True, most if it was crap, but I couldn't walk around in Jake's clothes forever.

"Yeah, about that…" Jake said.

"It's not still in your car?" I said. "Is it?"

"The thing is," Jake said, "it's missing."

I stared at him. "Your car?"

"No. Your stuff."

My jaw dropped. "You've got to be kidding. How'd *that* happen?"

He shrugged. "Happens more than you'd think."

Well, this was just great. That stuff was all I had. And worse, I had no money to replace anything. I blew out a long breath. What was I supposed to do now?

Jake leaned his head close to mine. "We'll talk about it later, alright?"

I slid my gaze to Bishop, who was watching us with a perplexed look. For some reason, it annoyed the snot out of me.

"What are you looking at?" I said.

"Got me," Bishop said, getting to his feet. He turned to Jake. "You got a coat she can borrow?"

I stared up at Bishop. "Why would I need a coat?"

"Because," he said, "it's cold out. Why else?"

Jake reached an arm over my shoulder, pulling me close. He looked up at Bishop and said, "Except, unlike you, *she's* not going anywhere."

Bishop turned his cool gaze on me. He waited. I glanced from him to Jake, who studied Bishop with open hostility.

Bishop broke the silence. "Luna, you ready?"

Actually, I wasn't. I wasn't naïve. I knew I'd have to leave eventually. But I didn't have to leave *now*. Did I?

Again, I looked toward Jake. Against my side, his muscles were tense. Still, when he spoke, his voice was surprisingly easy. "You wanna go with him?" he asked.

I felt my brow wrinkle. Did he want me to leave? I didn't think so, but I had to be realistic. How long could I really hang out here? I bit my lip and gave it some thought.

I was still thinking when Jake stood. "So you wanna go?" he said.

I did a double-take. "That's not what I'm saying." Slowly, I got to my feet. I moved close to him and lowered my voice. "Can we talk about this?" I gave Bishop a sideways glance. "In private?"

Jake turned to his brother. "You heard her," Jake said. He flicked his head toward the door. "Get out."

I gave Jake an exasperated look. "That's not what I meant." I looked to Bishop. "Can't you just step out on the balcony or something?" I returned my gaze to Jake and said in a hushed whisper, "Or maybe you and I could go talk in the bedroom?"

Across from us, Bishop made a sound of disgust.

I whirled toward him. "What's *that* supposed to mean?"

Bishop eyed Jake with obvious disapproval. "Nothing."

My gaze narrowed. "You meant *something*." With a sigh of frustration, I turned to Jake. When I saw him, I caught my breath. His body was rigid, and his eyes were blazing. But he wasn't looking at me. He was looking at his brother.

When Jake spoke, his voice was almost scary. He took a slow step toward Bishop. "Get out."

Bishop didn't move. "You gonna make me?"

Jake took another step toward him. "If it comes to that."

"Oh for God's sake," I muttered. I turned to Bishop. "Just go. Alright?"

"You heard her," Jake said. "She's staying. *You're* leaving. Alone."

Bishop still didn't move, and he didn't speak. He gave me a penetrating look, and the silence became deafening. Slowly, he turned his gaze on Jake. Around us, the tension grew so thick I could hardly breathe.

Desperate to end the standoff, I blurted out, "Know what I need?"

Both guys turned to look at me.

"What?" Jake asked.

"Um…" Oh crap. I didn't actually have an answer. My gaze bounced around the penthouse and landed on the open kitchen. "Waffles." I gave a vigorous nod. "Yup. Waffles. Definitely. With bacon. And uh, extra butter."

For a long moment, no one said anything. Jake glanced toward the kitchen.

But it was Bishop who first spoke. "Not a problem," he said. "We'll hit a breakfast place on the way back."

"Actually," I said, "I meant *homemade* waffles."

Bishop turned toward Jake. "You cook?" Bishop said.

"Sure, he does," I said. "He's really good at it too." One time, I'd seen Jake roast a hot dog at the beach. That counted for something, right?

Bishop was still giving Jake that dubious look. "Right," Bishop said.

"So, uh, anyway," I told Bishop, "you probably *should* get going."

His gaze drifted back to me. "Is that so?" he said.

"Yeah." I summoned up a smile. "But hey, you know what you should do?"

Next to me, Jake muttered, "Mind his own damn business?"

I gave Jake an annoyed look. "No," I said with more patience than I felt. "He should get some waffles to go." I turned back to Bishop. "You know that breakfast place you were talking about? You could swing by on the way back, and maybe get a bag of them or something."

Bishop's eyebrows furrowed. "A bag. Of waffles."

"Or whatever they put them in," I said. "Jeez. You could surprise Selena. You know, she's not a morning person, so, uh, she'd probably really like that."

From the look on Bishop's face, he wasn't in a waffly mood. "You want me to leave?" he said. "Is that's what you're saying?"

Jake stepped forward. "It's what *I'm* saying. Except I don't give a shit whether you pick up waffles or not."

I whirled toward him. "Shush!"

His eyebrows lifted. "Shush?"

"Or whatever," I said. I turned back to Bishop. "Don't forget the bacon," I said. "And extra butter. Selena *really* likes butter. You know that, right?"

With something like a sigh, Bishop reached into his pocket and pulled out a pen, along with a small white business card. He scribbled something onto it and held the card out in my direction. I reached out and took it. I squinted down to look. On the card, I saw nothing but a barely legible phone number.

"Anything happens," Bishop said, "you call me. I'm two hours away. But I'll be here in half that."

I stared up at him. "What? How?"

"What dickhead is trying to say," Jake said, "is that he thinks speed limits are optional." Jake turned to Bishop. "If she needs anything," Jake told him, "she'll be calling *me*. Not you. Now for the last time, get out."

I looked from brother to brother, trying to understand the dynamics of their relationship. I had siblings of my own, including a couple of younger brothers. I knew things could get complicated, but their level of animosity was totally foreign to me.

With a sound of disgust, Bishop turned to give me a penetrating look. After a moment, he said, "See you in a couple days."

"What?" I said. "What's going on in two days? Is there a wedding shower or something?"

Wordlessly, Bishop he turned toward the door and started walking.

"Hey," I called after him. "Just answer the question."

At the door, Bishop finally stopped. Slowly, he turned around. "You want the answer?" he said. "Ask Jake." And with that, he opened the door, strode out, and shut it, hard, behind him.

I whirled toward Jake. "What did he mean by that?" I asked. "Do you know?"

"Eh, he's a dick," Jake said. "He didn't mean anything."

I stared up at him. "You're lying," I said. "I can tell."

Jake's gaze shifted toward the door. "Forget it," he said. "He doesn't know what he's talking about." Returning his gaze to mine, he reached for my hand. As if shaking off the gloom, he gave me a crooked smile and said, "Waffles, huh?" □

CHAPTER 43

As it turned out, he didn't have waffles, or even a waffle-maker. But he did have bacon, orange juice, and pancake mix. Together in his gourmet kitchen, we whipped up stacks of pancakes and extra-thick bacon. Carrying it all to his dining room, we ate looking out over the riverfront skyline.

Funny, I'd known Jake for years. And yet, except for occasional snack food, I'd never eaten with him. Glancing out the window, I felt myself smile. I was doing a lot of new things with him.

Soon, I wanted to do some of those things again. My stomach fluttered. Maybe after breakfast.

"You have a killer smile," Jake said. "Anyone ever tell you that?"

"Me?" I returned my gaze to Jake, who looked sinfully tousled in the early morning light. "Not lately," I said. "But—" I made a show of hesitating. "—Wait a minute, you don't mean like a *serial*-killer smile, do you?"

He gave me a speculative look. "Now that you mention it…"

"Hey," I said, "I can assure you, I'm mostly sane." I took a tiny sip of my orange juice. "Or at least, that's what the voices tell me."

Before making breakfast, Jake had thrown on a black T-shirt to go with his black running pants. He looked fabulous, of course, but he would've looked even more fabulous without the shirt. I had the teeniest regret that he was wearing a shirt at all. Embarrassingly, I'd always fantasized about someday having breakfast with him half-naked.

I couldn't really blame him though. The shirt was my own fault. When he'd started frying up the bacon, I'd practically forced him to put on more clothes – and not only to keep myself from pouncing on him.

Mostly, I was worried about all that hot bacon grease. One wrong move, and any exposed skin would be in serious danger. Jake might not care. But I did, and not just for superficial reasons.

There was something about him that touched my heart. I couldn't help but wonder if anyone had ever looked out for him, *really* looked out for him. Knowing what little I did of his family, I seriously doubted it.

"Wanna know what the voices tell *me*?" Jake said.

"What?" I asked.

"That we need to go shopping."

"For what?" I asked.

He glanced down at my makeshift outfit. I was wearing the same clothes I'd borrowed from his closet. "I've gotta replace your stuff," he said.

"What do you mean *you've* got to replace it?"

"Only fair," he said, "since I lost it."

"Yeah, but I borrowed your T-shirt last night," I said. "And it got ripped. So I guess we're sort of even."

"That was only one shirt," he said. "And *I* ripped it, not you."

At the memory, I felt myself blush. I lowered my voice. "Can I confess something?"

"You'd better."

"I really liked that."

He gave me a slow, intimate smile. "Yeah?"

I swallowed and felt myself nod. "Of course, you wouldn't want to do that *all* the time. I mean, think of the clothes you'd go through."

"Or," Jake said, "think of the fun you'd have."

I laughed. "Well, there is that."

"About your stuff," he said, "let me replace it."

I glanced away and tried not to consider it.

"Come on," he said. "I'll feel bad if I don't."

The offer was shamefully tempting. Obviously, Jake could afford it. And I couldn't. But something about the idea didn't seem quite right. "But that really wasn't your fault," I said.

"Well, it sure as hell wasn't yours."

"And," I continued, "who knows? My stuff might turn back up." I hesitated. "Eventually."

"If you believe that," Jake said, "I've got a bridge to sell you somewhere."

I leaned forward. "Really? How much are you asking?"

"I dunno." He downed the rest of his orange juice. "How much you got?"

"Well," I said, looking down at my plate, "I do have this last piece of bacon…"

"Done." He reached across the table and speared the bacon with his fork.

I stifled a laugh. "Hey!"

He hesitated. "So, uh, you want it?"

"Oh, never mind." I rolled my eyes. "Take it, take it. Please."

He popped the bacon into his mouth and grinned over at me. "Sucker."

He looked so boyish that I had to smile. "Jeez," I said. "Guys and their meat." Instantly, my face grew warm at the obvious implication. "Uh, forget I said that."

"Not a chance," he said.

It felt good to joke around with him again. Somehow, the last twenty-four hours had been way too serious for my liking and probably for his too. Bishop's visit hadn't helped. But somehow, the act of making breakfast together had eased most of the tension, and I felt oddly content.

It was Sunday morning, and I was with an amazing guy in an amazing place. The previous night, I'd had the best sex of my life, and was eating my second-favorite breakfast food.

At this instant, life was good. I blew out a breath. But tomorrow was Monday. Reluctantly, I pulled my gaze from Jake and looked out the window, taking in the cityscape. What I really needed was a job. Actually, I needed *two* jobs, given the fact I had no clothes, no furniture, and no place to live.

To replace everything I'd lost, one job would never be enough.

Half of me wanted to give Jake hell for everything he'd cost me, especially on the job front. I still had no idea what he'd been thinking. But then, there was that other half of me. That half wanted to drag Jake to the bedroom and forget the real world existed at all.

When I returned my gaze to Jake, he was watching me with an expression I couldn't quite decipher. If I didn't know any better, I'd have said he looked content. But Jake was never content – not fully anyway, not for as long as I'd known him.

But then again, he *did* just have bacon.

Recalling the piece he'd swiped from me, I gave him a stern look. "You still owe me a bridge," I said.

"Alright," he said. "If they have one at the mall, it's yours. I'll add it to the other stuff I owe you."

"Seriously," I told him, "you don't need to do that."

"I know," he said. "But let me anyway. Alright?"

I bit my lip. "I dunno."

"Come on," he said, reaching for my hand. "It'll be fun. I always wanted to go shopping with a beautiful girl."

I looked heavenward. "Now you're just sucking up."

"Yeah." He gave my hand a squeeze. "But it doesn't mean it's not true."

"Oh get real," I said. "No guy wants to shop. Not really."

"Why not?" he said. "I can watch you try on stuff." Slowly, he rubbed his thumb against my palm. "Later, if I'm lucky, maybe I'll get to watch you take it off."

Instantly, my temperature shot up several degrees. "Okay, now you're just being unfair," I said.

"Yeah? How so?"

"How is any girl supposed to resist that?"

"Luna," he said, his voice softening, "you're not just any girl."

I swallowed. "I'm not?"

His gaze dipped to my lips. "No. You're not."

Just when I started to feel all warm and fuzzy, he added. "You're a smart-ass. And bratty as hell." His voice grew lower. "And so sweet that I want to drag you away and corrupt the shit out of you."

Oh wow. My lips suddenly felt way too dry. Without thinking, I brushed my tongue against my upper lip and managed to croak out, "You do?"

He nodded.

I glanced toward the bedroom. "Just so you know," I said, "you could corrupt me now if you really wanted to."

A slow smile spread across his face. "Yeah?"

I felt myself nod.

He pushed away from the table. "Now, you did it."

I blinked innocently up at him. "Did what?"

"Here," he said, "let me show you."

And so he did, right there in the dining room. By the time we finished, I was too blissful to argue about anything – not about shopping, not about my lost jobs, and not about the fact I knew all of this was temporary.

Soon, I'd be leaving. And he'd go back to whatever – or whoever – he was doing. The idea made me just a little sick to my stomach, but I wasn't a fool. So I kept telling myself only a *real* fool would give up the chance to enjoy this for whatever it was.

The way it looked, Jake was enjoying himself too. It was a win-win.

Right?

A couple hours later, we were showered, dressed, and ready to hit the mall. Jake was wearing dark slacks and a charcoal dress shirt that made him look half-dangerous and all delicious.

If I didn't love looking at him, I might have felt shamefully outclassed, given what I was wearing. Short of clothing options, I'd thrown on the same yoga pants and long-sleeved shirt that I'd purchased with Bianca.

Unlike our sham of a date at the museum, this upcoming shopping excursion felt more like an actual date, and I felt surprisingly jittery. I knew it was silly. After everything we'd done in the last twenty-four hours, a simple trip to the mall was hardly anything to be nervous over.

And yet, I *was* nervous, even if I was determined not to show it.

I was just lacing up my new black tennis shoes, when I heard the sound of a key card in the front door. I froze. So did Jake. A moment later, the door flew open, and there she stood – Bianca□

CHAPTER 44

Together, Jake and I stood looking at her. Bianca was dressed in high red heels and a skimpy red dress that was way too sexy for a chilly Sunday morning. She threw back her shoulders and said, "Alright. Where is it?"

Jake gave her a cold look. "Where's what?"

"My dress." She looked toward me. "You told me to pick it up today. Remember?"

"Yeah. I guess," I said. "But honestly? I didn't think you'd actually do it."

She pursed her lips. "And why is that?"

"Well, for starters," I said, "because I haven't had a chance to get it cleaned or anything."

Next to me, Jake's gaze zoomed in on the key card, still in Bianca's hand. "Forget the dress," he said. "Where'd you get that?"

"You gave it to me," she said. "Remember?"

His jaw tightened. "No."

"Well, you did," she said. "I don't know why you're acting all surprised about it. I used it just last night." Bianca turned toward me. "Or didn't you bother to tell him?"

I turned to Jake. "Oh hey," I said, "when Bianca stopped by, she used her own key."

Bianca made a sound of frustration. "I didn't mean *now*," she said. "I suppose you didn't give him my message either."

"What message?" I asked. "And why would I *have* to give him a message when you talked to him yourself?"

With a long-suffering sigh, she turned to Jake and said, "I'm terminating our arrangement."

I stared at her. "You never gave me that message."

"Yes, I did," she said. "I told you that I'm working for Vince Hammond now. Remember him? The guy you were drooling over last night?"

"Oh please," I said. "I was not."

"Whatever." Again, she turned to Jake. "I'll be sending you my final invoice. And you know what? Forget the dress. I'll add it to the bill."

"Wait a minute," I said. "Didn't he already pay for that dress?"

She turned to give me a little smirk. "Well, he sure paid for *yours*. Didn't he?" A nasty edge crept into her voice. "Tell me. Did he get his money's worth?"

My face grew warm. He *had* paid for my dress. And if she was talking about sex, he did, in fact, get his money's worth. But so did I, a few times over. But that hardly seemed the point.

Either way, the reminder still stung. It didn't help that Jake and I were literally on our way out the door to do even more shopping. Maybe that wasn't such a good idea after all. What was I, anyway?

"Bianca," Jake said in a barely controlled voice. "Whatever you wanna say to me, go ahead, say it, but you're not dragging Luna into this."

"Well isn't that sweet," she said.

I looked from Bianca to Jake. Obviously, they had a history together. And obviously, that history extended well beyond their business relationship. "Come to think of it," I said, "I just remembered that, uh, I need to call my sister." I gestured toward the guest room. "I'll just, uh, be in there."

"Hang on," Jake said. "I'll walk you."

"Oh for heaven's sake," Bianca said, "it's just down the hall."

Jake gave her a cold look. "Or," he said, "you can leave now. Your choice."

"Fine," she muttered. "I'll wait."

Feeling slightly ridiculous, I started heading toward the guest room with Jake beside me. When I opened the door to the guest room and walked inside, he followed after me and shut the door behind him.

I glanced at the closed door. "I'm not sure I'd leave her out there alone," I said. "I mean, she seems pretty mad. What if she trashes something?"

"Forget that," he said. "There's something I've gotta say."

"What?" I asked.

He reached for my hand. "I'm sorry. The thing with Bianca, it's complicated."

"Really?" I said. "I had no idea."

"I'm gonna take care of it," he said. "So don't worry."

"I'm not worried," I said in a voice that was hardly convincing.

He pulled me close, gathering me into his arms. Into my hair, he said, "This'll just take a few minutes. And then we'll go. Alright?"

I nodded against him, soaking up the feel of him, the scent of him. I wanted to melt into him and forget everything. I especially wanted to forget that another girl was waiting for him to discuss who-knows-what.

But a moment later, he was gone. And then, the yelling started. Or at least, Bianca was yelling. As for Jake, he wasn't saying a whole lot, at least not from what I could hear. What was he doing, anyway? Letting Bianca rage at him, so she'd get it out of her system?

If so, Bianca was definitely rising to the challenge. I heard phrases like arrogant jackass, reckless hothead, callous heartbreaker, and too many more to dwell on.

Desperate for a dose of sanity, I grabbed my cell phone and called my sister. When she answered, I breathed a sigh of relief and said, "Hey, it's me."

"About time you called back," she said. "I was almost ready to hop in my car and track you down."

I tried to laugh. "Well, you wouldn't be the first one today."

"What do you mean?" she asked.

"Didn't Bishop tell you?"

"Tell me what?"

"He stopped by this morning."

"What?" she said. "Where?"

"Here," I said. "At Jake's."

"Oh shut up," she said. "He did not."

"Wanna bet?"

"Damn it." She gave an irritated sigh. "You're serious, aren't you?"

"Yeah. Didn't he mention it?"

"Well, not really," she said. "But he *did* show up with waffles. It was really weird, now that I think of it."

So he'd actually gone and done it? He'd stopped to pick up waffles for my sister? For some reason, it almost made me smile. "Weird bad?" I said. "Or weird good?"

"Well, the waffles were great," she said. "Get this. He even remembered the extra butter. Isn't that sweet?"

"Yeah. That's Bishop," I said. "Sweet."

"Oh come on," she said. "You just don't know him like I do." I heard fumbling on the phone. "Hang on. I think he's out of the shower."

Oh crap. He was there? Now? Probably, I should have asked

about that in the first place. This definitely wasn't a conversation I wanted *him* to be part of.

A second later, I heard Selena call out, "Hey, why didn't you mention your little trip this morning?"

I heard Bishop's voice call back, "I was just about to."

Selena groaned. "Oh cripes, not this again."

Again, I heard Bishop's voice, closer now. It was low, flirtatious even. "Hey, you were the one distracting me. Remember?"

Oh God. With everything else going on, this was the last thing I wanted to hear. "Hey," I said, "I've gotta go. I'll talk to you later, okay?"

"No. Wait," she said. "Why don't you come for a visit?"

Things were complicated. Too complicated. But I didn't want to discuss it. At least not now. So I stuck with a simple reason. "Because I don't have a car anymore."

"You don't?" she said. "What happened to it?"

"It's a long story," I said. "I'll tell you later."

"Then let me come get you," she said. "Come on. If you want, I'll leave right now."

I heard Bishop's voice in the background. "You mean *we'll* leave right now."

"Oh stop butting in," she told him in a hushed tone. "Let *me* talk to her, alright?"

"It's *my* brother," he said.

"Yeah," she said. "And it's *my* sister." I heard fumbling again, and a noise that sounded a lot like a door thudding shut. "Luna?" she said.

"Yeah, I'm still here."

"Sorry about that," she said. "So, can I come and get you?"

"Well, the thing is," I said, "I don't really have a place to stay."

"Oh stop it," she said. "Yes you do. With me." Her voice

grew coaxing. "Come on. It'll be fun. I haven't seen you in forever."

I bit my lip. "I dunno. Maybe in a few days, alright?"

Outside the guest room, Bianca was practically screaming now. In a way, she sounded almost exactly like Maddie, except Bianca's words were a whole lot bigger and slightly less profane.

And, Bianca wasn't naked. Well, not that I knew of anyway.

"That girl yelling in the background," Selena said. "Who *is* that?"

"It's someone Jake does business with," I said. "That's another long story."

Too bad I didn't even know the story, not all of it anyway. But that did remind me of something. "Hey," I said, "A question. By any chance, do you know someone named Debbie?"

"No," she said. "Do you?"

How to put this? I tried to remember what Bishop had said – something about Debbie turning up naked in Jake's bed? Had Jake stolen one of Bishop's girlfriends? Was *that* the reason they didn't get along?

I was dying for more details, but I didn't want to upset my sister, so I tried to be vague. "I think she might've dated Jake. Or Bishop." I paused. "Or both. It sounds like she might've hung around their house or something?"

"Oh. *Her?*" Selena said. "No. If it's the person I'm thinking of, she didn't date either one of them."

Well, not as far as Selena knew, anyway.

"So who was she?" I asked. "Did you ever meet her?"

"Not really," Selena said. "She only lasted a few months. She was pretty rough, and a lot older than I was. But I guess that's to be expected, huh?"

"Why's that?" I asked.

"Because," Selena said, "that was their *dad's* girlfriend." □

CHAPTER 45

I heard a sharp intake of breath. It was my own. I flopped back onto the bed and stared up at the ceiling. So Jake had slept with his dad's girlfriend? That was disturbing on too many levels to count.

No. That couldn't be true. This morning, Bishop must've been talking about someone else.

On the phone, I heard Selena's voice. "Luna? Are you there?"

"Yeah."

"What's wrong?" she asked.

"Nothing."

I was still trying to add things up. Selena had met Bishop when she was how old? Eighteen. I did the math. If Selena was talking about the same Debbie, Jake would have been how old at the time? Twenty-one. Definitely old enough to know better.

Wasn't there anyone he wouldn't sleep with?

I returned my attention to Selena. "Hey, can I ask you something else?" I said. "Has Jake ever hit on you?"

"Me? No. Never. I hardly know him." She laughed. "Why would you even ask such a thing?"

"Just curious." I closed my eyes, hoping to block out my own ugly thoughts. It didn't help. "Sorry, I need to go," I said.

"Can I give you a call in a few days?"

"Oh, alright," she muttered. "But if I don't hear from you soon, I'm tracking you down. I mean it."

I had to smile. If I knew my sister, she'd do it too.

After we hung up, I didn't move. Bianca was still raging. I wrapped a pillow around my head, trying to muffle the noise. It only reminded me that two nights ago, I'd done practically the same thing with a different pillow in a different place, when Maddie and Jake had been screwing like porn stars in the adjacent bedroom.

Jake had made Maddie scream too. Of course, Maddie's screams had sounded a whole lot happier than Bianca's.

The recollection didn't make me feel better, especially when Bianca's screeching picked up volume. Just when I thought I'd go absolutely insane, I heard a door slam so hard, I swear, the bed shook. And then, everything was silent.

I flung aside the pillow and sat up. I listened. I heard nothing. Was she gone? Or had they killed each other?

I heard a knock on the guest room door, followed by Jake's voice. "Luna? You in there?"

Where exactly did he think I was? Hiding out in some closet again?

Not this time. Embarrassment aside, I'd learned that lesson the hard way. There were some things a girl was definitely better off not knowing.

I pushed myself off the bed and stood. I took a deep breath and made myself smile. "Yup, come on in."

Jake pushed through the door and stopped short at the sight of me. "Are you okay?" he asked.

I nodded. "Yup. I'm good. How about you?"

His eyebrows furrowed. "You want the truth?" he said. "Or the same bull you're giving me?"

"Actually," I admitted, "I'm not sure how to answer . Maybe

you should go first."

"Alright." He shoved his hands in his pockets and leaned against the far wall. "I'm mad as hell."

"At who?" I asked. "Bianca?"

"And me." He made a sound of disgust. "And Vince Hammond."

I squinted over at him. "Vince? That sports agent? Why him?"

Jake's expression darkened. "Who do you think put Bianca up to that?"

"I don't know," I said. "I just figured maybe you and Bianca had that kind of relationship."

"Yeah? What kind is that?"

"Volatile." I swallowed. "You know. Break up. Make up. That sort of thing."

"Well, we don't," he said.

"Oh."

"That scene today?" he said. "That was new."

"And you're blaming Vince?"

"I know how he works." Jake pushed away from the wall and strode toward me. He stopped just outside arm's reach. "*You* don't."

I looked up at him. "What do *I* have to do with anything?"

"Tell me," Jake said. "When he stopped by, was he Mister Charming?"

"What?" I said. "He was nice, if that's what you're asking."

"Nice? Let me tell you something. That guy? He's not nice." Jake glanced away. "Any more than I am."

"Oh for crying out loud," I said, "that's not even fair."

His gaze returned to mine. "Yeah? Why not?"

"Because," I said, "you can't lump both of you together like that. When he stopped by, he *was* nice. And actually, I think *you're* nice too."

At this, Jake laughed, a hard sound that rang hollow in the quiet room. "Luna," he said, "I'm not nice. And the sooner you get that, the better off you'll be."

I wanted to argue. But something made me stop. Nice guys didn't start fights and film them for fun. They didn't cost people endorsement deals and laugh it off like nothing. My stomach clenched. They definitely didn't have sex with their dad's girlfriends.

Stop it, I told myself. That whole girlfriend-thing probably wasn't even true. It couldn't be. I studied Jake's face, looking for some kind of clue. I didn't know what to say. So I said nothing.

In front of me, his gaze softened. "Forget all that," he said, closing the distance between us. "Forget Vince. Forget Bianca. Forget my damn brother." He wrapped his arms around me and pulled me close. I knew I should fight it. But honestly, I didn't want to. So I leaned into him, soaking up the feel of him as I tried to push aside my doubts.

He spoke into my hair. "There's something I should've said right off."

"What's that?"

"I'm sorry," he said. "I would've told her to get the hell out. I should have. Wanna know why I didn't?"

I nodded against him.

"I didn't want her coming back." His voice was softer now. "Not now. Not with you here."

Did that mean he wanted her to come back *later*? When I was long-gone?

"Baby, what is it?" he asked.

I said nothing. If I were smart, I'd push away. I'd call my sister and be gone before dark. Instead, I burrowed deeper into his embrace. I didn't want to move. Not now. Not ever.

But that was my own stupidity talking. I recalled what those two guys in the mall had told me. Jake didn't do the girlfriend thing. In a way, that was funny, right? Because apparently, he *did* do somebody's girlfriend. His dad's, in fact.

On second thought, that wasn't funny at all.

Damn it. Why couldn't I stop thinking about it?

I heard Jake's voice low in my ear. "Luna?"

Lost in my own thoughts, I was only half listening. "What?"

"If you've got something to say, just say it."

"Okay," I said, letting that dreaded question tumble from my lips. "Who's Debbie?" ☐

CHAPTER 46

Next to me, Jake's body froze. "What?" he said.

This time, I made myself push away. "Someone named Debbie," I said. "Who is she?"

When Jake said nothing, I continued. "It's just that Bishop mentioned her, so…" I let the sentence trail off, hoping Jake would pick up the thread.

He didn't. "So?" he said.

"So I was just wondering. That's all."

In front of me, Jake's posture remained rigid.

I tried to keep my tone light, teasing even. "So, did she really fall naked into your bed? That had to be exciting, huh?"

He looked toward the door. "Ready to go?"

"Where?"

"To replace your stuff."

I stared up at him. Okay, maybe the Debbie thing was none of my business, but the way he was reacting, it was only fueling my curiosity. Worse, it was confirming my darkest fears. "So you're not going to answer the question?" I said.

He gave me a hard look. "Like you've answered mine?"

"What question?

"Questions," he said. "As in more than one." He spoke slowly and clearly. "What happened?" His jaw tightened. "To your clothes. To your stuff. To your apartment."

"As far as my clothes," I said, "You tell me. *You're* the one who lost those."

"I'm not talking about the crap in your suitcase."

"It wasn't crap," I said, stretching the truth more than a little.

"Right." He crossed his arms and waited.

"Fine," I said. "You wanna know what happened to my other stuff? Okay. It was stolen, just flat-out disappeared. And the stuff that *wasn't* stolen? It was ruined. Ripped to pieces, trashed. Almost nothing was salvageable." I took a ragged breath. "Not even my furniture, as crappy as it was."

"This was in your old place?" he asked.

"Yeah. And before you ask, I reported it too. Not that it did any good."

"Why not?"

I threw up my hands. "Because there was no way to tell who did it. Or why. And I didn't have any renter's insurance, so…" I looked away. "You know what? Forget it."

"No," he said. "So? What'd you do?"

"I moved," I said. "The same day actually."

"In with Maddie?"

"Yeah, I mean, I saw her ad on the internet. The place was cheap. And already furnished, sort of, so, I figured I'd stay there a while and save up some money."

"Any idea who was behind it?" Jake said.

"Well, at first, I was sure it was Rango, so…" I glanced away.

"So…?" Jake prompted.

"So," I continued, "as you seem to know already, I started giving him a taste of his own medicine."

"Meaning?"

"Well, I had that book with his passwords. So I started

posting things."

"Like what?"

"Funny things mostly, under Rango's name." I almost smiled. "It made him *so* crazy."

"I wouldn't look too happy about that if I were you."

"Hey, he had it coming."

"Maybe. But that's a good way to get the wrong kind of attention."

I gave him a snotty smile. "Says the guy who beats up people for money."

His expression froze. "Not just 'people.' He said. "Assholes. There's nobody I picked a fight with who didn't have it coming."

"Yeah. Sure."

"And I never swing first."

"Well aren't you the noble one," I said.

"No," he said. "And I never claimed to be."

"Whatever," I said. "I answered *your* questions. Now what about mine. Who's Debbie?"

"First, I've got one more."

"No way," I said. "It's *my* turn."

He continued as if I hadn't spoken. "When you heard Bishop talking about her, what exactly were you doing?"

"What?"

His voice hardened. "Okay, *where* were you?"

Oh. Yeah. I'd been skulking in his closet, eavesdropping on a private conversation. My mouth opened, but somehow, my lips couldn't seem to form an answer.

"I thought so," he said.

"Sorry," I mumbled. "I guess I overheard it."

"Yeah. I guess you did." He glanced toward the door. "So are you ready to go? Or not?"

I *so* didn't feel like arguing. But somehow, I couldn't see us waltzing off to some shopping mall either.

"No, I'm not ready to go," I said. "And I don't think you are, either."

"Is that right?"

I threw up my hands. "Okay, you caught me. I *was* listening in. But trust me, it's not the kind of thing I normally do."

"Uh-huh."

"It's true," I insisted.

"Is it?"

"Okay," I said. "I get it. I know it was crappy. And I'm sorry. If you don't want to talk about the Debbie thing, well, I guess that's your business." I crossed my arms. "And I won't bother you about it anymore." I hesitated. "If that's what you really want."

"Good," he said. "You ready to go?"

I gave an exasperated sigh. "In case you're not aware of this fact, when someone apologizes to you, you're supposed to say something like 'that's okay', or 'hey, don't worry about it.'"

"That's okay. Don't worry about it. Now, you ready?"

"No," I said. "Not when you're still mad about it." *And not when I'm still dying to know.*

"Since we're still asking questions," he said, "I've got another one."

"What?"

"Why didn't you tell me about Vince?"

I shook my head. "Tell you what, exactly?"

"That he was here last night."

I shrugged. "I don't know. I guess I should have. I meant to."

Jake's voice was flat. "You meant to."

"Oh for crying out loud," I said. "In case you forgot? You and me? We got a little distracted last night. Remember?"

"If you're trying to change the subject," he said, "forget it."

"There's a subject?" I said.

"Yeah. Vince."

"What's wrong?" I said. "Are you worried he stole something? Because you'll be glad to know I didn't let the guy out of my sight."

"Glad?" he said. "I'm supposed to be glad?"

"Jeez, what are you worried about?" My voice grew sarcastic. "That he took the good silver?"

"You think I give two shits about…?" Jake's eyebrows furrowed. "What the hell is good silver?"

"I don't know," I said. "It's just an expression. I think it means nice silverware."

"Okay, I don't give two shits about silverware."

"Then what is it?" I said. "Cash? Coins? Something else?"

"Not some *thing*," he said. "Some *one*."

"Who?"

Jake's voice grew deadly serious. "You." □

CHAPTER 47

I stared up at him. "What are you talking about?"

"The 'thing' that Vince wants to steal," Jake said, "is you."

"Oh stop it," I said. "He does not." I forced out a laugh. "I mean, he already has Bianca, right?" I lowered my voice with mock sincerity. "I think his work here is done."

"You think it's a joke?" Jake asked.

"Of course it's a joke. I've met the guy like two times."

"Yeah," he said. "You did. And if you think he's not interested, you're nuts."

"Fine. Then I'm nuts."

"And," Jake said, "he knows you're important to me."

"How would he know anything?"

"He's smart," Jake said. "He knows."

"How?" I repeated.

"He knows *me*."

"Yeah? Well here's what *you* need to know," I said. "Vince showed zero interest in me last night."

Jake's gaze met mine. "Right."

"It's true," I said. "I mean, he was friendly. But not *friendly*-friendly."

"You disappointed?" Jake said.

"What's that supposed to mean?"

"The way it sounds," Jake said, "you showed interest in *him*."

"Get real. I did not."

"Uh-huh."

"Oh come on," I said. "Is this because Bianca said I was 'drooling' over him? Seriously? You're gonna believe her? Over me?"

Jake glanced away. "Forget it."

"No," I said. "I want an answer. Who do you believe? Me? Or Bianca?"

Jake said nothing, and I felt my temper rise. I liked him. I liked him so much, it hurt. And probably, I had always been at least a little in love with him. But enough was enough. Maybe it *was* time to call my sister for that ride.

Looking for my phone, I turned away.

Jake's voice, quieter now, carried across the small distance. "You," he said.

I didn't bother to look at him. "What?"

"I believe *you*."

"Yeah. Sure you do." I scanned the nearby bed and spotted my phone on the far pillow.

"Luna," Jake said.

I whirled toward him. "What?"

His dark gaze met mine. "I'm sorry."

"Yeah, me too," I said, turning back toward the bed.

I felt a hand on my elbow. "Just listen," he said.

With a sigh, I turned to face him.

"I'm an asshole," he said. "I know that." He pushed his free hand through his hair. "But do me a favor. Pretend I'm not. Okay?"

I gazed up him. Standing there, he looked so tough and so forlorn, with his muscle-bound body and haunted eyes. I didn't know what to say.

Somehow, I managed to speak. "I don't even know what

you mean by that."

He let out a long breath. "I mean," he said, "let's get the hell out of here. Forget Bianca. Forget Vince." His voice softened. "Forget all the stupid shit I said."

Desperately, I wanted to. It would be so nice to hit a rewind button, to go back to this morning – before Bishop, before Bianca, before talking to my sister, and before the Vince thing, whatever it was.

As if sensing my weakness, Jake moved closer. He leaned toward me until our lips might have touched. "Say yes," he said.

I felt myself swallow. I wanted to say yes to a lot of things. I felt the threat of a smile.

He moved a fraction closer. His voice was very quiet. "Come on. Say yes. You know you want to."

He was right. I did want to. But unfair or not, I wanted something in return. "If I forget everything *you* said, will you forget about *me* hiding in your closet?"

Finally, his lips brushed mine. "Done."

An hour later, we were strolling through the same mall I'd visited with Bianca. But this time, I was actually having a good time. Okay, a great time.

As we walked from store to store together, I had to laugh. "You know what?" I told him. "I can't believe we're actually at the mall."

"Why not?" he asked.

"Because when I was in high school, this would've been my ultimate fantasy."

He gave me a sideways glance. "Shopping?"

"Actually," I admitted, "it would've been shopping with *you*."

His eyebrows rose. "So, you wanted to *shop* with me?"

In truth, I had wanted to do a lot of things with Jake. Some of those things, I had done this morning. And last night too. And if my luck held out, I'd be doing those things again before

I slept. Part of me wanted to those things right now, maybe in the back seat of his car, or in some abandoned dressing room.

What was it about Jake that brought out my inner hussy?

I gave him a sheepish smile. "I didn't *only* want to shop with you."

He grinned over at me. "Yeah?"

The guy way too smug for his own good. "Yeah," I said. "I wanted to do each other's hair too."

The smugness disappeared. "Please tell me you're joking."

Jake had nice hair. It was dark and thick with a mere whisper of a wave. Earlier today, it had drifted through my fingertips like silken magic. I wanted to mess his hair up, not style it, or braid it, or brush it, or color it. But Jake didn't need to know any of that. The way I saw it, a little fear might do him some good.

"And after that," I told him, "I figured we could give each other makeovers and talk about boys."

He stopped walking. "Come here," he said, pulling me close.

Laughing I fell into him, savoring the feel of his strong arms wrapped around my waist. Around us, other shoppers circled past, but I couldn't seem to make myself care.

He leaned down to whisper in my ear. "Lemme tell you something," he said.

"What?"

"If you talk about another 'boy,' someone's going to be very unhappy."

"Really?" I pulled away to blink up at him. "Who?"

Jake gave me a cocky grin. "Him."

With an epic eye-roll, I grabbed his hand and tugged him forward. "That's it," I told him. "We're getting facials too."

In the end, we stuck with shopping. And the more we shopped, the guiltier I felt. My old pair of sorry suitcases had held nearly nothing. And the stuff that *had* been in those things?

It was mostly crap. It was cheap, second-hand, or both.

In contrast, the replacement stuff was expensive, brand-name, and stylish. No matter how many times I tried to steer us toward cheaper stores or at least toward the clearance racks, Jake wouldn't hear a single word of it.

Within a couple of hours, we were loaded down with way too many festive shopping bags filled with everything I'd been missing and then some. There were jeans, sweaters, shirts, pants, skirts, shoes, a couple dresses, and enough lingerie to make me blush, especially when Jake threatened to muscle his way into the dressing room to watch me try it on.

Laughing as he tried to drag me into yet another store, I pulled against him. "No," I said. "Seriously. We need to stop."

"Why?" he said, giving me a gentle tug forward. "You tired?"

"It's not that," I said. "But come on." I glanced down at all the bags. "This is way too much, and you know it."

He propelled us forward anyway. "How do you know what I know?"

I knew he was spending a lot of money. And I knew I'd never be able to repay him. And yet, I also knew he didn't expect me to.

In some ways, it was absolutely wonderful. In other ways, it just didn't seem right. But for the last couple of hours, I had argued nearly to the point of awkwardness. If I argued any further, I'd just be ruining the fun for both of us. Plus, he'd threatened to make me walk back if I gave him any more trouble.

I recognized a bluff when I saw it. But it was such a sweet bluff that I couldn't call him on it. So I smiled up at him and tried a different approach. "For one thing," I said, "I know you haven't bought anything for yourself."

He flicked his gaze toward the nearby store. "I will," he said. "In there."

I glanced at the sign above the entrance. "But that's a woman's store," I said. "They don't even sell guys' stuff."

He grinned. "I know." He tugged me forward. "Now come on." □

CHAPTER 48

Inside the store, he scanned the displays as if looking for something in particular. He stopped at an elegant display of silk blouses in a wide array of colors. He pulled out a pale blue one and held it against my skin. He shook his head and returned it to the rack.

For all his size and masculinity, he was reminding me of a toddler in a toy store. I had to laugh. "What exactly are you looking for?" I asked.

"I'll know it when I see it." He reached for a different blouse. This one was creamy white with a classic cut and little pearl buttons all the way down the front.

He held it up in front of me and nodded. "That's the one," he said.

I raised my eyebrows. "Is it now?"

He handed the blouse over. "Try it on. We'll see." He held up a hand. "No, wait."

"For what?" I said.

"You need a skirt," he said. "Something black. And short."

"Actually," I said. "I have one of those. Remember?" I'd been wearing a short black skirt the morning he'd shown up at Maddie's apartment.

He gave a slow nod. "Yeah. I remember."

That reminded me of something. "Where *is* that skirt, by the way?" I hadn't seen the thing since taking it off to shower a couple days earlier.

"Probably at the cleaners," he said. "It doesn't matter. We'll get you a new one."

"I don't need a new one," I said. "The old one's fine, really."

He flashed me a grin. "Hey, this stuff is for me. Remember?"

I gave him a dubious look. "You're planning to wear a skirt?"

"Sorry, no more questions," he said.

"You don't *look* very sorry."

He shrugged. "I've been thinking about this a while."

"How long?" I asked.

He stopped to give me a look that, I swear, made my toes tingle and core ignite. He leaned close, and his voice was nearly a caress. "Since yesterday morning."

The words were completely innocent. And yet, for some reason, the store was feeling a whole lot hotter. I almost wanted to fan myself. No. I definitely wanted to fan myself. With his shirt. He'd just need to take it off and–.

From just behind me, I heard a crisp female voice say, "Can I start you a dressing room?"

I whirled around too fast, nearly knocking over a nearby mannequin. Color shot to my face, and I stammered out, "Oh. Yeah. That'd be great. Thanks."

The clerk reached out for the blouse. "Here, let me take that for you."

"She'll need a skirt too," Jake told her. "Something black." His gaze dipped to my legs, still clad in those yoga pants. "Short, but not too short. Let's leave *something* to the imagination." He grinned over at me. "Right?"

Oh God. I was imagining all sorts of things right now.

Wordlessly, I nodded.

A few minutes later, inside the dressing room, I studied my reflection in the mirror. I was wearing the new clothes that Jake had picked out. I gave them a good, long look. The outfit was infinitely respectable and yet somehow a lot sexier than I would have imagined.

Now, I only needed to show Jake. Before entering the dressing room, he had made me promise to give him a look. Almost embarrassed, I opened the door to the dressing room and poked my head around the corner. Jake was sitting in one of two chairs just outside the shallow dressing room hallway.

He looked up, meeting my gaze. "Do I get to see the whole thing?" he said. "Or just the collar?"

I gave him a flirty smile. "I don't know. Don't you want to leave *'something* to the imagination'?"

"Not *that* much," he said. "Smart-ass."

I moved forward, revealing the whole outfit. Jake gave a slow nod. The sales clerk appeared around the corner and stopped to look. "It looks like you have a winner," she said.

"Well, technically, it's for him," I said. "I'm just modeling it."

Ignoring the taunt, Jake turned to the sales clerk. "Got any scissors?" he asked. "She's gonna wear this out."

"I am?" I looked down at my tennis shoes. It suddenly occurred to me that this might explain why a few stores ago, Jake had insisted on buying me some black heels for no apparent reason.

When the clerk left to retrieve some scissors, I lowered my voice and told Jake, "You're awful devious. You know that, right?"

He reached into one of our shopping bags and pulled out the exact shoes I'd been thinking of. "Don't you know it," he said.

I was just slipping into the new shoes when the clerk

returned with an oversized pair of scissors and started removing tags. When she finished, Jake accompanied her to the register while I ducked into the dressing room to grab the clothes I that *had* been wearing.

When I finished gathering them up, I sidled up to Jake at the register and paused. The clerk was ringing up second outfit exactly the same as the one I was now currently wearing. I gave Jake a perplexed look. "What's that for?" I asked.

Jake shrugged. "You seemed to like it. I figured you'd want a set for you, too."

"Oh," I said, conscious that the sales clerk was listening. "Thanks. That's really thoughtful." Even if it made absolutely no sense.

After Jake signed for the purchase, we headed straight to the car and hit this amazing Italian restaurant on the way back. Looking around the place, with its upscale décor and even more upscale patrons, I could see why my yoga pants weren't exactly appropriate.

We laughed all the way through dinner, about silly things ranging from the idea of him actually wearing that little black skirt to the pros and cons of schoolmarm-themed attire.

So far, I was having the best day of my life. It was funny too, because the day hadn't all been terrific. Parts of it had stunk pretty bad, actually. But the parts that were good? Well, those more than made up for it.

We were halfway through dessert when a stranger appeared at our table. It was an elderly lady in upscale, conservative clothes. I braced myself, wondering if I'd been laughing too loud at what Jake had just been telling me.

He had spent the last few minutes giving me a blow-by-blow, literally, about the first time he'd gotten thrown in jail for fighting. The story shouldn't have been funny. But the way Jake told it, even going so far as to mention that he'd lost a meatball sub in the cop car, I just couldn't stop laughing.

But now, looking at the lady standing beside our table, I clamped my lips shut and tried to look respectable. In college, I had worked at enough restaurants to know there always seemed to be that one obnoxious table, where people laughed way too loud and weren't nearly as funny as they thought they were.

Were *we* that table? God, I sure hoped not.

But when the woman started to speak, I knew that something else was going on entirely. □

CHAPTER 49

The woman leaned over our table. "Excuse me," she said. "I'm sorry to interrupt, but I couldn't help but notice..." She turned to Jake. "You're that Jake person. Aren't you? You know, the guy who does all those fight videos?"

"It depends," he said with a grin that somehow managed to look boyish. "You're not looking for a fight, are you?" He held up both hands. "Because I don't want any trouble."

She practically giggled. "You are *so* bad," she told him. She turned toward me. "Isn't he?"

Reaching for my wine glass, I gave a long, dramatic sigh. "You have no idea."

Turning back to Jake, she lowered her voice. "Well, the thing is," she said, glancing around, "I just wanted to tell you that I'm *glad* you kicked some Chainsaw ass."

Sputtering, I almost choked on my wine. At the choking sound, the woman's gaze swiveled back to me. "Well, I am," she said, "and I'm not sorry for it either." Her eyes narrowed to mere slits. "Did you see what that fucker did last Saturday? Shameful – that's what it was."

She turned back to Jake and said, "Next time, kick his ass harder."

"Yes ma'am," Jake said.

Somewhere behind me, I heard a female voice call out, "Grandma!"

I turned in my seat and spotted an attractive girl about my own age. She was giving the older woman an exasperated look. When the girl saw me looking at her, she winced. "Sorry," she said as she approached our table. "She's real, uh, sociable."

"What Chloe *means* to say," the woman said, "is that I call 'em like I see 'em." She gave Chloe the steely-eye. "Someone's gotta do it. Damn politicians won't. Fuckers are all liars and crooks, if you ask me."

Across from me, Jake was nodding. "Can't argue with that," he said.

For the first time, Chloe's gaze landed on Jake. She froze. "You're Jake," she said.

The girl's grandma poked her in the side. "I know," the older woman said. "I was just telling him that." She lowered her voice. "But I think he already knew."

I glanced at Jake. He was giving the girl an odd look, like he thought he might know her from someplace. I wanted to groan. This was never good. I already knew way too many of Jake's former flings. Then again, she didn't look like a fling. Maybe she was a fan?

Chloe was still giving Jake that perplexed look. "Did you get our invitation?" she asked.

Jake leaned back in his chair. "So you *are* that Chloe," he said. "Yeah, I got it."

"Well, you'd better come," she said. "It wouldn't be the same without you."

The older woman looked from Jake to Chloe. "What the hell are you talking about?" she said.

Chloe reached for the woman's elbow. "I'll tell you at the table." Before hustling the woman away, Chloe turned back and said, "Nice meeting you both."

I watched them go and then turned to Jake. "So you know her?"

Jake shook his head. "Nope."

"But she sent you an invitation?" I said. "To what?"

"Her wedding."

"Oh stop it," I said. "Why would she send you a wedding invitation?" I felt the color drain from my face. "Oh my God," I said. "Is this one of those weird stalkery things, where she thinks she's marrying *you*?"

At this, Jake burst out laughing.

"It's not funny," I said.

"No. It's not," He said. "But trust me. She's not a stalker. I've met her fiancé. That's all."

"Oh. Well, that's nice." I hesitated. "Isn't it?"

"Yeah," he said. "It's nice." And then, as if eager to change the subject, he said, "Hey, you know why everyone's mad at the Chainsaw?"

I shook my head. "No. Why?"

"Get this," Jake said. "Last Saturday, the guy 'accidentally' spikes a football into the stands, hits this ten-year-old kid who's wearing the opposing team's jersey."

"That's terrible," I said. "On purpose?"

"No." Jake's voice grew sarcastic. "Not on purpose. The ball slipped, that's all."

"Was the kid hurt?"

"Nah," Jake said. "It knocked him over though. Chainsaw thought it was hilarious."

"What a turd," I said.

Jake's eyebrows lifted. "Yeah?"

"Oh come on," I said. "He is."

"You see me arguing?" Jake said. "Everyone hates him. Even the fans."

"Is that why you picked a fight with him?" I asked.

"Nah, he picked the fight with me. Remember?"

"You mean the one I saw?"

"Eh, the one before that."

I didn't bother to hide my skepticism. "By any chance," I said, "did you happen to, oh, I don't know, provoke him in any way?"

Jake grinned. "There might've been some provoking."

"I knew it."

"Hey," Jake said. "I'm good at two things – pissing people off and fighting. Why not put it to use, right?"

The logic made sense in a Jake sort of way. But I couldn't quite agree. "You're not good at *only* two things," I told him.

"Is that so?"

I nodded. "In fact, there's a third thing you're particularly good at." Across the table, I crooked my finger for him to come closer. When he did, I added, "but I'm not saying you couldn't use a little more practice. Like soon."

A slow smile spread across Jake's face. "Yeah?"

I nodded. "Definitely." □

CHAPTER 50

Within fifteen minutes, we were out of the restaurant and on the road. Night had fallen, and Jake navigated the nearly empty highway while I kept him company from the passenger's seat.

He was driving a different car than the one he'd used to pick me up from Maddie's. Probably, that car was still in the shop. This one was shiny and black with a grey interior and kick-ass sound system.

With the music on low, I glanced toward the rear of the car, where we'd stashed the shopping bags. "I still can't believe you didn't get yourself anything," I said.

He gave me a sideways glance. "But I did," he said. "Remember?"

I looked down at my new outfit. "Oh come on," I said. "This?"

"Yeah, that." He turned his head to give me a long, appreciative look. When he returned his gaze to the road, the hint of a smile played across his lips.

This time, when we neared Jake's building, he passed the front turnaround and circled around to the side, entering a concrete parking garage under the building. He pulled into a numbered spot and popped the trunk.

A couple moments later, he was pulling shopping bags out

of the trunk.

Standing beside him, I said, "Here, let me carry some."

"Not a chance," he said, grabbing the last bag and holding it out of my reach.

I laughed. "You do realize you're spoiling me something awful?"

"Good," he said. "Now come on." He flicked his head toward a wide metal doorway with an exit sign hanging just above it.

Together, we walked toward it, chatting about nothing in particular. Probably, I was talking *too* much, because honestly, I was almost afraid I'd jump him right in the parking garage.

I gave him a long, sideways look. He was my real-life fantasy, dark and sexy, and slightly dangerous, in spite of his expensive clothes and designer watch. My lips parted, and my breathing grew shallow. Abruptly, I stopped talking.

We were quiet until Jake broke the silence by saying, "I've got a question."

"Yeah? What?"

"Just how much practice do you think I need?"

"Huh?"

"In the restaurant," he said, "you said I needed practice."

I felt myself smile. "I didn't say you *needed* practice. I just said you *could* practice, you know, if you wanted to."

Next to me, Jake made no response as we entered the building and walked toward the elevators.

I cleared my throat. "But you don't have to," I said, "I mean if you're tired or something."

His voice held the hint of teasing. "So *you're* tired?"

"No," I blurted out. "Definitely not."

He gave me a wicked grin. "No?"

With an effort, I tried to sound slightly less desperate. "I mean, well, I'm a night owl, so I'm up for whatever."

"Good," he said. "Want a tour of my office?"

"What?" Unsure what had just happened, I gave a little shake of my head. "You mean your home-office? In your penthouse?"

"No," he said. "My regular office."

"You have an office?" I said. "Why?"

"Why not?" he said. "I've got stuff. And people. They've got to go someplace, right?"

Trying to concentrate on more than the idea of getting him naked, I made myself ask, "What kind of stuff?"

"Computer stuff mostly," he said. "Servers, software, work stations, a small graphics studio, that sort of thing."

I almost had to laugh. "I can't believe I'm actually talking about computers with you."

"You know much about computers?" he asked.

I shook my head. "Nope."

"Me neither," he said. "Thus, the people."

"And now," I said, "I can't believe you just said 'thus'."

"Just seeing if you're paying attention."

Oh, I was paying attention, alright. Just not to anything business-related. But that did remind me of something. "Speaking of computers," I said, "who hacked into my email account? You never did tell me."

"You can thank Trey for that."

"Somehow, I can't see myself thanking him."

Jake gave a low laugh. "Give it time. You want the tour or not?"

We'd just made it to the elevators. What I really wanted was him. Like now.

I wanted us to be naked. I wanted to reach out with my fingers and trace the contours of his muscles and tattoos. And then I wanted a whole lot more. But Jake had been such a great sport about shopping that there was no way I'd be saying no to a tour, if that's what he really wanted to be doing. Plus, I was genuinely interested.

"That sounds great," I said. "I can't wait." I glanced back toward the parking garage. "So where's your office? Are we heading back to the car?"

"Nah." Still holding the bags, Jake leaned forward and pressed the elevator up-button with his elbow. "It's here in the building."

"Really?"

"Yeah. I'll show you."

In front of us, the nearest elevator door slid open, and we stepped forward. Inside, Jake used his elbow again to press the button for the floor just below his penthouse. Once the elevator started moving, we stood side-by-side, facing the elevator doors while I tried not to fling myself at him.

I snuck a quick glance in his direction. He looked relaxed, casual even. I tried to look relaxed and casual too, as opposed to the sex-starved idiot I was on the inside.

In front of us, the numbers on the control panel changed with every floor and then stopped at the floor he'd pressed. When the elevator doors opened, Jake motioned for me to go first.

Breathlessly, I stepped out of the elevator and looked around. The place didn't look like any office I'd ever seen. Mostly, it was all windows and wide open spaces, with marble floors and clusters of nicely arranged furniture positioned here and there.

The lights were still off, but there was more than enough light to get the basic feel of the place. I looked around. The window-blinds were open, and lights from the city streamed in from all sides. "It's beautiful," I said, "but not exactly what I was expecting."

Next to me, Jake set down the bags. "I know the feeling," he said.

I looked over at him. "But you've been here lots of times, right?"

He met my gaze. "I wasn't talking about the office."

A soft breath escaped my lips. "Oh."

He moved closer, and his casual demeanor vanished. "Want to know why I brought you here?" he asked.

My breath caught. "Sure."

His gaze travelled the length of me. "Want me to *tell* you? Or *show* you?"

How did a girl answer such a thing, especially when he was looking at me like that? Cast in shadows, his angular face showed no hint of that boyish streak that I'd seen in the store.

I gazed up at him. "You could do both," I said, "if you wanted."

CHAPTER 51

Through the shadows, he loomed closer, and his lips brushed my ear. "You see what you're wearing?" he said.

I glanced down at my new outfit. When I spoke, my voice was nearly too breathless to be heard. "Yeah."

"This is what I'm gonna do." He reached out and trailed a finger lightly down my neck, toward the center of my cleavage. "You see that nice, respectable shirt you're wearing?"

Mutely, I nodded.

His finger trailed lower, grazing over those pearly buttons of the formal blouse. "I'm going to rip that thing off your hot little body, button by button."

My breath hitched. "You are?"

His voice was low, hypnotic. "I am." He kissed my earlobe. "And then, I'm going to take that lacy bra of yours and rip it aside, so I can get a good, long look at you." His finger was still trailing lower. It was nearing my naval. He continued. "And when my eyes have had their fill, wanna know what I'm gonna do next?"

Wordlessly, I nodded again.

"You see that armchair by the window?"

Listening to his voice, hearing the things he was saying, I was growing hotter and wetter with every word. Somehow, I managed to whisper, "Yeah. I see it."

"I'm gonna carry your sweet ass over there, and I'm gonna bend you over that armrest, and I'm gonna lift up that new skirt of yours and yank down your panties…"

Oh. My.God. He had barely touched me, and I felt in danger of climaxing any second.

His finger trailed lower, skimming over my naval and onto the fabric of the new black skirt. "And then, when I have you just the way I want you, I'm gonna grip those sweet hips of yours and make you mine until you forget your own name."

I could hardly breathe. Or maybe I was breathing too much. I tried to speak. The only sound that came out was a soft moan.

He pulled his lips from my ear. Like a powerful predator, he circled to the front of me. Catching my breath, I looked up. Our gazes locked and held. He was so beautiful. And so primitive. And so thrilling. I wanted to remember this forever. I *knew* I would remember it forever, no matter what happened next.

His gaze dipped to my blouse. I braced myself, wondering if he'd actually live up to that insane promise. But all he did was reach up with both hands to caress the sides of my face. Slowly, he lowered his lips to mine. I sagged against him, lost in the feel of his lips and the motions of his tongue.

Too soon, he pulled away, leaving me utterly lost. With his hands still caressing my face, he moved a fraction backward. Slowly, his hands slipped down my face, over the sides of my neck, and down to my shoulders.

Mesmerized, I drank in the sight of him. His lips were parted, and his eyes were hungry. In his coiled muscles, I saw passion battling with self-control. My heart racing, I felt his warm fingers slide under the neckline of the blouse. I caught my breath.

Suddenly, as if he couldn't wait an instant longer, he gave

the fabric a soft yank. I heard a button pop and fabric give way. His eyes grew hungrier, and my breath hitched. He gave another soft yank, and second button went flying.

My knees were weak, and my heart was racing. He yanked again, and third button succumbed to the force. When I whimpered with need, he gave a vicious yank at the thin fabric. I heard fabric tearing and buttons popping. I heard a low groan. Maybe mine. Maybe his. Maybe both. Cool air brushed over my stomach, and I stifled a shiver that felt achingly hot.

I watched breathlessly as his eyes devoured me like I was his last meal on Earth.

His voice was ragged when he said, "You're so sweet. So perfect." He reached up and yanked aside the lacy fabric of my bra. I felt cool air on my nipples, and heard his low exhalation of breath.

I glanced down, seeing what I had already felt. With the fabric pushed aside, somehow the concentration of lacy support was raising my breasts higher, as if begging for his attention. With a low murmur, he cupped them in his warm hands and worried the nipples between his fingertips.

I should've been embarrassed. I could only imagine how I looked – half naked in a torn blouse and a bra that covered next to nothing. But I wasn't embarrassed. I was hungry. For him.

I wanted to tear at his clothes and get a good, long eyeful of his glorious muscles and tantalizing tattoos. I wanted to run my hands over his skin. I wanted to touch him everywhere and make him want me like I wanted him.

I reached up with both hands and gripped the neckline of his dress shirt. Following his lead, I yanked the fabric aside, and half of the buttons went flying, giving me a nearly perfect view of his chiseled chest, along with a sneak peek at his amazing abs. I yanked again, and his torso was utterly exposed. I reached out and trailed a hand over his pecs and downward until I skimmed his flat stomach.

I inched my hand lower, over the waistband of his pants, and lower still, until I felt the outline of his massive erection. Through the fabric of his pants, I gripped his length and ran a palm over its contours. I felt a thrill of triumph when he gave a low moan that sounded an awful lot like my name.

His hands were moving now too. One of them skimmed my stomach and reached up to lift my skirt. He skimmed the inside of my thighs and stopped when he reached the front of my ever-dampening panties.

Through the smooth fabric, I felt the tantalizing touch of his finger as it brushed against that special spot, rubbing and coaxing until my knees felt like jelly, and I was slick with wanting him. I was grinding against him now, desperately ready and wanting more.

Unable to wait an instant longer, I moved to unbutton his pants. He stepped away, leaving me cold and hungry. I gave another whimper.

And then, almost before I knew what was happening, he plowed forward to throw me over his shoulder. A half-moan, half-giggle escaped my lips as he took long, powerful strides toward the armchair.

As he moved, I felt his hand reach under the skirt, and then under my panties. His warm palm cupped my bare ass, petting and caressing as he moved us forward. It was almost too much – the thoughts of him, the feel of him against me, the sensation of my hair dangling over his back as we moved – I needed him now, before I went absolutely insane.

When we reached the armchair, he lifted me over his shoulder and half-tossed, half-laid me, face-down, over the chair's wide, cushiony arm. I turned my head to look back at him and tried to take a mental picture, something I could pull out later when this night was long gone. Silhouetted against the city windows, he looked a lot more like a conquering warrior than a guy from my old neighborhood.

My feet, still in those heels, slid against the marble floor, as if looking to lend at least a little stability to my vulnerable position.

"Give it up," he said, "you're not going anywhere."

Like I'd want to.

He prowled closer, and I felt his hands at my hips, skimming the bunched-up fabric of that short black skirt. With one forceful motion, he shoved the skirt up completely above my waist and then yanked down my panties, leaving the thin fabric straining, taut against my thighs.

With one hand, I reached behind, looking to push the panties downward and kick them off.

Gently, he stopped my hand. "Don't move," he said. "I want to see you just like this."

Lost in the moment, I swear, I couldn't have argued with anything he wanted, so I didn't even try. When I heard the sounds of a zipper, and felt his erection tease against my opening, I let out a moan of need.

Using my heels as leverage, I moved my hips upward, hoping he'd give me what I so desperately wanted. Instead, I felt his fingers drifting up the inside of my thigh until they reached their intersection. I felt a fingertip move higher and give that hardened little knob a long circular stroke that soon had me squirming against him and panting for more. And more.

It was utterly maddening. I wanted him inside me, and I wanted his touch. Desperate for both, I moved my hips backward. When he pulled back, leaving me no more satisfied than I'd been just a moment earlier, I whimpered with longing.

How could he wait, when he knew I was dying for him?

Desperate for anything he was willing to give, I wriggled my hips forward and ground against his fingertips. Finally, when I thought I couldn't wait another instant, I felt his erection tease my opening once again. But this time, instead of pulling back, he surged forward, entering me with one powerful motion, claiming me, filling me, making me moan out his name.

That was nearly all it took. I peaked hard and fast, shuddering with pleasure as his fingers and pelvis drove me over the top and then some.

As if free from constraint, Jake moved to grip my hips with both hands. He drove into me, harder and faster, until he too reached that moment of sweet oblivion. I heard my own name mingled with the sounds of his pleasure, along with the sounds of my own.

When we fell together, loose-limbed onto the armchair in a hot, quivering heap, I half-wondered if I'd wake up next day and learn this was all a dream.

I sure as hell hoped not, because if this *was* real, I definitely wanted to do this again. □

CHAPTER 52

A couple hours later, we were sprawled in his penthouse, watching the city lights through the open window-blinds. We had showered together and thrown on some lounging clothes. For him, it was running pants with no shirt. For me, it was new lace panties and another oversized T-shirt from Jake's closet.

Snuggled against him on the sofa, I looked down at our clothes. "Hey look," I said, pointing downward. "Together, we make up a full outfit."

Jake gave me a sleepy smile. "Yeah?"

"Yeah," I said. "You have the pants. I have the shirt. See?"

"Maybe I should have both," Jake said.

I laughed. "Now you're just being selfish."

"Selfish?" he said, running a hand over my hips. "Or smart?"

I burrowed against him and heard myself sigh.

"What?" he said.

I groaned. "Tomorrow's Monday."

"So?"

"Well for *me*," I said, "that means I've gotta start looking for a new job." Actually, I needed to find two jobs, but that was beside the point. I pulled back to look at him. "Hey, can I ask you something?"

"What?"

"I don't want to fight or anything," I said, "but why did you quit my jobs? I mean, they weren't my dream jobs, but still..."

"Screw those jobs," he said. "Come work for me."

I practically laughed. "Doing what?"

"For one thing," he said, "it looks like I need a new event planner."

"Are you talking about Bianca's job?"

"Sure, why not?"

"For starters, she wasn't even your employee, not technically, anyway."

"She was close enough," Jake said. "And your degree's in the same thing, right? Come on. I could use the help."

Liar. I was the one who needed help, and he damn well knew it. Still, the offer was way too tempting. In one fell swoop, I'd regain almost everything I'd lost over the last few weeks.

As if sensing weakness, Jake added, "And one thing about Bianca, she wasn't cheap."

I stiffened. Had Jake and Bianca lain across this very same sofa? Had he offered *her* the exact same deal? Had *she* been bought and paid for, only to be discarded the moment someone new came along?

The old Luna would have jumped at this chance. The new, mostly reformed Luna, was a little more cautious, and with good reason. If I agreed, Jake would practically own me. Even now, I had nearly nothing to my name except the things he had purchased.

I bit my lip. "That's a really nice offer."

"So take it."

"I can't," I said. "I need to find my own job, and besides, you never answered my question. Why would you burn my bridges like that?"

"Maybe I wanted to keep an eye on you."

"But why?" I said. "Because of my stupid ex-boyfriend?"

"Hell no," he said, "Rango's a pussy."

I almost laughed. Rango was no pussy. I didn't bother to hide my amusement. "Is that so?"

He cradled me closer. "Maybe I just want you nice and close. Is that so bad?"

"Jake, I'm not stupid," I said. "You showed up at Maddie's place out of the blue and practically dragged me out of there. I think I deserve to know why."

He said nothing.

"Be honest," I said, "Is this all because Rango sent you those crazy texts?"

"Which ones?

"You know which ones. The ones where he said he was looking for me."

Jake still said nothing.

"Come on. Tell me," I said. "I'm not going to stop asking."

After a long silence, Jake said, "Alright, here's the thing. Those messages weren't from Rango."

I felt my brow wrinkle. "They weren't?"

"No."

"Wait a minute," I said, "You *knew* that's what I thought. Didn't you?"

He said nothing.

"Seriously," I said, "why didn't you correct me?"

"Maybe I didn't want to scare you."

"Scare me? Why would I be scared?" My voice rose. "So who, exactly, was texting you about me?"

He stroked my hair. "Baby, let it go. Everything's fine."

"No, it's not," I said. "Tell me. Who was it?"

Jake blew out a long breath. "It was a friend of mine, some guy who works for Rango's boss."

"Rango has a boss?" I said. "Who?"

"You don't wanna know."

"Yes, I do."

"No," he said. "You don't. But I'll tell you this. That little black book you 'borrowed'? It's not Rango's, and it's not just some random notebook the guy had lying around."

"Yeah, you mentioned that," I said, "but I still don't know what you meant."

"I meant," Jake said, "that the book belongs to Rango's boss. Who is *not* a pussy, by the way. And he's not happy it's missing."

"What?" I stammered. "Why?"

"The way it sounds," Jake said, "it's got account numbers, passwords, financial notes, things the guy doesn't exactly want passed around. You looked at the thing, right?"

"Not really," I said. "Mostly, I just copied down a couple of Rango's passwords and left the book hidden away."

"Is that why you took it?" Jake said. "For Rango's passwords?"

"It's one of the reasons." I cleared my throat. "But, uh, mostly it was because he took my car."

"You have a car?" Jake said. "The way I heard it, you were taking the bus."

"I was. But I *had* a car. You see, something happened where I needed some money fast—"

"What?" Jake said. "Why?"

"That's not important," I said. "The point is, Rango gave me this title-loan. And after we broke up, he wouldn't give me the title back." I winced. "Or the car."

"You serious?" Jake said. "What kind of asshole-boyfriend makes his girl sign over the damn car title?"

"It wasn't like that," I said. "When this first started, he wasn't my boyfriend."

"Is that right?"

"Yeah," I said. "But he was part-owner of this title-loan

place near my old apartment. It was fine. More or less. But after the breakup, the whole loan thing went to crap. The car was gone, and the title wasn't mine anymore."

"I'm surprised you didn't sue him," Jake said.

"Why?" I said. "The lawyer would cost more than the car. And the car wasn't exactly new. The whole thing was a total mess."

"So you took that notebook?"

"Hell yeah, I took it," I said. "Rango was practically in love with the thing. He looked at it all the time. That's why I wouldn't give it back, even after all those weird things started happening." My voice grew misty. "I loved that car. It was the first one I ever owned. And Rango wouldn't give *that* back, so..." I swallowed. "Anyway, that's the story."

"Tomorrow," Jake said, "we'll get you a *new* car."

I had to smile. "No," I said. "We won't. I'm done with that sort of thing."

"I wasn't talking about some title-loan," Jake said.

"Jake, seriously," I said, "you can't get me a car. You've done too much already."

"No such thing," he said.

"Thanks," I said, "but the answers still no." Maybe I didn't have a lot of things, but I still had my self-respect. And there were limits on what kind of help I'd be willing to accept, even from him.

Still, it was a sweet offer. I smiled against his chest. All things considered, it had been a good day. An amazing day, actually.

Looking back, I'm glad I enjoyed it, because less than twenty-four hours later, everything started going to crap. □

CHAPTER 53

The next morning, I woke in Jake's bed to find him gone. I vaguely recalled him mentioning some early morning errand. But honestly, most of the previous night was such a wonderful blur, that the details were a little foggy.

I stumbled out of bed, took a quick shower, and threw on some of the new casual clothes from our shopping trip. I had no car and no computer, but I did have a smartphone. So I sacked out on Jake's sofa and started scrolling through some of the more popular help-wanted sites in search of a new job.

I'd been searching less than a half-hour when I heard a knock at the door. When I pushed off the sofa and looked out the peephole, I saw one of the last people I would have expected – Vince Hammond.

Puzzled, I squinted through the peephole for a better look. This time, he was alone, at least as far as I could tell. He was dressed in a business suit and holding a white sheet of paper loose at his side

When he knocked again, I reluctantly opened the door and stuck my head out. "Sorry," I told him, "but Jake's not here."

"You think I want to see *him*?"

I glanced around. "Well, this *is* his place."

"Maybe. But I'm here to see *you*."

Instantly, snippets of that awful argument with Jake came flooding back. Against all logic, Jake had claimed that Vince wanted me. At the time, I'd been sure Jake was nuts. Now, given Vince's statement, I wasn't so sure.

"Me?" I said. "Why?"

Vince grinned. "I've got a proposition for you."

"Look," I said, "whatever it is, the answer's no."

He lifted an eyebrow. "Shouldn't you, oh I dunno, listen to it before you shoot me down?"

"Nope."

At this, he actually laughed. "Why not?"

"Because Jake wouldn't like it." The answer was stupid, and I felt a little silly using it. I mean, I was an adult, capable of making my own choices. But honestly, I didn't know what else to say.

"Aw come on," Vince said. "Humor me, alright?"

"Why should I?"

"Because I'm here to offer you a job."

"A job?" I said. "What kind of job?"

"Something in our P.R. department."

"Look," I said, "I'm not naïve."

"Meaning?"

"Meaning, if this so-called P.R. position is real—"

"Which it is."

"*If* it's real," I continued, "you could go on the internet right now and find a hundred resumes within minutes. Why me?"

"For one thing," he said, lifting his sheet of paper. "I already did that. I found me a great candidate right here."

I looked down at the paper. The text on it looked oddly familiar. "Is that my resume?" I asked.

"I don't know," he said. "Is your name Luna Moon?"

"Unfortunately."

"I looked over your qualifications," he said. "You've got the degree. You've got just enough experience. You're perfect." He grinned. "And, you came highly recommended."

I didn't bother to hide my skepticism. "By who?"

"Bianca."

"Very funny."

"It's not a joke," he said.

"That's what *you* think," I said. "Either way, the answer's still no."

"Just hear me out," he said. "We do billions in revenue a year. We're a good company. We represent some of the biggest names in sports entertainment. We've got a great team. You'd like it there."

My gaze narrowed. "Where exactly is 'there'?"

He gave a small shrug. "Here in the states, we've got offices in New York, L.A., satellite offices all around the country, including here. It's just a few blocks away, in fact. You wouldn't even have to move."

I tried to laugh. "Well, I'd have to move out of here, that's for sure." I glanced around. "Speaking of which, Jake will be back any minute, so…"

"No he won't," Vince said. "He's got a meeting 'til noon."

"And you know this *how*?" I asked.

"I've got my sources."

"Bianca again?"

"Sorry," he said, "I don't kiss and tell."

"Right," I said. "Well anyway, this has been interesting and all, but I've got to go." I started to close the door.

Vince held up a hand. "Wait."

I crossed my arms and waited.

"I know what you're thinking," he said.

I gave him a dubious look. "Do you?"

"Sure," he said. "You're thinking this is a setup. That the offer's a scam. That if Bianca starts bad-mouthing you, you'll be gone with no notice." He met my gaze. "But that's not the way I roll."

It was almost funny, because he *had* known exactly what I'd been thinking. Then again, all things considered, it wouldn't be too hard to figure out. "Want to know what *I* think?" I said.

"Sure, hit me."

"I think that you want to get back at Jake for how much money he's cost you. I think you've already hired away Bianca, and now you want to put a little more salt in the wound by recruiting the girl you *think* is Jake's girlfriend. I think you want to hit Jake where it hurts, and you want to use me to do it."

At this, Vince laughed. The sound was oddly pleasant and missing the malice I'd been expecting. "Hell yeah," he said. "That's what I want."

My mouth fell open. "Huh?"

"You think I'm gonna deny it?"

"Well, actually, yeah."

"Why would I?" he said. "You're right. I *am* trying to hit Jake where it hurts. The guy's cost me a lot of money. And if I don't start hitting him back, he'll cost me – and my clients – a whole lot more."

"So I was right?" I said. "The job *was* a fake."

"Nope," he said. "It's a real offer and a real job. And if you're worried about job-security, we can sign a contract." He gave me a speculative look. "Or I'll give you a nice signing bonus, make it worth your while."

If it weren't for loyalty, I might have almost been tempted. But I was loyal. To Jake. Not to Vince. "Thanks," I said, "but the answer's still no."

"Just think about it." He reached into his pocket and pulled out a printed business card. He handed the card over. "Here. In case you change your mind."

Reluctantly, I took the card. "I won't," I said. "But thanks. I guess."

Somewhere behind Vince, I heard the ding of an elevator. A moment later, the elevator doors slid open, and I spotted someone else I hadn't expected to see this morning – Trey. And if I wasn't mistaken, those things with him were my two missing suitcases. □

CHAPTER 54

Following my gaze, Vince turned toward around to look. Together, we watched Trey walk toward us, lugging the two slightly mangled suitcases with him. When Trey reached Jake's door, he turned to Vince and said, "Man, you must really want your ass kicked."

Vince looked only mildly amused. "By you?"

"Hell no," Trey said. "By Jake."

"I'll take my chances," Vince said.

"Whatever," Trey said. "It's your funeral." He looked toward me. "Hey, I brought up your suitcases."

I glanced down to study them. "Yeah, thanks. I can see that. But I thought they were missing. Did they just turn up?"

Trey gave me a puzzled look. "Well, they turned up in the storage closet downstairs, if that's what you mean."

"Here?" I said. "In this building?"

"Yeah," Trey said. "I figured Jake forgot to bring them up, so here they are."

I stared at them. So they weren't lost? Or stolen? Had Jake hidden them away on purpose? I shook off the distraction and turned back to Vince. "Anyway," I told him, "thanks for stopping by, but I think it's time for you to leave."

Next to me, Trey spoke up. "Yeah. Run, while you still can."

"Oh stop it," I told Trey. Turning back to Vince, I said, "But you really do need to go."

"Alright," Vince said, "I can take a hint." He turned away and began walking toward the same elevator that had just delivered Trey. When he had almost reached it, he called over his shoulder, "When you change your mind, call me."

"Thanks, but I won't," I said.

Trey, still lugging those suitcases, elbowed his way past me into the penthouse. "Jake's gonna be so pissed," he said.

"Why?" I asked.

"Because he hates that guy. You shouldn't have let him in."

"I didn't let him in," I said. "In fact, I hardly opened the door."

"Next time," Trey said, "hit him with some mace. Keep him from coming back."

I rolled my eyes. "I'll think about it." Eager to change the subject, I asked, "So, were you just in the neighborhood?"

"Nah, I was working downstairs. At Jake's office."

At the memory of what Jake and I had done in that office, I felt my face grow warm. "Oh. That's nice," I said.

"Yeah, I'd better head back," Trey said. "But if Vince stops by again? You know what you should do?"

I gave him a look. "Aside from the mace?"

"Yeah. Aside from that. You should tell him to piss off."

I laughed. "Why would I do that?"

"Because," Trey said, "that's what Jake would do."

"Except I'm not Jake," I reminded him.

"Yeah," Trey said, "but he'd still like that."

"Uh, thanks for letting me know."

"No problem."

After Trey left, I sank down on the floor and opened the beat-up suitcases. All my stuff was in there, just like I remembered, including the piles of panties, still covered in floor-crud. Shuddering, I shut both cases and tried not to think about it.

Whenever Jake returned, this was definitely worth a discussion. I just didn't know what kind of discussion we'd be having. I had a pretty strong hunch that the suitcases were never lost in the first place. What I didn't know was whether Jake's deception was a good thing or a bad thing.

It was sweet and scary all at the same time. I had to smile. Kind of like Jake.

I left the cases out in the open and returned to my phone, intending to resume my job search. I was surprised to see I had a missed call, along with a new voicemail, both from the same unfamiliar number. Checking my phone, I realized that I'd forgotten to turn on my ringer this morning.

I'd need to do better, especially now that I was looking for a job. Thinking of Vince's offer, I felt myself smile at the total absurdity. Half-distracted, I scrolled to the new voicemail and hit play. As soon as I began to listen, my smile faded.

The message was from Maddie, and she sounded half-crazed. "Listen up, Anna, or Luna, or whatever the hell your name is," she said. "I don't know what shit you're into, but I sure as hell don't appreciate you dragging me into it."

Listening, my eyebrows furrowed. What on Earth was she talking about?

As the message continued, the less I understood. "You know what happened here last night?" she said. "Someone broke in. They trashed the place. They ripped up Monica's – or should I say *your* – room." Her voice broke. "Everything's destroyed, even the furniture, and *I'm* sure as hell not paying for it."

What?

"And one other thing," she said, "the next time you want a man, go out and get your own. Whore."

When the message ended, I yanked the phone away from my ear and stared down at the screen. My hands were trembling. The message felt like pure poison. I wanted it gone – gone from my phone and gone from my memories.

Maddie had been a crappy roommate. And if Jake was right, she was a lot worse than that. Still, there were things in that message, ugly things, that I couldn't quite deny. The last thing, in particular, made me feel just a little bit sick.

With a shaky finger, I reached out to erase the thing. And then I hesitated. There were parts of that message I didn't fully understand. But I had a sickening feeling that a certain someone just might.

Had Jake known that would happen? And if he did, why hadn't he warned Maddie? Obviously, he liked her well enough to have sex with her. But he didn't like her enough to warn her of potential danger? The thought was so cold, it gave me a shiver.

And on an infinitely more personal note, one question kept returning over and over. Why was I here, really?

Was all of this one big favor? Was it Jake's way of keeping me safe and distracted all at the same time?

I tried to convince myself I was being stupid. I told myself that Jake really did want me here. And as far as Maddie's message, it meant nothing. She was unhinged, that's all.

But no matter how hard I tried, my worst fears came crashing back again and again.

Sometime soon, it would be me in Bianca's – or worse – Maddie's shoes. I'd be kicked to the curb and treated with cold contempt. Except, unlike them, I'd also be homeless and unemployed. The clothes on my back weren't even mine.

I glanced at my dented suitcases filled with cast-off clothing. Suddenly, I felt cheap and ridiculous. What was I doing here? Playing house? Living out an adolescent fantasy? Pretending I was something I wasn't?

I was still trying to sort it out when I heard a key card in the door. I looked up just in time to see the door fly open. And there he stood, Jake, looking royally pissed off. □

CHAPTER 55

Jake slammed the door behind him. He looked around. "Where is he?"

Startled, I shot to my feet. "Who?"

"Vince."

"He's gone," I said.

"So he *was* here?"

"Yeah." I made a sound of annoyance. "Who told you? Trey? God, what a tattle-tale."

Jake's voice was flat. "A tattle-tale?"

"Yeah. Totally," I said. "Because I would've told you myself. And, just so you know, I didn't let Vince inside, if that's what you're worried about."

"You think *that's* the problem?"

"Well, obviously, there's some sort of problem."

His jaw clenched. "You could say that."

"Oh for crying out loud," I said. "Whatever you're thinking, that's not it." After all, it wasn't like Vince had propositioned me. Well, not sexually anyway. "Get this," I said. "He offered me a job."

Jake gave a hard laugh. "A job. Now *that's* funny."

Funny how? Did Jake think I wasn't qualified or something? Okay, I *knew* Vince's job offer had nothing to do with me. But did Jake really have to be so scornful about it?

My gaze narrowed. "Why is that so funny?"

"Because," Jake said, "a couple minutes ago, someone called my cell."

"Yeah? So? What'd they say?"

"They claimed," Jake said, "that they just saw you."

"Where?" I looked around the penthouse. "Here?"

"No. In the elevator." His jaw tightened. "Giving Vince a *blowjob*."

My jaw dropped. "What?"

In front of me, Jake said nothing.

"Who said that?" I demanded. "It wasn't Trey, was it? Because that's not funny."

"No," he said. "It wasn't Trey. And you're right. It sure as hell wasn't funny."

Suddenly, a horrible thought occurred to me. "Wait a minute. You didn't think it was true. Did you?"

Jake glanced toward the front door. Just outside that door were the doors to the elevator. What exactly was going through his head?'

"Jake," I snapped. "I'm waiting for an answer."

As if shaking off an ugly image, he turned toward me. He shook his head. "No."

"No, what?"

"No." His voice was quieter now. "I didn't think it was true."

I gave him a good, long look. "Are you sure about that?"

His expression softened. He strode toward me and wrapped me in his arms. "Baby, I'm sure."

In spite of the turmoil, or maybe because of it, I leaned into him, suddenly exhausted. "Then why were you so mad?"

He spoke into my hair. "Because I wanted to kill him."

I pulled back to look up at him. "Vince?"

"No." A dose of sanity seemed to return, and I saw the

barest hint of a smile. "Okay. Maybe him too. But mostly that dick who called me." The smile disappeared, and his voice became raw. "And that wasn't the only thing he said."

Oh God, there was more? My stomach churned as I asked, "What else did he say?"

"Things I'm not gonna repeat, that's what."

That was probably a good thing, because honestly, I wasn't sure I wanted to know. "And you have no idea who it was?"

"No."

I gave a weak laugh. "It was probably Bianca, disguising her voice or something."

"No. It wasn't her."

"How can you be sure?" I asked.

"Because when I got that call, I was with Bianca."

I stepped back from his embrace. "What?"

"Just finishing up some business, that's all."

For some reason, this set my teeth on edge. "After that scene yesterday?"

"It's done," he said. "So don't worry about it."

"You know what?" I said. "You say that way too much."

"What? Not to worry?"

"Yeah," I said. "Because maybe, there are some things that I *should* worry about. And maybe when you hide stuff from me, it just makes me worry more."

"Hide stuff?" he said. "Like what?"

Where to begin? The thing with Debbie? Jake's shady connection to Rango's boss? That weird phone message from my old roommate?" But all of those things were way too complicated to say in a sentence or two. So I pointed to something simple – the suitcases. "Well, like those for example."

Jake looked toward the cases. He said nothing.

"They were never lost," I said. "Were they?"

He returned his gaze to mine. "You want the truth?"

"Obviously," I said, "since I'm asking."

"Alright. Here it is." He glanced at the pair of suitcase. "Back at Maddie's place, when you were packing that stuff, I saw the look on your face."

"What look?" I asked.

"You hated that stuff. Every damn thing you threw in there."

"Not *all* of it," I said.

"And it made you feel bad. And then I felt bad. So I decided to fix it."

At his crazy logic, something in my heart melted. "That's really sweet," I said. "But you didn't need to hide them."

"You sure about that?"

"Yeah. Positive."

"Uh-huh," he said. "Suppose I wanted to buy you things for no good reason. Suppose I wanted to dress you up and watch you smile. Suppose I wanted to wipe that worry from your face—"

"I look worried?" For some reason, I hated hearing that. Never in my life had I been a worrier, and I didn't want to become one now. Still, the last few weeks had definitely taken their toll.

In front of me, Jake didn't answer. He was right, of course. I was worried right now, especially after Maddie's phone message.

Jake's eyebrows furrowed. "What is it?" he asked.

With a sigh, I pulled my phone from my pocket. "There's something you need to hear."

Silently, he waited while I scrolled through the screens to reach my voicemail. When I found Maddie's message, I set the phone on speaker-mode and hit play.

As that message played, I studied Jake's face, hoping to see some reaction. There was none, until it reached the part about someone trashing my old bedroom. His jaw tightened, along with the muscles in his neck and forearms. But his face remained oddly expressionless.

It wasn't until the very end, when Maddie called me a whore, that I saw his composure break. "You just got this?" he asked.

I nodded.

"Come here," he said, reaching out for me. When I didn't move, he stepped forward and gathered me into his arms. I didn't resist. I couldn't. I didn't want to.

He squeezed me tight. "You know it's not true, don't you?"

I leaned against him. "Which part?"

"The last part. And I'm not gonna say it. Because it's not what you are."

"I know," I sighed. "But still…"

"What?"

"She does have a point."

"No. She doesn't."

I pulled away to look at him. "But what about the other stuff? About someone trashing my bedroom? Does that surprise you?"

He shrugged.

I stared at him. "Don't tell me you *knew* that was going to happen."

"'Know' is a pretty strong word."

"So you, what, *suspected*, that was going to happen?"

When he didn't answer, I took another step backward. I stared up at him. "What about Maddie?" I asked.

"She's full of it," he said. "Just like I told you."

"I mean," I said, "why didn't you warn her?"

"Because no one's looking for Maddie."

As we spoke, something else was dawning on me. It was something I didn't want to think about. But I couldn't seem to stop myself. Amidst all the other questions, there was something I absolutely needed to know.

"Jake?" I said.

"What?"

"Why exactly am I here?" ☐

CHAPTER 56

In Jake's penthouse, the question lingered. I turned away and sank onto his sofa. Jake remained standing. He said nothing.

"Seriously," I said. "Why am I here? Is it only for me? For my safety, I mean?"

"Does it matter?" he said.

"Of course it matters."

"Why?"

"Do I really need to spell it out for you?"

"Go ahead." He made a forwarding motion with his hand. "Humor me."

"Okay," I began, "let's say that everything in my life was fine. Let's say no one was 'looking' for me, or for anything like that. What then?" I glanced around. "Would I even be here?"

When my gaze returned Jake, I knew the answer. And from the look on his face, so did he. The silence stretched out beyond the point of discomfort, but I refused to break it.

Finally, he spoke. "You want the truth?"

Did I? I wasn't so sure. Bracing myself, I nodded anyway.

"No," he said. "You wouldn't be here."

My heart sank. I knew it. I had known it all along. So why had I let myself get caught up in some stupid fantasy? This wasn't real. I had known it wasn't real. I looked around the penthouse. My gaze landed on my two crappy suitcases. I felt so adrift, so lost, and more than a little foolish.

And then Jake spoke again. "But," he said, "that only means one thing."

"What?" I asked.

"I wouldn't know what I was missing."

Bleary-eyed, I looked up at him. "Huh?"

He looked around, letting his gaze drift from one luxury to another. "It's different with you here," he said. "The place is different. I'm different. Everything's different."

Something in his voice made my heart give a little flutter. "You said that when I first got here," I said. "But you never said what you meant."

He remained standing, and part of me wondered if he'd turn around and walk out the door. But he didn't. Instead, he took another long look around and asked, "You know how long I've been living here?"

"How long?" I asked.

"Maybe a year, year-and-a-half. But you know what?"

"What?"

"It's never felt like home."

"Never?" I said.

His gaze met mine. "Not until you showed up."

The words felt like a dream. Yet somehow, I managed to say, "Technically, I didn't show up." I smiled through my confusion. "You practically dragged me here. Remember?"

"Best thing I ever did."

I caught my breath. "Really?"

"Really," he said. "But when all this is over, there's something *you've* got to do."

"What?" I asked.

His voice was almost a whisper. "Leave."

I did a double-take. "What?"

His muscles tightened, and when he spoke again, it was like the words were wrenched from his gut. "I said..." He visibly swallowed. "You've got to leave."

Dumbstruck, I stared up at him. "What exactly are you saying?"

He pulled his gaze from mine and looked out toward the panoramic skyline. "It's all messed up," he said. "My life. Me." He blew out a ragged breath. "And you see how things end up with the girls I—" He stopped short, as if unwilling to continue.

Sudden anger made me blunt. "With the girls you 'screw'?" I stood. "Is that what you were gonna say?"

"No." he said. "Not with you."

I crossed my arms. "Really? But isn't that all just semantics?"

"No. Because you're not like them." His voice hardened. "And I don't want you to be."

Somehow, it felt almost like an insult. "What do you mean?" I asked.

"I mean," he said, "I don't want to lose you. I don't want you to hate me." His voice grew quieter. "And more than anything, I don't want to hurt you."

Well, that was rich. "Then why are you saying all this?"

"Because it needs to be said."

I stared at him. "First you offer me a job, then you give me this pretty little speech, and then you tell me to leave? That is *so* messed up."

"I know," he said. "But it wasn't a speech. It was the truth. And about the job? It's still yours if you want it."

The arrangement sounded all-too familiar. I made an ugly sound. "Oh, so *I* can be the new Bianca? The psycho ex, still on the payroll?"

"She's not my ex," he said. "We had a couple nights of fun. No big deal."

Somehow, that didn't make me feel any better. A couple

nights of fun. That sounded familiar too. "You're insane," I said. "You know that, don't you?"

"Hell yes, I know that. You think I *want* you to leave?"

"Yeah. Actually I do." My voice rose. "Because you just told me to." I took a long, steadying breath. "You know what? Forget it. I'm sorry."

"Why are *you* sorry?" he asked.

"Because," I said, "it's not like I expected to stay. I don't even know why I'm arguing about it."

I glanced at the nearby suitcases. Well, at least I was already packed. That was good, right?

Jake said something too quiet for me to make out.

I turned toward him. "What?"

His eyes were haunted. "I never meant to sleep with you."

God, how humiliating. "Oh. That's nice."

"No. It's not. None of this is nice."

"I was being sarcastic," I said.

"And *I'm* not," he said. "Look, I know you don't believe this, but you're important to me. And I don't want to screw this up. Luna, you're too good for all this. You know it. I know it."

"Oh," I said, my tone growing snotty, "so it's not me, it's you? Is that what you're saying?"

"Luna," he said, "listen."

"No," I said. "What is this? A pre-emptive strike? Like you're breaking up with me in advance?"

"Luna," he repeated.

"What?"

"I love you." □

CHAPTER 57

His words, said so quietly, echoed off the high walls. I stared at him. "What?"

"You heard me."

I shook my head, trying to clear the cobwebs. "You can't mean it."

"Why not?"

"Aside from you telling me to leave?"

He didn't answer.

"Okay." I pushed a hand through my hair. "How about the fact I've been here like two days?"

"You're forgetting," he said, "I've *known* you for years."

And for too many of those years, I had longed for him. I'd adored him. And yes, maybe I had even loved him in my own childish way. But all this time, he had never shown the slightest bit of interest.

"But you never even noticed me," I said. "Even when I wasn't a kid anymore."

His was voice just above a whisper. "I noticed."

"So what was the problem?" I asked. "Was it because I was underage?" I summoned up a hollow laugh. "You know, jailbait?"

"Jail never scared me."

"So what was it?" I said.

"For one thing," he said, "I was twenty-some years old. You were in high school." He glanced away. "I've always been an asshole, but even I have my limits."

"But I'd have been eighteen in a few months," I pointed out.

"Yeah? And on your eighteenth birthday, wanna guess where I was?"

"Where?"

"In jail."

"For what?" I asked.

"The usual stuff, some fight at the house. The point is, it wasn't just the numbers. Not then. And not now. The other night, you asked me a question. Remember what it was?"

I had asked too many questions to count, not that I'd gotten any answers. "You'll need to narrow it down more than that," I told him.

A single word fell from his lips. "Debbie."

Oh yeah. Her. The girl Bishop had mentioned. "Forget it," I said, suddenly fearful of what he might say. "I don't need to know."

"That's where you're wrong," he said. "Debbie? She was my dad's—" He gave a hard laugh. "—I guess you'd call her his girlfriend."

My stomach clenched. "So it's true. You—"

"No. Not quite."

Not quite? What did *that* mean? "But somehow, she ended up naked in your bed?"

"Not 'somehow,'" Jake said. "I invited her."

My heart sank. "So you really liked her?"

"Hell no," he said. "I hated her guts. She was a drunk, a cheater. She used to hassle the piss out of my brothers."

"But if that's true," I said, "why would you proposition her?"

"Because I wanted her gone."

I stared at him. "I don't understand."

"She was bad news," Jake said. "And we had plenty of *that* on our own. And Debbie? She used to goad the shit out of my dad. She'd get him all worked up." Jake glanced away. "All liquored up too. And this one night, they start hassling the piss out of Joel."

"The youngest, right?"

"Yeah." He was a tough kid, but there was something about it that just wasn't right."

"With Debbie?" I asked.

"Shit, with everything," Jake said. "So I'm thinking, 'What's the best way to get rid of this skank?' And I think, 'I know. I'll sleep with her. Make sure my dad catches us too.'"

"Wow," I breathed, "that is so messed up."

He made a scoffing sound. "You think?"

"So what happened?" I asked.

"So, I talk Debbie into paying me a visit. Not that it took a whole lot of convincing."

That, I could definitely believe.

"So anyway," Jake said, "Long story short, my dad walks in, and Debbie's laying there on the bed. She's drunk off her ass and naked as hell. And my dad's going nuts. And Debbie starts blubbering that nothing happened. She says she just fell into the wrong bed, all kinds of bullshit. And my dad, he doesn't believe her, especially when I say, 'Yeah. I fucked her. And it was like screwing sandpaper."

As awful as it was, I stifled a laugh. "You didn't."

"I did."

"So what happened then?" I asked.

"So my dad? He does the usual thing, tries to kick my ass. And Debbie? She's clawing the hell out of my back. A couple of my brothers jump into the mix. Remember Joel? He ends up with twenty stitches and a broken arm."

"Oh jeez," I said. "I always wondered how that happened."

"Now you know," Jake said. "I did him *some* favor, huh?"

"Hey, your intentions were good." I pushed myself off the sofa and reached for his hand. "Jake, you are *not* the villain of this story."

"In *this* story?" he said. "There's nothing *but* villains."

"Oh come on, you're no villain," I said. "You did it for love. For your family, I mean. And honestly, it wasn't that bad. I mean, you didn't actually sleep with her, right?"

"Hell no," Jake said. "She was trash. Probably had a dozen social diseases."

"But they all think you did? Still?"

"Sure," Jake said. "I never denied it. Probably never will."

"Why not?" I asked.

Jake gave a humorless smile. "My dad? Like I said, he liked to beat on us. I was the oldest, so no problem for me. I could take it just fine. But after I 'screwed' his girlfriend?" At this, Jake actually grinned. "It kept him good and pissed at me for a year. Left him no time for my brothers."

"Oh my God," I breathed. "That's so awful."

"Yeah, a regular freakshow, huh?"

"No. Not you," I said. "The situation."

"Right."

He met my gaze, and his voice grew ragged. "So when I tell you I love you, that doesn't mean it's a good thing. Don't you get it?" He gave a hollow laugh. "Even when I try to do the right thing, it turns out wrong."

I studied his face. His words said one thing, but his face said another. I couldn't let it go. And not only for my sake. "Oh come on," I said. "The Debbie thing was years ago. Ancient history."

"It's not about Debbie," he said. "For every story like that, I've got a million more." He leaned over me, and I felt the promise of a kiss. "I meant what I said. I do love you. I've loved you for years. But I hope to God that you never love me back."

"But why?"

"Because I ruin everything I touch. And I don't wanna ruin you."

"Jake," I said, "look at this place. You're successful. You're famous. Girls literally throw themselves at you. I don't think you're seeing yourself clearly. You haven't ruined anything. You've built something to be proud of. Why can't you see that?"

"I see it." He looked around. "But you know what you *don't* see?"

"What?"

"Behind all this, there's a long string of people who hate my guts. And you what?"

"What?"

"I don't care."

"You don't?"

"No," he said. "I can't afford to."

"Why not?" I asked. "Because of the money?"

"I don't care about the money," he said. "I mean, yeah, it's nice. But that's not why I do it."

"So why?" I asked. "For fun? Fame?" I tried to laugh. "The girls?"

His gaze met mine. "There's only one girl I care about." His voice softened. "And she deserves a lot better than me."

My head was reeling from the whiplash of emotions swirling around the room. He claimed to love me, but he wanted me to leave. He *had* to be lying, whether to himself, or to me, because both things couldn't be true at the same time.

Could they?

As if reading my confusion, he moved forward and reached out for me. There was something so lost about him that I couldn't stop myself from falling into his arms. To comfort him? Or to comfort me? Probably both.

Melted against him, I spoke against his chest. "Jake?"

"Yeah."

"That thing you said, that you, uh, love me?"

"Yeah?"

"Just how many girls have you said that to?"

"Including you?" he asked.

Against him, I nodded.

His answer was a long time in coming. But when it did, it took my breath away. "One."

I pulled away to meet his gaze.

The script called for me to say I loved him too. Did I? I had idolized him forever. I had spent countless nights lusting after him. And now, I wanted to wash away his torments and somehow make him whole and happy.

Was that love? It sure as hell felt like it. But I refused to say it – not for fear of embarrassment, and not because he didn't want me to love him. It was because if I admitted to such a thing, even to myself, I'd never be able to leave, whether he wanted me to or not.

It was because regardless of those pretty words, I still couldn't believe him. If he truly loved me, he'd never ask me to leave. And if I truly loved *him*, I wouldn't be *able* to leave, whether it was supposedly for my own good or not.

Still unsure of what I might say, I opened my mouth, but before any words came out, Jake lowered his head to seal my lips with a kiss so desperate that it made me forget almost everything else.

I shouldn't have done it. But when he carried me away to his bedroom, I didn't utter a single word of protest. I couldn't have, even if I tried.

Tenderly, we made love that whole afternoon. I knew I

shouldn't have. But I couldn't help that either. And I didn't want to help it.

As we lay naked together, I kept expecting him to take everything back, to tell me he never wanted me to leave – or as much as I would have hated to hear it – to tell me he didn't love me at all.

None of that happened.

So I knew what I had to do. The only question was, did I have the will to do it?

THE END

Coming in Spring 2015

JAKE ME

Jake Bishop can take a punch, but can he take the chance of losing Luna, the one girl who melts his heart? She's still in danger. He's still afraid of ruining her. Together, they're one hot mess looking for a place called home. Will they find it with each other? Or go down in flames, trying?

Other Books by Sabrina Stark
Unbelonging (Unbelonging Book 1)
Rebelonging (Unbelonging, Book 2)
Illegal Fortunes

ABOUT THE AUTHOR

Sabrina Stark writes edgy romances featuring plucky girls and the bad boys who capture their hearts.

She's worked as a fortune-teller, barista, game-show contestant, and media writer in the aerospace industry. She has a journalism degree from Central Michigan University and is married with one son and two kittens. She currently makes her home in Northern Alabama.

ON THE WEB

Learn About New Releases & Exclusive Offers
www.SabrinaStark.com

Follow Sabrina Stark on Twitter at
http://twitter.com/StarkWrites

Made in the USA
Lexington, KY
01 September 2015